# WHAT TO DO
# WHEN YOU MEET
# CTHULHU

# WHAT TO DO WHEN YOU MEET CTHULHU

## A GUIDE TO SURVIVING THE CTHULHU MYTHOS

BY RACHEL GRAY

EDITED BY WILLIAM JONES

2010

*What To Do When You Meet Cthulhu* is published by Elder Signs Press, Inc.

This book is © 2010 Elder Signs Press, Inc.

This book is © 2010 Rachel Gray; all rights reserved.
Cover art © 2010 by Steven Gilberts; all rights reserved.
Interior illustrations © 2010 by Bryan Reagan; all rights reserved.
Cover and interior layout by Deborah Jones.
Edited by William Jones.

FIRST EDITION
10 9 8 7 6 5 4 3 2 1
Published in October 2010
ISBN: 1-934501-18-2

Printed in the U.S.A.
Published by Elder Signs Press
P.O. Box 389
Lake Orion, MI 48361-0389

www.eldersignspress.com

*For my mother, who taught me how to read,*
*and for Jerry, who taught me how to write.*

ACKNOWLEDGMENTS

The author wishes to thank Susanna, Kevin, and Charles, who, as always, came through when they were needed the most. Thanks to the talented artists Steven Gilberts and Bryan Reagan. And a very special thanks to my editor, William Jones. Without your guidance, editing, and advice, this book would never have come to fruition.

# Contents

# Introduction

Welcome to *What to Do When You Meet Cthulhu!* This book hopes to serve as a handy guide that will help you navigate through the eldritch world of the Cthulhu Mythos.

Jammed into this tome is information for all readers—both those who are new, and those unfamiliar with the Cthulhu Mythos. In fact, for readers who are in their Mythos infancy, you may not even know what "Cthulhu Mythos" means, let alone how to pronounce "Cthulhu." Not a problem! By the time you're done reading this, you'll be armed with a cornucopia of delightful facts which you can relate to your friends. After all, everyone wants forewarning of the world's inevitable destruction at the hands of the Great Cthulhu.

Or perhaps, you're already familiar with the Mythos. You'll still find this tome useful—the Mythos facts loaded in this book make a handy reference, whether you're trying to answer a trivia question about Wilbur Whateley or simply doing your best to be prepared for the inevitable end of the world.

Either way, we'll begin with the question . . .

---

# So What Is This Cthulhu Mythos, Anyway?

The Cthulhu Mythos is replete with ancient ideas about the world around us—a world we only think we know and understand. Lurking beneath humanity's naïve conception of reality is a darker world, one filled with unimaginable creatures, fearsome god-like entities, and untold powers. Comprehending all of this is a herculean undertaking, and usually leaves the one who undertakes the task with a brain transformed into a gooey mess. With that in mind, let's start with some brain-safe basics:

In the 1920s, a young writer named H.P. Lovecraft penned several stories and a few novellas that slammed the world into the shadowy face of an alternate universe—a universe which exists around us, and isn't normally visible to humans without some bumbling about, or the help of weird gadgets.

Through his illuminating words, H. P. Lovecraft guided readers through the world of the Mythos and the terrible things prowling within its dark recesses. That very well could have been the end of the matter. But Lovecraft took it further—he opened up his stories to other writers, allowing them to expand upon his ideas, what we today call the Cthulhu Mythos. And from there, the Mythos grew, ever so cleverly seeping into popular culture.

Throughout the years, people have insisted Lovecraft's Cthulhu Mythos is fiction, and simply jumped out of Lovecraft's astounding imagination. But the believers amongst us, who have studied the origins of Lovecraft's writing in great detail can see the truth revealed in his writings.

Unbeknownst to most readers, Lovecraft was a gifted historian, and a prophet. During his time, he catalogued the dangers dwelling in our world, and predicted the coming of the End Times.

H.P. Lovecraft 1890–1937

Proof of Lovecraft's prophetic nature is apparent once you understand that many of his stories were revealed to him in dreams. Well, some call them dreams, others might call them "visions."

## A CTHULHU MYTHOS OVERVIEW

So now you understand the origins of the Cthulhu Mythos. However, summarizing the entire Cthulhu Mythos is difficult and daunting. The breadth of the material has been expanded for decades, and now encompasses an endless range of deities, creatures, and artifacts. But if one were to put it in a nutshell, and we're going to for now, it would be something like this: The Cthulhu Mythos describes a mysterious world beyond the comprehension of most humans—a world of such cosmic scale, humanity is but an insignificant speck in comparison. This uncanny universe

### WHAT TO DO WHEN YOU PRONOUNCE CTHULHU

The question often arises: How do I pronounce this bizarre word with way too many consonants? According to H.P. Lovecraft, the origins of the word are definitely not human; however, opinions differ on how to pronounce it. The most common pronunciation is:

KAH-THOO-LOO.
Now you try it.
Gesundheit.
Have a tissue.

While you'll occasionally encounter a person with a different pronunciation (such as a cultist of Cthulhu), know that the way you say Cthulhu is equally valid. After all, the human mouth isn't capable of correctly uttering this alien sound. Still, we make the best of it.

belonging to the Cthulhu Mythos is inhabited by great deities known as Other Gods (sometimes referred to as Outer Gods). All in all, because of humanity's cosmic insignificance, the Other Gods care little about our comings and goings. If a dim-witted human manages to summon the attention of an Other God, intentionally or otherwise, the consequences are usually horrific for the unlucky sot, and sometimes for the rest of humanity (though to the Other God, it's less significant than swatting a fly).

So it is safe to say that as long as humanity keeps to itself, threats from the Other Gods remain minimal. Still, a greater terror looms closer to home.

Long ago, alien creatures known as Great Old Ones descended from the skies to inhabit the Earth. They dominated the planet for many eons, until a mysterious cosmic event forced them underground, and underwater. It's not clear whether this event was a simple change in climate, or more significant cosmic forces at work. It's always hard to understand the motives and plans of alien minds. Yet, regardless of the reason, the Great Old Ones relocated underground. Some of these mysterious entities constructed massive cities and civilizations beneath the surface. Others, such as the enormous, tentacled Great Cthulhu, ended up taking a long nap; or, sometimes it is described as slumbering in a state of hibernation—waiting for when the "stars are right"—the time when the Great Old Ones can reclaim the planet as their stomping ground. Was Cthulhu bored, or did he simply need to catch-up on his sleep? While no one is really sure, one thing is certain: When he awakens, things will take a turn for the worse.

But don't think that the Cthuhlu Mythos is limited to a giant dreaming entity. Sure, it is named after Cthulhu, but there is much more within the Cthulhu Mythos. Nasty witches. Time-traveling aliens. And, of course, an abundance of tentacles. We'll cover all of it in plenty of detail . . . once you're ready.

## How to Use This Book

The best way to use this book is to open it to the first page, read the words, and turn the pages to get to more words (for those fancy eBook things, you access those additional words via a finger swipe or button click. Please refer to the appropriate user's manual). But, on the off chance you were not looking for that type of instruction, here is another approach to using this book:

*What to Do When You Meet Cthulhu* is designed to maximize your Mythos knowledge and increase your ability to defend against the creatures of Lovecraft's universe. With the aid of this guidebook, you'll travel to many popular and nefarious Mythos locales: Arkham, Dunwich, Kingsport, and Innsmouth are a few of the favorite destinations. But you'll also be transported beyond these notable spots. This guidebook will carry you across the sea, around the world, and to the mysterious universe we inhabit during slumber—the Dreamlands. We'll make stops in multiple realities and dimensions. So many fun things to see and do . . . that is until you go insane. But no need to worry about that now.

During your journeys, you'll encounter the vast array of terrifying creatures and curious personalities occupying the world of the Cthulhu Mythos, and learn how to defeat them—or use them to your advantage.

The best way to prepare yourself for the Mythos dangers surrounding you today, as well as for the imminent "End of the World" lurking just around the corner, is to absorb this material in an orderly, start-to-finish fashion the first time through (please refer to the first paragraph of this section should you need further details on how to proceed).

If you're in a hurry, or you waited until the End

## OVER HERE!

Throughout this book, you will see Mythos information boxes, such as this one. These information boxes contain everything from survival tips, to How-Tos, to quick snippets about H.P. Lovecraft and his Cthulhu Mythos. And, of course, handy information on how to postpone your inevitable destruction at the hands of an overpowering creature you can never hope to defeat.

Times are already upon you, then try sleeping with the book under your pillow, in which case the knowledge contained within will pass into your mind via osmosis. Warning: Learning though osmosis may cause headaches, drowsiness, insanity, and complete confusion about what was actually supposed to be learned (it works differently for everyone). But, on the upside, it saves reading time (results vary based upon pillow density, quality of sleep, and skull thickness. Osmosis may not be right for you. Always remember to consult a supernatural physiologist before starting osmosis).

Then again, you might not be into the whole end-of-the-world thing. Or maybe you don't put much stock in the "reality" of the Cthulhu Mythos. Not a problem. This book offers a crash course in Lovecraft's creations. With the dark knowledge gained from this tome, you'll possess a new arsenal of quickly-amassed Mythos knowledge for use at parties, guaranteed to astound your friends (and crush your enemies). Or, if you're not into regurgitating facts at the party scene, this book can be used as a reference as well. It's filled with handy facts and places of interest. In general, *What to Do When You Meet Cthulhu* assists anyone, although it is probably more useful for those yearning to visit the lands of Lovecraft's imagination.

So what does that mean? The Mythos information in this book provides background and details from Lovecraft's stories in addition to helpful Mythos survival tips. Not only can you impress all your friends by recounting what happened in "The Shadow Over Innsmouth," you'll be able to tell them how to avoid a Deep One attack!

This wonderfully illustrated and detailed text focuses upon the Cthulhu Mythos stories of H.P. Lovecraft. Though additional authors have further expanded his universe, and may be mentioned or referenced, the bulk of the creatures, items, and places in this guidebook stem from the original visionary himself. And for both the neophyte and the sanity-hardened veteran, that is more than enough knowledge to prepare for the unseen universe folded over our world, and the end of all things—although, the "end of all things" pretty much trumps books, scrolls, and any amount of knowledge. Screaming might be the only option left at that point.

## WILL THIS BOOK REALLY DRIVE ME INSANE?

If you're a sharp reader, you might have noticed a few prior references to "going insane" in the previous sections. Or, perhaps a rumor or two found its way to you, filling your head with the fear that knowledge of Cthulhu Mythos affects a person's sanity. I'd love to assure you this isn't true. But, unfortunately, it is. General observations have revealed that the greater a person's knowledge of the Cthulhu Mythos, the crazier you become. But why squabble over aesthetics, or quibble about the depletion of sanity versus knowledge gained. In the grand scheme, a little "craziness" is a minuscule price for such valuable knowledge. Really, that's the best way to look at it.

However, it can be argued that too much of a good thing is "not so good." So, to help protect your mind, the doom-laden facts of this book are wrapped in soft, cottony cushions of light, airy, jolly descriptive goodness. This tactic will help ease you into the concepts contained in this guidebook. Even so, you should understand that no matter how the Mythos is presented, a horrific and destructive end awaits all of us shortly, at the hands (or tentacles) of Cthulhu. A little corrosion of the mind now might even make things appear a touch delightful in the end.

Best of luck!

## IN SUMMARY . . .

As you progress through this book, the skills, tools, and knowledge needed to ultimately deal with (or run away from) the great godlike creatures dwelling in the Cthulhu Mythos will be honed. Once you've studied enough and fortified your repository of sanity-shattering, brain-bursting knowledge, you'll be ready to find out What to Do When You Meet Cthulhu!

INTRODUCTION

# Arkham

*He was in the changeless, legend-haunted city of Arkham, with its clustering gambrel roofs that sway and sag over attics where witches hid from the King's men in the dark, olden years of the Province.*

—H.P. Lovecraft, "Dreams in the Witch House"

Welcome to the town of Arkham, a city with a long, and strange, history. Nestled upon the Miskatonic River, Arkham is H.P. Lovecraft's most popular literary location. Not only did Lovecraft often return to Arkham within his tales, it also appears in works by countless authors. Even DC Comics' favorite character, *Batman*, was not unfamiliar with Arkham—many of his insane, menacing rivals were said to be housed within the walls of Arkham Asylum— although DC Comics makes it clear that their "Arkham" is not connected to Lovecraft's "Arkham." Just a coincidence I guess. Or, in other words, all that *Batman* nonsense is just crazy-talk. The Arkham Asylum is a place of fiction. *Batman's* villainous jokers never set foot in Lovecraft's Arkham or in its actual asylum— Arkham Sanitarium.

H.P. Lovecraft's Arkham was founded in the late 1600s. Arkham is the residence of choice for countless ghouls, witches, horrors unseen, floating colors, and plenty of things far worse— namely college students. Don't underestimate these critters—one of them managed to reanimate the dead and cause quite a bit of trouble in and about Arkham.

In any case, if you want to learn how to survive the perils of the Mythos, the best place to start is Arkham. Or, you might be considering enrollment at the town's pride and joy, Miskatonic University, in which case you'll still need to consult this chapter if you want to survive four years at such an unusual, and sometimes deadly university . . ..

## MISKATONIC UNIVERSITY

Like any other college town, Arkham bustles with the innocuous activities of campus life. Football games. Tailgating parties. midterm exams. Periodic monster attacks. When trouble stirs in Arkham, as it often does, Miskatonic is usually at the center of the maelstrom.

Despite a lengthy history of trouble, the university has gained honor, recognition and prestige over the years. Although many argue that Miskatonic's distinction derives from its ill-fated expeditions, unique faculty, students, and mysterious library archives.

21

## MISKATONIC LIBRARY ARCHIVES

### THE NECRONOMICON

This world renowned tome is one H.P. Lovecraft's most famous creations. Mythos fan or not, most everyone has heard about it, and even a few are in search of it as you read this. The *Necronomicon,* or the "Book of Dead Names," was penned by the mad Arabic author, Abdul Alhazred. One of the few copies in existence dwells in the Miskatonic University library archives. The book's contents in its entirety are not known by a solitary human—such a vast mass of Mythos knowledge would pulverize the human brain. But the tome does contain great magic. Powerful spells used to get inside a person's head. Formulas to summon gods. Descriptions of the great beasts lurking about.

The *Necronomicon,* and its variations, appear throughout literature, film and popular culture. It's no coincidence that the powerful grimoire generating trouble in the *Evil Dead* movie series is *Necronomicon Ex-Mortis.* And there is the similarly-titled and

equally powerful *Book of the Dead* in the delightfully Lovecraftian film, *The Mummy*. When librarian Evelyn Carnahan states "No harm ever came from reading a book," prior to flipping it open, any Lovecraft fan or scholar knows it's time to take cover.

## THE BOOK OF EIBON

Appearing in many Lovecraft tales, the *Book of Eibon* is attributed to author Clark Ashton Smith, one of Lovecraft's contemporaries and friends. In this tome, Eibon, a wizard from the ancient, mythical land of Hyperborea, chronicles his lifelong adventures and journeys to distant lands. Eibon discovered powerful magical spells during his travels, recording them in *The Book of Eibon*. Unfortunately, only tattered fragments of the book remain. It is sometimes referred to as "The Black Book." Its creation by Smith was a nod to Lovecraft's *Necromonicon*.

## UNAUSSPRECHLICHEN KULTEN

Another popular tome, this time created by Lovecraft's friend, Robert E. Howard. This mysterious volume appears throughout the Mythos. The German name roughly translates to Unspeakable/Nameless Cults—at least that's what Howard was going for. The book itself focuses on various cults around the world, as well as their practices and rituals. Since most of the Mythos monsters have unspeakable names, it follows that their cult names are equally unpronounceable. So this title works well. Or, it might be that these cults are so notorious, so dangerous, so deadly that it is best to leave their names unspoken. So perhaps it's best not to write any jingles with names from this book—just in case you get on the bad side of one of the cults. And that's pretty much that—there isn't much more to say about *Unaussprechlichen Kulten*—otherwise it would need to be renamed *Speakable Cults*.

## THE FACES OF MISKATONIC

Plenty of notable folks have graced the halls of New England's most (in)famous university. This section provides a brief description of some of Miskatonic's more well-known students and faculty, as well as where to find them in this guidebook.

### HENRY ARMITAGE

Henry Armitage served as the head librarian at Miskatonic University for many years. He delved into the university's copy of the *Necronomicon* on occasion. Maybe a few too many times. He was a fount of knowledge in his day, and has become a legend in the Mythos. Read more about Armitage in the *Dunwich* chapter.

### ALBERT WILMARTH

Professor of Literature at Miskatonic, and debunker of legends regarding strange, crab-like flying creatures spotted in Vermont. Although his debunking skills turn suspect when he actually encounters the crab-like race called the Mi-Go. Wilmarth's adventures appear in the *More Mythos Monsters* chapter.

### PROFESSOR WILLIAM DYER

This geology professor directed the unfortunate Pabodie Expedition to Antarctica. The Pabodie Expedition is covered later in this chapter. You're not quite ready for that yet.

But if you really want to skip ahead, there is a *Miskatonic Expeditions* section just a few pages from this spot.

### HERBERT WEST

One of Miskatonic University's most famous medical students is Herbert West. He is well known for a number of risky experiments—notably his experiments on the dead. Or, perhaps better put, once he was done experimenting with them, the not-so-dead, "undead." Read more about Herbert West in the *Need a Doctor?* Section of this chapter. And honestly, don't go skipping around these pages too much. A little information in the wrong order can spell disaster. Of all people, Herbert West can testify to that.

### WALTER GILMAN

Walter was a Miskatonic student specializing in non-Euclidean calculus and quantum physics (it just sounds thrilling already). As a student, he decided to room at the local boarding-house, cleverly dubbed the Witch House (Walter obviously didn't give much thought to names). For more details on how that adventure went down (although you can probably guess it didn't end up good for Walter), visit the *Where to Stay in Arkham* section in this chapter.

## WHAT TO ASK WHEN YOU
## INTERVIEW FOR A UNIVERSITY

1.  Have any strange colors have been seen in the town? (If the answer is "yes," ask: Just what is a *strange* color?")

2.  Are there any dead people walking the streets? (I mean "dead" as in zombies, not the type of dead drifting around malls—then again . . .)

3.  Do you have a copy of the *Necronomicon?* (Anyone with a copy can't be trusted, so this means that if the university has a copy, either "yes" or "no" as an answer are equally dangerous. Really, who would admit to having a copy? And if someone does, then the person is clearly insane. If someone lies and says, "no," well, then he or she knows you *know* about the book, and the end result is likely to be death or torture or sacrifice—on your part. This means you need to study the person's face when he or she answers. You'll find the truth there. A confused expression is mostly likely a "no." This is a good sign.)

4.  Are any students enrolled here named Herbert West? (I'll explain later why this is important. For now, know that it is significant, and it is related to question #2.)

5.  Describe the psychological state of your dean. Is he:
    a.  dead,
    b.  in an asylum,
    c.  all of the above?

(Sure, this seems silly, but when looking for a good university, the above answers are important. Above and beyond the strangeness that goes on at Miskatonic University, the academic world is filled with unfathomable, unwritten rules and guidelines that often lead to the death or insanity of a faculty member. Sometimes it leads to the death, reanimation, and then institutionalization of said member. It's best to get this knowledge up front).

CONTINUED . . .

## RANDOLPH CARTER

Antiquarian, writer, prophet, and former student of Miskatonic, Randolph Carter bears an uncanny resemblance to H.P. Lovecraft. The numerous adventures of Randolph Carter are detailed throughout this book, and heavily in the *Dreamlands* section.

## NATHANIEL WINGATE PEASLEE

A professor of political economy, Peaslee suffered from a five-year case of amnesia—and it wasn't related to his topic of study. It turns out, his blackouts were more than medical curiosity, or trauma from an overload of statistics and unimaginable laws of economics. You see, Peaslee's brain was inhabited by a time-travelling creature from the Great Race of Yith. Although this does make one wonder: Why would an alien inhabit a professor of political economy? Anyway, there's more on Peaslee and his alien companion later in this chapter.

## ASENATH WAITE

There are few females depicted in H.P. Lovecraft's fiction. One is an evil witch (think "Witch House"), and the other one is just an evil . . . person. Asenath Waite dabbled in magic and studied medieval metaphysics at Miskatonic before charming fellow Miskatonic graduate Edward Derby into marriage. It turned out Asenath really knew how to get inside someone's head.

More on her abilities in the *Wife Swap!* section in this chapter. Yes, there is a "Wife Swap" section in this book. It just goes to show how forward thinking Lovecraft was—he had the basic premise of the modern reality show decades before they appeared. Or maybe television producers have been reading the writings of H.P. Lovecraft all along. Either way, as I told you, don't go flipping through the pages too early. The section will arrive soon enough, and who knows what other surprises await before then.

## EDWARD DERBY

Edward Derby majored in English and French literature at Miskatonic, finished his degree at the early age of nineteen, and then devoted himself to the study of "subterranean magical lore." At thirty-eight, he met the wicked and alluring Asenath Waite. And again we are at the *Wife Swap!* Section. I would like to add that literature seems to

## WHAT TO ASK WHEN YOU INTERVIEW FOR A UNIVERSITY (CONTINUED)

6. What is the ratio of local inhabitants who are living in the local asylum, versus those who have not been placed inside the local asylum? (If the number inside the asylum exceeds those outside the asylum, you are probably at Miskatonic University or an Ivy League university—not much difference.)

7. Do you have a copy of the *Necronomicon?* (Just making sure they didn't lie to you the first time.)

8. If you had to put a number to it, how many ghouls live beneath the city? (This is a closed question. It catches a person off guard, forcing a number to pop into his or her mind. Obviously, a sour expression with a counter question of "What are you talking about?" is what you're looking for.)

9. Why does a small college town have an asylum? (Nothing much to elaborate on here. The question isn't a poser, and a bit self evident.)

10. Do the number of graveyards in town exceed the number of car dealerships? (Many people believe there is a link between car dealerships and graveyards. There is no hard evidence to back this up, but as a rule of thumb, any location is better if it has more car dealerships than graveyards. In fact, this might make a good topic of study to consider at the new university: "The Correlation of the Dead and Car Salesmen." Try pitching that one to your doctoral advisor.)

get a bad rap in the Cthulhu Mythos—but that isn't true. After all, Edward went on to study "subterranean magical lore." I'm certain there's a pun in there. Anyway, he was clearly finished with literature and looking for a little more adventure.

## ALLEN HALSEY

Dr. Allen Halsey served as Miskatonic's dean during Herbert West's years in medical school. The two quarreled over West's questionable medical practices regarding dead bodies—is there really a debate there? There's more on these two in the section *Need a Doctor?*

## WHERE TO STAY IN ARKHAM

Of course, the only way to learn about Arkham is to visit Arkham. So the first thing you need is somewhere to stay . . .

## THE WITCH HOUSE

Reduced to rubble long ago, legends brew about the Witch House boarding house in Arkham. The new boarding house on the site doesn't have the same charm, but it offers excellent rates. If you room there, make sure to ask for the Gilman Room.

In "Dreams in the Witch House," H.P. Lovecraft reveals the unique history of Arkham's most unique boarding house. The Witch House gains its name from its original inhabitant. Stay with me. You see, Keziah Mason owned the boarding house in the late seventeenth century, until the good people of Salem nabbed her for the Salem Witch Trials (no reality television in those days, so entertainment was live). She readily confessed her witchy ways, but it didn't much matter. She "inexplicably" escaped from the Salem Gaol not long afterward, leaving the folks in Salem with an abundant supply of angst, branding irons, rope, chains, letters to be stitched onto clothing, and far too much kindling for fires. True, some people claimed that her disappearing act proved she was a witch, but without any active witch hunters, there was little the folks of Salem could do—except to accuse someone else not so witchy, making it easier to follow through with the accusations.

## WHAT TO DO WHEN YOU SELECT YOUR SCHEDULE AT MISKATONIC UNIVERSITY

1. Avoid any class that has non-Euclidean in its title. Think about it. What good can come from studying non-Euclidean geometry? Actually, what good can come from studying Euclidean geometry? Unless you're one of those engineer-types.

2. If you have a class that assigns the *Necronomicon*, drop it. The class, not the book. You shouldn't be that close to the book in the first place.

3. Find out if the class has a student named Herbert West. If so, drop the class just to be safe.

4. If your professor's last name is Marsh, and the class is on swimming, consider track instead.

5. If the dean of your department is in the asylum, consider another department.

6. When signing up for class, ask about the rats in the walls. If they say there's no problem, it's time to leave.

7. If your art class is taught by someone named Pickman, consider taking a pottery course instead.

8. If you've signed up for a class and learned it will have a field expedition as part of the curriculum, drop it (no one ever survives these expeditions).

9. If your major is in Library Studies, consider another major—although don't make it literature.

10. If you're a Comparative Lit major, and you're asked to work on the *Necronomicon*, drop the class. Seriously. You shouldn't be that close to the *Necronomicon*. I mean, if you want to study Comparative Literature, you don't belong at Miskatonic University to begin with. Pick a new major or leave town.

## WALTER GILMAN, MATH STUDENT EXTRAORDINAIRE, STUDENT IN NEED OF LODGING

While attending Miskatonic studying non-Euclidean calculus and quantum physics, Walter Gilman decided it sounded fun to board at Arkham's most famous boarding house. Not his smartest decision. Clearly Gilman was book-smart, but not a practical guy—after all, he was excited about boarding in a *Witch House*.

Gilman believed Keziah Mason had not been a witch. Instead, she was a misunderstood mathematician who mastered the unusual angles and geometry of her spooky house (typical student of mathematics). This allowed her to travel between dimensions and transcend time.

Now, since Gilman was a math major, he was likely suffering from Student Syndrome—you know, where every medical student becomes a hypochondriac (well, except for the ones interested in reanimating the dead), and every first-year electrical engineering student lectures incessantly about how

### MYTHOS SURVIVAL TIP: CHECK THOSE CORNERS!

Strange angles and arcane geometry appear throughout the Mythos. If you find an item, artifact, room, or even *city* with strange angles and corners that seem like they don't obey the natural laws of physics, that's because they *don't*. If you're wondering what a "strange angle" is, think Salvador Dali or M.C. Escher.

But back to encountering anything with strange geometry. Drop the item/artifact and escape the room/city as quickly as possible. While prowling through a Dali landscape or an endless Escher stairway seems entertaining on the surface, it isn't. Nothing good comes of these ventures, and most likely it will end in insanity. Just remember this rule: When in doubt, run!

electrical circuits work. Well, Gilman obviously wanted to glamorize his field of study, and make it seem more mystical than it really was—honestly, it seemed mystical enough already; remember, Gilman didn't have a calculator yet. Way too much time on his hands.

Anyway. Gilman found the perfect room in the Witch House, chock-full of weird curves and angles (hmmm). The room, by the way, was easy to snag, since the boarding house's waiting list was completely empty, due to the house's high Creepy Factor.

## WEIRDNESS IN THE WITCH HOUSE

Not surprisingly, Gilman didn't solve the house's mysteries. But he did discover more about Keziah Mason when she crept into Gilman's dreams—a trick Freddy Krueger learned later. Each night, the witch and her unsightly rat-like familiar, Brown Jenkin, visited the student in his slumbers.

As Gilman's dreams grew increasingly disturbing, his antsy behavior drew attention. His professors dismissed his nervous behavior to overzealous study habits, urging him to lay off the books for awhile. Think about that one for a minute; his professors thought he was *studying too much* and *urged him to study less.* Yet another reason to consider Miskatonic University. Where else can you find professors telling you to have more fun and cool it on the studying?

Eventually, Gilman found himself entangled in the dream-kidnapping of a young child, who was clearly intended to be sacrificed. His dreams spilled into reality when Gilman read about the kidnapping in the daily paper. And when Gilman deftly thwarted Mason's attempt to sacrifice the child, Brown Jenkin finished the job for his witch-master.

Gilman didn't fare better, his body was discovered in the Witch House not long afterward, heart bored out in a very rat-thing-like fashion.

Later, the skeletal remains of a rat-like creature, found in the rubble of the demolished boarding house, indicate there may be some truth behind the Witch House rumors. Not to mention tales of scuttling heard in the walls of the new boarding house.

And the unsettling feeling, reported by many guests who awaken in the night, that a small, furry creature had just been snuggled against their neck.

## RODENT PROBLEM?
## NO PROBLEM!

Brown Jenkin, Keziah Mason's familiar, was sent straight from the devil to do Mason's dirty work. The furry, white-fanged creature was the size of a rat. But the creature's face resembled a human's visage, as did its hands. It subsisted on a diet of Keziah Mason's blood. Haunting the Witch House, the creature nuzzled up to the guests at night, and apparently nibbled on a few, such as poor Walter Gilman.

Suddenly, having a rat problem in your house doesn't seem so bad, does it?

### MEALS INCLUDED

When traveling to Arkham, be judicious in choosing a place to stay. Not every spot in Arkham is as delightful as the Witch House. For instance, in the tale "The Picture in the House," a traveler takes a shortcut to Arkham, only to get caught up in a nasty storm. Striving to find cover from the rain, he takes shelter in an abandoned house. Inside, a strange book titled *Regnum Congo* catches his attention. It contains a disturbing picture from a butcher's shop of the Anzique cannibals. That's right, even cannibals have butcher shops.

And things didn't get better for the traveler.

When an old man shuffled downstairs, the traveler realized the house wasn't as abandoned as he thought. The elderly fellow appeared friendly enough, but when he saw the *Regnum Congo,* things turned weird.

The old man started rambling about the book, the strange

## THE BLACK MAN

In addition to Mason and Brown Jenkin, a mysterious figure known as "The Black Man" appeared in Walter Gilman's dreams. No, Lovecraft wasn't trying to be politically incorrect, although he was arguably a racist. But in this case, The Black Man is one of the many forms of Nyarlathotep, one of the famous deities of the Cthulhu Mythos.

As a guideline, know that regardless of the form, Nyarlathotep is always up to no good. In this case, he was sacrificing young children, which should fit anyone's "no good" category. Unfortunately for Nyarlathotep, he serves as a messenger and/or guardian between other deities, which keeps him very busy. This might explain why he's so bitter, and always getting into trouble.

But like most dark, godlike entities, Nyarlathotep is keen on being admired, and as a result, cults constantly crop up, worhshipping him. The Black Man heads up a witch-cult, and enlisted Keziah Mason to do his bidding.

The great deity is one of the few that appears so readily, and so often, to humans. As the Black Man, or in any of his other 999 forms (imagine this guy's closet), he often appears to influence the deeds of mankind, or create general mischief. He has an outfit for every occasion, and a diabolical scheme to go with it.

Anzique folk, and their cannibalistic ways. All of it gave the old guy a peculiar *hankering*, he explained, to try something more than just sheep for dinner. But, no worries—he assured the traveler he'd never actually try anything like . . . human flesh. Although the blood dripping from the ceiling seemed to say otherwise.

As Luck or Fate would have it, there was a fortuitous bolt of lightning which struck the house at that very moment. This finished any speculation on the traveler's behalf as to whether he'd stay for dinner.

The crazy old man was not seen again. It seems the universe doesn't like cannibals much. Either way, it's best you don't stop at any abandoned houses outside of town. Just in case there are no approaching thunderstorms.

## WHAT TO DO WHEN YOU'RE ASLEEP

As Walter Gilman demonstrates, dreaming causes serious problems in the confines of the Cthulhu Mythos. You'll learn more about the dangers of dreaming in later chapters, but for now, here are a few handy tips to stay out of trouble:

1. Consider learning lucid dreaming techniques. Lucid dreaming allows a person to remain "aware" during the dream-state. There are plenty of resources on the web you can use to learn about lucid dreaming. Use them!

2. Set a timer. If you never fall into REM sleep, you can't dream. Sure, you'll eventually go insane and die from lack of REM sleep, but you won't get involved in child sacrifices that way. And this very important if you live on a street named "Elm."

3. Sleep aids are your friend! Sure, you still dream while under the influence of sleep aids, but if you're zonked-out enough, odds are you won't remember your dreams in the morning, anyway.

CONTINUED . . .

## IT'S A BIRD, IT'S A PLANE, IT'S A . . . COLOR?

One of the most *colorful* tales from the outskirts of Arkham is "The Colour Out of Space." Covered by a giant reservoir today, tales abound of a "blasted heath" at the original site—a five acre farm, long abandoned, where trees grew stunted, and the land was gray and desolate.

Eccentric elderly hermit Amni Pierce delighted in telling the surveyor, sent from Boston to assess the reservoir site, all about the blasted heath. A meteorite crashed to Earth in the late 1800s, landing on Nahum Gardner's farm. Globules within the rock were of a queer new color, never before identified. A troupe of professors and scientists quickly converged to slice up the meteorite into manageable chunks and test the heck out

---

### WHAT TO DO WHEN YOU'RE ASLEEP (CONTINUED)

4. Or, try the opposite approach—stock up on caffeine and energy drinks, and avoid sleeping altogether.

5. Try thinking about a pleasant scene, or memory, prior to falling asleep. Dreaming about sunny fields and sandy beaches will make you less likely to suffer a Freddy Krueger moment.

6. Try sleeping on an uncomfortable bed. The more your sleep is disturbed, the better.

7. Encourage your spouse/significant other/best friend who always sleeps on the couch to take up snoring.

8. Work the late shift. Nothing ever happens to people who dream during the day.

9. Take up sleepwalking.

10. Eat a large, spicy, fatty meal just prior to bedtime. This will definitely produce bad dreams. Still, it's a known quantity. You're better off being chased by a giant hamburger than being consumed by a Mythos creature.

---

of it. But the strange material defied analysis.

If all of this sounds a bit familiar to the film *The Blob*, well then it's probably because it is similar. That's not to say the writers, director, and producers of the classic horror film intentionally borrowed from Lovecraft, but nonetheless, Lovecraft did have a strong influence in popular culture, so sometimes his influence seeped into other works without the knowledge of the creators. In other words, sometimes a tentacle is just a tentacle, and sometimes it's the influence of H.P. Lovecraft. You decide. Anyway, back to the uncanny events in Arkham . . .

## THE DYING FARM

Stories circulated about strange happenings at Nahum Gardner's farm. The land produced oversized crops that would win a "largest cabbage" contest hands down. But they were gray and tasteless (Lovecraft used "grey" instead of "gray"), and the crops were not fit to eat—except when used in Vera Mariner's local, legendary, award-winning "Tasteless and Not Fit to Eat Cabbage Soup" recipe.

Things grew even more bizarre as nearby flora and fauna twisted into gray (Lovecraft used . . . nevermind, you get it), diseased shapes. Nahum Gardner's children also started acting odd—running about,

### STRANGE SPELLINGS

Regardless of your nationality, and how you spell "color" or "colour," you might be wondering what's up with the spelling in H.P. Lovecraft's fiction. Yes, he was American. Typically this means he would use American standardized spelling. But Lovecraft favored the British style—he was from New England after all. He also enjoyed archaic words, and an abundance of adjectives. Sometimes all of this combined presents a touch of confusion to the reader. But worry not. Lovecraft was very much aware of what he was doing, and the end result was an overall eerie and alien effect to his prose styling, which worked well with his topics.

## WHAT TO DO IF A COLOUR OUT OF SPACE LANDS ON YOUR FARM

1. Consider moving. Think about it; you're living in Arkham. Things are not going to get better. If in doubt, visit the local university.

2. Do not drink the water or eat the plants, but feel free to continue selling them, at your discretion. Such behavior is not uncommon in Arkham. In fact, it seems somewhat expected.

3. Immediately put the house up for sale. Don't wait for the land to become a pallid gray/grey hue. Speed is of the essence here.

4. If the Colour is in your well, do not try chemicals, such as bleach. It's a creature from space that appears to be a strange, never-before-seen color. Not a load of laundry. Besides being ineffective, you are likely to irritate it.

5. When extracting the Colour from a well, try using a pool-cleaner to capture the globules. It might also be handy to simple call in a pool cleaning service, just to avoid contact with the entity dwelling at the bottom of your well. Sure, the service will be reluctant, after all they clean pools, not wells, but here is where a bit of bribery might come in handy. But do not utter a word about the prior events or what's in the well, just proffer plenty of cash. Everyone likes cash.

6. To properly dispose of the Colour, deposit it in your neighbor's well. Preferably the one who cheats every year in the pumpkin-growing contest. On second thought, make it a neighbor a good distance away—if that neighbor wins the farm market contests also, then all the better. Ideally, choose a neighbor with an inground swimming pool. Offering to pay to have the

CONTINUED . . .

## What to Do if a Colour Out of Space Lands on Your Farm (Continued)

neighbor's pool cleaned will help move the "Colour" from your place to his, and you already have a pool cleaning service in your hire.

7. Always make sure you remove *all* globules of Colour. There's nothing worse than exacting revenge on a neighbor with a Colour Out of Space, only to find out you still have a Colour Out of Space problem. In fact, it is a bit embarrassing.

8. Contact the state government and see if they want to build a reservoir on your property.

9. Ask your best friend to descend into the well and retrieve the Colour for you (if you're feeling magnanimous, you might want to suggest they rent a Haz-Mat suit)

10. Ignore the Colour—once it has leeched the land and killed everything around it, the problem will go away on its own.

maniacally screaming and yelling (although today such behavior seems to be taken as normal). Then they started dying.

Nahum insisted one of the colorful globules dwelled at the bottom of his well, feeding off the environs, sucking the life from everything around it.

When Amni and the authorities arrived at the farm to check things out, the landscape around the well was gray (uhh . . .) and blighted, disintegrating into dust. The family was dead. It appeared Nahum's suspicions were correct about the greedy, gorging globule at the bottom of his well. After leeching the area, the alien color was ready to move on. With a spectacular shimmering show, it burst forward from the site and into the sky. And that was the end of it.

Almost. Some people believe a bit of the "Colour" creature remained. And the area did remain devoid of life, gray( . . .), and blighted. Other than that, it really was the end of it.

The surveyor sent out to survey the reservoir reported back to Boston, and must have given the site a clean bill of health, because the Arkham Reservoir sits there today. And it's probably the source of Arkham Springs sparkling bottled water.

## What Not to Try in Arkham

Known for its crisp, distinctive taste, Arkham Springs Bottled Water is captured at the source, and bottled right in Arkham. It has quickly become one of the best-selling bottled waters in the New England region. Distilled using a proprietary process developed at Miskatonic University, Arkham Springs water is the purest and cleanest you'll ever find. And it has a natural sparkle!

Also available in colorful, eco-friendly bottles, locally manufactured!

## WIFE SWAP!

Sure, this concept is depicted innocuously in television reality shows today, in which your horrible spouse is temporarily traded for someone else's horrible spouse. In the end, it usually turns out your horrible spouse is not so horrible. At least, in comparison with the new, even more horrible spouse, who has accomplished monumental achievements in the art of the horrific.

So your ghastly spouse returns, and the two of you live dreadfully ever after.

If you think that's bad, imagine this scenario: your best friend's wife swaps brains with your best friend, and won't give his body back. The only way to stop her is to put six bullets in *his* head.

Tough one to explain to the judge, there. And I'll bet someone's already working on that reality show.

ARKHAM

In Lovecraft's story, "The Thing on the Doorstep," Daniel Upton and Edward Derby find themselves in this predicament. They were the best of friends. That is, until Derby fell for the attractive and unfriendly Asenath Waite. I'm not sure what was up with Derby, after all Asenath was a bit creepy—she allegedly spent a lot of time studying magic and the arcane at Miskatonic University. She wasn't fond of Upton, either. But one thing led to another, and Derby proposed to Asenath. Soon after the wedding, Derby and Upton's friendship withered (this is also a problem for gamers who don't marry "gaming spouses." However, I don't think Lovecraft used them as a model—mostly because they didn't exist yet).

## How to Tell if You're the Victim of a Mental Wife Swap

1. Lipstick on your collar and it's not your girlfriend's shade (think about it).

2. Your friends observe you've been talking a lot about your "feelings." Or your friends no longer talk to you.

3. When you're lost, you feel inclined to stop and ask for directions.

4. You keep renting "chick flicks."

5. You have a sudden aversion to professional sports.

6. You have a sudden attraction to professional sports.

7. You're pretty sure you were not wearing those high heels fifteen minutes ago.

8. Your buddies in the local poker game keep asking you to bring more of those great blueberry muffins.

9. You're in Camp Edward. Worse, you're in Camp Jacob.

10. The number of gifts you're purchasing for your wife go from zero to anything higher than zero.

After a few years, Derby suddenly attempted to renew his friendship with Upton. And all was not well with Derby. In Upton's and Derby's discussions, Derby dropped hints about his wife, revealing his fears of Asenath. He suspected Asenath used her arcane knowledge and powerful magic to possess him. And the frequency of her mind-inhabitation sessions were increasing. Yes, she was time-sharing Derby's mind. It's a bit like borrowing a neighbor's car, or maybe your spouse's car to be more exact. And in this case, everyone who sees you inside the car mistakes you for your spouse—well, that's because you are in your spouse's body. Or car. Or . . . oh, nevermind.

Not surprisingly, Upton didn't buy it. Clearly, Derby was suffering from hallucinations. And those complete changes in personality and demeanor—which occurred increasingly in their conversations—were nothing to be concerned about. Here we begin to see that Upton wasn't the fastest car in the race. Or maybe he simply enjoyed speaking to a different version of Derby on occasion. It's like having two friends in one.

## I See Dead People

Eventually, even Upton became suspicious. And all it took was the decaying, gurgling corpse of Asenath Waite dragging itself onto Upton's doorstep, handing Upton a politely written, though smudged note (with decomposing corpse bits). In retrospect, Upton didn't really seem like that close of a friend to Derby. I mean, he'd rather believe Derby was "confused" and hallucinating than accept his outlandish claims (remember, we're in Arkahm). But when a decrepit corpse finally arrives at his door, *then* he's convinced. Until then Derby didn't even get the mildest benefit of the doubt.

Anyway, the note explained what the corpse could not. Derby's body was up at Arkham Sanitarium, permanently possessed by Asenath. But even Asenath wasn't Asenath, really. Long ago, her father Ephraim Waite escaped death by possessing the young girl, taking advantage of her weak will (is this a form of cross dressing?). Ephraim was the true villain behind all of the body-swapping shenanigans.

Derby had murdered Ephraim/Asenath to escape his/her constant

41

possession attempts. But Ephraim/Asenath's powers exceeded death. He/she permanently possessed Derby, from beyond the grave.

So, the note requested, if Upton would be so kind, would he please go up to the sanitarium and shoot Derby's former body in the head, thank you very much, hope all is well, have a great evening, see you later.

So, finally proving himself a true friend, Upton did as requested, and killed Derby. Now that's what friends do for each other. Keep it in mind. This nugget of knowledge will help you later when the world starts to fall apart. Remember keep your friends close, and make sure they are good friends—the kind who'll make sacrifices for you . . . should the need arise.

## NEED A DOCTOR?

Try Dr. Herbert West, Reanimator, whose exploits are covered in the coincidentally-titled "Herbert West—Reanimator." Herbert West is Arkham's most famous medical personality and is always on the prowl for new patients.

On first glance, you might be worried about West's medical training. But don't be concerned about his complicated medical history. "Technically" West was banned from Miskatonic. But only due to trivial "ethical" concerns of the persnickety dean, Dr. Allen Halsey. Apparently the dean wasn't fond of West injecting the medical school cadavers with his reanimation serum. This means there is a great chance Herbert West didn't receive an actual diploma, nor was he board certified. So the "doctor" part might be stretching things a little.

Anyway, the blond-haired, blue eyed, innocuous-looking West took up residence in an abandoned farmhouse in the town of Bolton, just outside of Arkham. He worked with his trusty assistant (and close friend) who chronicled their adventures (remember the close friend requirement from Derby's experiences?). You might say the two of them were just like Watson and Sherlock Holmes. Well, close, anyway. If Sherlock Holmes had been an insane doctor obsessed with reanimating the dead, and Watson his equally insane assistant, then you've got a dead-on match.

In West's day, dead bodies were difficult to come by. By being clever, West acquired them from a nearby potter's field, allowing him to continue his gruesome experiments. After some trial and error, West and his assistant saw their first "success"—they injected West's refined reanimating fluid into a freshly-dead body. The corpse gurgled a horrid, inhuman cry as it awoke. Horrified, West and his assistant ran, screaming, from the house. Really, what else were they expecting? They were trying to reanimate the dead.

Given their reactions, you'd think this would be enough to deter future experiments. Nope.

## NOT FRESH ENOUGH

By the time the two experimenters returned to their house, they found the dead guy was dead again. West assumed his failure stemmed from the fact that his corpses suffered from a *freshness* issue. The bodies were not fresh enough—he needed to get his hands on them just as the victim expelled his or her last breath.

So his trials continued, as did his quarrels with Dr. Halsey, Dean of the Medical School. The grumpy dean refused to allow West access to Miskatonic's resources (makes you wonder what type of resources they had). Nonetheless, West yearned to prove his genius to Halsey, and win the man's respect. A horde of

ARKHAM

### NOW ACCEPTING PATIENTS!
# DR. HERBERT WEST, M.D. (ALMOST)

Now treating patients with any ailments! Dr. West's special elixir helps you forget all of your aches and pains.

**Requirements**: Must be dead, near dead, or very unwell
**Location**: Bolton, just outside Arkham
**Hours**: Between 10pm and 4am daily

By appointment only (unless you are just about to die, in which case, please stop by as soon as possible)

fresh, reanimated dead people stomping about town would do the trick.

As luck would have it, an outbreak of typhoid descended upon Arkham. West was beside himself with joy. Sure, the university suffered and nearly closed. Plenty of people died. Arkham residents lived under a shroud of terror. But for West, typhoid offered a wealth of bodies, free of embalming fluid, ready for reanimation. And oh, how fresh!

Eventually West's nemesis, Dr. Halsey, succumbed to typhoid, depriving poor West of his well-deserved vindication. But West made the best of it. He hijacked Halsey's body, reanimating him.

Finding himself snatched from the claws of death, Halsey showed his appreciation by mauling West, and setting out upon a typical zombie rampage about town. Eventually, a band of searchers captured the undead dean, and unsure of what to do with him, they tossed Halsey into Arkham Sanitarium.

After such a harrowing experience, and nearly being discovered by the authorities, you'd think West would halt his reanimation experiments. Okay, maybe you wouldn't. He does seem a bit like the obsessive type. And thinking things through really wasn't his forte.

Instead, a bandage-covered West simply muttered to his assistant, "Damn it, it wasn't quite fresh enough!"

## THE BOXER

Clearly West needed "exceedingly fresh" dead people. Just his luck, a boxing match nearby delivered a "still-warm" body/victim to West's door. The unfortunate boxer received a knockout punch of the permanent type.

West quickly injected the boxer with his serum. Then West settled back and waited. Nothing happened. So West and his assistant hauled the corpse off to the potter's field. Everyone makes mistakes.

The dynamic doctor duo's impatience returned to haunt them. The boxer made a last minute comeback, appearing on West's doorstep for a visit—politely knocking on the door, although he was gnawing on a child's arm. Horrified by the zombie's actions, West unloaded six bullets into the creature.

## WHAT NOT TO DO WHEN YOU'RE A REANIMATOR

1. Don't reanimate unfresh corpses. This tidbit comes right from the Reanimator himself.

2. Don't reanimate the dean of your university, who is likely to go on a rampage. In the end, this causes myriad academic problems for you, and most likely you'll never get that diploma.

3. Just leave dead boxers out of it—they've been hit in the head enough, and will be unstable when reanimated.

4. Never assume that the dead man you just reanimated is still dead! Think carefully about the concept "reanimated dead person" before you leave his body behind. For some reason, the dead are never grateful, and leaving a string of revivified corpses spells trouble for you in the future.

5. Don't set up a practice in your hometown, under your name. This helps avoid dead people from finding you. Honestly, if you do this, you might as well have a big arrow pointing at your house added to all local maps, and maybe a billboard on the highway saying: This way to the Reanimator's house. The bottom line is, if you are playing with dead things, try to be discreet.

6. Lock your doors. Simple, but amazingly efficient when dealing with the undead.

7. If you've locked your door, don't answer it if a zombie comes knocking.

8. Before starting this whole "experiment with the dead," consider a chemical to reverse the process. This would be called a *safeguard*. Maybe it sounds outlandish, but

CONTINUED . . .

> ## WHAT NOT TO DO WHEN
> ## YOU'RE A REANIMATOR (CONTINUED)
>
> when an Undead Tactical Strike Force decides to launch an assault on you, it'll be worth the time spent.
>
> 9. You're alive—they're dead. Do the math. It's well known that dead people resent the living, particularly the living that reanimated them.
>
> 10. If you're the assistant to a Reanimator, leave. That's it, just leave. Dr. Reanimator is injecting every dead thing he stumbles across, and things will go bad soon enough. Don't wait around. Move to another town, change your name (see above for precautions).

By this point it might appear that West would realize the whole reanimation thing wasn't working out. His biggest success ran riot about town, and was now incarcerated in the asylum. His other success consumed babies. Clearly West's career choice needed to be reconsidered.

## WHAT'S THAT SMELL?

After a long and much needed vacation away from West's House of the Dead, the assistant returned to find an exuberant West. And, what a surprise, a dead body.

A weary traveler paused at the farmhouse to ask directions (sound familiar?), and just *happened* to keel over from heart trouble. Such a lucky break for West, who injected him full his brand-new *special* embalming fluid, one guaranteed not to interfere with later reanimation attempts. It simply kept the bodies fresh, just how West liked them.

But when West revivified the corpse, the assistant recoiled in horror as the victim screamed, "Help! Keep off, you cursed little tow-head fiend—keep that damned needle away from me!" It seems West had decided to help the traveler "pass along." Some people might brand this as murder, but it was in the name of science and the creation of zombies. And really, travelers in or around Arkham should know better than to stop at a random house.

## THE GREAT WAR—AN OPPORTUNITY FOR WEST

Clearly, the macabre Dr. West is beyond hope. He's never going to get over his obsession with the dead. And the whole killing people thing, well, it even put off his friend—and close friends are important when it comes to the Mythos.

Terrified and disgusted with his mad mentor, West's assistant nearly walked away from the undead business entirely. *Almost.* Then West went off to war. The assistant's morbid curiosity got the best of him, and he followed West (see *More Experiments in Providence* in the *Providence* chapter to discover why you should always be there for your best friend—especially if he is a self-obsessed, insane scientist).

The gruesome front lines of war provided near-unlimited opportunities to procure dead bodies. And West cleared a bit of time in his busy schedule to train Major Sir Eric Moreland Clapham-Lee, D.S.O, in his reanimation techniques. But Clapham-Lee suffered a ghastly accident, nearly severing his head clean off.

Highly intelligent in his former life, freshly dead, and nearly decapitated, Clapham-Lee was West's ideal subject. And that's what friends are for: horrific experiments. Besides, if the experiment went sour, what threat was a disembodied head?

Always a man of detail, West placed the Major's head in a vat and the body on the table, then West injected the corpse with his reanimation serum. The body twitched to life.

Then the head in the vat started screaming. Honestly, it seems that West just couldn't get a break to save his life ... or to reanimate someone else's.

West and his assistant didn't stick around to find out what happened next, as shells whistled from the sky, destroying the building as they fled. The two men escaped unharmed, and assumed Clapham-Lee had been reduced to bloody pieces. Really. That's what they thought. Even though they'd been wrong every time before, they still convinced themselves that nothing bad would come of this.

## Undead Revenge!

So not only is West beyond hope, but his twisted assistant is clearly beyond reason. After the war, the two returned to Bolton, living happily ever after, reanimating corpses here and there. Until the ungrateful and perturbed Clapham-Lee "unexpectedly" returned, insistent on spoiling the party.

To everyone's surprise, the undead major managed to escape the shelled building (albeit without his head). Then he assembled his own reanimated army. His Undead Tactical Strike Force descended upon West's farmhouse, disemboweling *and* decapitating the crazy doctor (the Major wasn't going to make the same mistake West continually made; he left no room for error). Then, without notice, the strike force disappeared into the night, leaving behind West's dead and mutilated body. This put West's friend and assistant in a bit of a pickle. Everyone knew the assistant disliked West, and when authorities arrived, West was very much dead and the frumpy assistant was alive. So with Herbert West's gruesome end at the hand of his reanimated friend, and his assistant's uncertain future in the eyes of the police, things worked out pretty well when it comes to the Cthulhu Mythos. The world didn't come to an end, and there were no cults hunting anyone down. All in all, the "bad guys" got their just rewards, and only a few reanimated dead remained on the prowl.

## It's Time For the Great Race

I know what you're thinking—up to this point, Arkham sounds like any other boring New England town. Just in case you're not impressed with everything else you've heard, how about tales of time-traveling, mind-stealing, cone shaped aliens.

### It's a Matter of Political Economy

One of H.P. Lovecraft's extraordinary tales was about an ancient alien race that occupied human minds. It is in the story, "The Shadow Out of Time," where we find Nathaniel Wingate Peaslee, professor of political economics. In 1908, he collapsed during class. While this was common for the students in political economy, it caused concern when the professors did it mid-lecture.

Peaslee recovered, but his personality and demeanor changed entirely (again, *never* a good sign). Apparently, the change wasn't for the better—his wife, and most of his children, ceased contact with him. Undeterred, Peaslee quit his comfy university job, traveling about, exploring and learning.

After some time, a startled Peaslee awoke, back to his old self, in the year 1913, with no memory of his exploits for the past five years. Or so he claimed.

---

### WHAT TO DO WHEN FAMILY/FRIENDS EXHIBIT CHANGES IN PERSONALITY OR DEMEANOR

It cannot be stressed enough that changes in personality/demeanor should never be ignored. They can be signs related to the Cthulhu Mythos, and are often related to (or mistaken for):

1. Possession

2. A curse

3. Possession due to a curse

4. Cult influence

5. Influence from a strange, magical artifact

6. Abundant alcohol consumption

7. The release of a new MMORPG

8. An indication that a murder plot is underway

9. Revivication (also known as "zombie-ism")

10. Mid-life crises

If you believe your friend or family member is suffering from a change in personality or demeanor, get him to Arkham Sanitarium *immediately*. The sanitarium offers a team of specialists, trained specifically in personality/demeanor issues. They are standing by to treat your possessed, cursed, cult-influenced, artifact-addled friend or family member. Although they'll just send him home if he's drunk.

---

## WHAT TO DO IF YOU THINK
## YOU HAVE AMNESIA

Just wake up from yet another three-hour blackout? Not sure how you got to the corner of 54th Street and 3rd Avenue? Unless there's a bottle of whiskey in your hand, it could be that be that your missing memories are Mythos related. Ask the following questions to help identify what type of Mythos-related amnesia you have:

1. How long did the blackout last? Is it more than a few years? If so, you've likely been inhabited by a member of the Great Race.

2. Do your friends and family hate you? This is another indication you were a victim of Yith inhabitation.

3. If the blackout was less than a few years, what was your condition when you snapped out of it? Were you wearing different clothes? In an unfamiliar location? If so, you may be the victim of a mind-swapping spell.

4. Think back to what you were doing prior to amnesia. If you found a strange artifact, it may have caused memory loss.

5. Were you reading a strange tome, such as the *Necronomicon?* If so, consider yourself lucky that you escaped with nothing but a case of amnesia.

6. Do you recall being hit on the head? If so, you're likely suffering from plain old amnesia.

7. When you came to, was Herbert West standing over you with a syringe? If so, it's likely you received a mild sedative. You're lucky to be alive.

8. In fact, do you know Herbert West at all? If so, he's probably *attempted* to drug you several times. Again, lucky to be alive.

CONTINUED . . .

## WHAT TO DO IF YOU THINK YOU HAVE AMNESIA (CONTINUED)

9. Do you vaguely recall seeing a strange, tentacled creature, prior to your amnesia bout? If so, your amnesia is likely *insanity*-induced. Roll with it.

10. Did you find yourself standing in the center of a mass of people clad in black robes, brandishing sacrificial knives, and chanting? Relax, you don't have amnesia. You've been drugged, and are about to become the victim of a sacrifice. Sit back, and enjoy the show. Things could be worse.

### STRANGE DREAMS

Eventually, a gaggle of experts attributed Peaslee's blackout to amnesia. Over time, Peaslee resumed his normal life (although without his wife, children, and job). But dreams and nightmares continued to plague him. He mostly dreamed of a vast, alien city. Researching amnesia cases similar to his own, Peaslee discovered a common memory amongst amnesia victims—remembrances of the Great Race of Yith.

This question might have suddenly popped in your head: What is the Great Race? If not, then go over the previous checklist on demeanor/behavior changes. And for those who are wondering, the Great Race ventured to Earth from beyond the stars in ancient times. They possessed advanced technologies and abilities—and could switch consciousness with another creature, at will. Pretty snazzy when you think about it.

It turns out the Great Race, or as they are also called, Yith, enjoy taking over human minds. When hosting a "mind party" for a Yith, victims usually find themselves in the large, cone-shaped bodies of their alien kidnappers, inside the vast city of the Great Race. These mind-trapped victims are free to wander about, exploring the ancient city and its immense libraries. But as they don't have the ability to comprehend anything, it turns out to be a great waste of time. Still, humans who have been taken over by a Yith often share these common visions of a great, alien city, just like the dream Peaslee had.

Believing there was more to all of this than a simple case of amnesia, Peaslee published accounts of his dreams in a psychological journal to help other amnesiacs. Surely, these common hallucinations, experienced by so many amnesia victims stemmed from some sort of weird medical phenomenon. It seemed perfectly reasonable to Peaslee—until a mining engineer in Western Australia recognized some of the ancient ruins and markings described in Peaslee's article.

## ANCIENT EXCAVATIONS

With such spectacular news, and no friends to keep him home, Peaslee quickly arranged an expedition, to Western Australia. There he discovered the decayed city of his dreams. He concluded, the mass "hallucinations" of so many amnesiacs stemmed from physical memories. And the more he saw of the location, the more he remembered.

Memories of the great city flooded into Peaslee's consciousness as he ventured into the ancient ruins. Unfortunately, his recollection returned as slowly as his common sense. One night, during a bout of insomnia, he decided to trek through the ancient ruins, by himself, in the dark—with no remembrance of the giant flying polyps that also dwelled underneath the city. These polyps had been driven underground when the Yith arrived on Earth, and fought repeatedly with the Yith. Eventually the polyps won the fight, though they opted to return to their subterranean homes. The entrances to the polyps' caverns below were now long abandoned and unguarded. As Peaslee tramped about, kicking up rocks and dust, he heard a shrill, inhuman whistle sounding from the depths. Smartly, he ran, and escaped the city before becoming a flying polyp's midnight snack.

Peaslee devoted his future efforts to ending excavations in the ancient city of the Great Race of Yith. Here he had little success. Yet, things could have been worse. Other than the occasional piercing scream in the middle of the night, or the odd missing scientist, nothing world-ending came of the ancient city expeditions. Again, in the grand scheme of the Cthulhu Mythos, this is getting off easy.

## THE GREAT RACE OF THE YITH

The Great Race, or Yith (if you find that eaiser to say) hail from a distant planet known as Yith—not very creative for supra-geniuses. Since the Great Race of Yith have mastered time travel, they can be wherever they want, whenever they want (which is strange, since they are always notoriously late for parties).

But the Great Race's neatest trick is popping into another creature's head. Plus, they can go forward or backward in time when they do so. Entire race dying out? Not a problem for the Great Race. They simply project their consciousness backward in time and inhabit new bodies. Oh, and don't let the whole "Great Race" thing confuse you. What the Yith really meant to say was "Great Species." The term "race" is typically an artificial sub-classification within a species. To make things clear here, just think of them as aliens—which they are, even if they're a bit off with their terminology.

Anyway, the Yith traveled through space and time by hurtling their minds at Earth. They ended up in Earth's ancient history, inhabiting ten-foot tall, cone-shaped creatures native to the planet at the time. And life wasn't easy, because there was a whole race (species) of flying polyps out to kill them here on Earth. Yes, deadly flying polyps. But when you're the masters of time (not quite Time Lords, that's another work of fiction) then getting away from vicious polyps isn't typically a problem.

In the meantime, the Yith like to skip around time, jumping in and out of human minds. Typically, the victim of the mind swap ends up in the Yith's body (compared to the Great Race, Asenath Waite's brain-trading abilities described in Wife Swap are a parlor trick).

These enormous creatures delight in amassing knowledge. So while renting space in someone else's brain, they

CONTINUED . . .

## THE GREAT RACE OF THE YITH (CONTINUED)

devote themselves to learning all about the current culture and history. With this knowledge they expand their amazing, ever-growing library. And in case you're wondering, it is a printed text library. They're not fond of eBooks.

When a Yith is done with its human host, it zips back to its original body, wiping clean the mind of the victim. When all is said and done, it feels like nothing ever happened—on the human side.

Well . . . almost nothing, if you don't count the five years you can't remember, your family left because you went crazy, and your friends all hate you. What seems like a flaw to a human mind is simply a trivialty to a Yith. They don't buy into the "need a close friend" rule. As a human, you should. Close friends come in handy during a pinch. So make sure you have quite a few—just in case a Yith decides to send a few running.

### MISKATONIC EXPEDITIONS

In addition to its library archive, Miskatonic's notoriety stems from its famous expeditions. Miskatonic often funded extended trips to collect specimens, acquire ancient artifacts, and test advanced gadgets in the field.

Most expeditions went down the same way—a group of scientists and professors headed to a remote location to investigate something seemingly mundane such as rock samples. They stumbled across a great and horrible discovery beyond human comprehension. One or more scientists and/or professors either went insane, were horrifically murdered, or both. Miskatonic's most notorious mess-up, "The Pabodie Expedition," spanned the entirety of these problems.

### THE PABODIE EXPEDITION

Not one to keep in a solitary setting, H.P. Lovecraft penned a novella about the Antarctic titled "At the Mountains of Madness."

## WHAT TO DO IF YOU'RE BEING INHABITED BY AN YITH

So, you've noticed large, missing blocks of time, and mysterious memories of an ancient city. You have a strange feeling, like an itch in the back of your head, as if someone else took up residence there, the night before.

If you think a member of the Great Race inhabits you intermittently, try the following:

1. Handcuff or tie yourself to immobile furniture.

2. Lock yourself in the attic, or a closet, and throw away the key.

3. Act crazy and get yourself thrown into a sanitarium.

4. Go live in a remote, isolated location so the Yith has nothing to do, and no reason to return to your body.

5. Take muscle relaxants or other medications that will make your rubbery body useless to the Yith.

6. Dress up as a clown—that will make it tough for the Yith to explain.

7. Cause a ruckus while you're in the Yith city, and get yourself branded a troublemaker.

8. Enlist in the military.

9. Eat a high-fat, high-cholesterol diet, and don't exercise. This will make it harder for the Yith to get around. Even if you don't prevent inhabitation, at least you'll enjoy yourself.

10. Leave notes around your apartment for the Yith, politely asking it to leave (or, at the least, clean up after itself)

While it did involve an expedition from Miskatonic University, the locus of the tale takes place at the bottom of the world. The novella has the flavor of a few later films, the most recognized being John Carpenter's version of *The Thing*. Even though the film was based on John Campbell's famous tale "Who Goes There?," Carpenter's revisitation brings some of Lovecraft's imaginings into the mix.

It was 1930 when Professor Frank H. Pabodie led an investigation to Antarctica, presumably to collect some rocks and try out his new-fangled lightweight drill.

Pabodie's team arrived at the campsite and set about their rock-collecting, new-fangled drilling activity. Nearby, an enormous mountain range loomed—larger than anything the expeditionary force had set eyes upon, even the Himalayas. And everyone knows ridiculously large mountain ranges simply beg for expedition members to crawl over and find out what's on the other side (here's a hint: more ice, water, and rocks).

Caving to temptation, a small expeditionary party headed

## MYTHOS SURVIVAL TIP: YOU DON'T NEED TO KNOW!

The common misconception, when it comes to Mythos knowledge, is the more you know, the better. Of course, you must absorb every fact in *this* book. But in general, curiosity should not to be satisfied when it comes to the Cthulhu Mythos.

Don't peer inside the antique, leather-bound tome. Resist temptation, and refrain from staring into the strange, glowing globe on the pedestal. Most importantly, don't venture out to discover the terrors awaiting you beyond the giant, Antarctic mountain range.

If you ever have a nagging doubt about picking up a strange, shiny object, or embarking upon an expedition, trust your instincts. Stay behind and grill up the hot dogs for the rest of the expeditionary team. The ones who return, that is.

out and explored the enormous mountain range. Of course they couldn't report back to the main camp and admit they found more ice, water, and rocks. Instead, they excitedly informed the remainder of the group about an enormous, ancient city, nestled upon the other side of the mountains.

The rest of the group remained dubious about the ancient city. But accounts of the large, fossilized remains of ancient creatures, dragged back to the mountain explorers' temporary camp, were harder to dismiss. Even more exciting (and unfortunate) for the explorers, the remains resembled creatures described in the *Necronomicon*—large, barrel-shaped beings known as the Elder Things.

## DISAPPEARANCES AND DEAD PEOPLE

It wasn't long before the main group lost contact with the expeditionary party. Again, if you've seen the movie *The Thing*, where strange, tentacled creatures just *dripping* with Cthulhu Mythos goodness are discovered in the ice and innocuously left to thaw, you can probably guess how this ends.

Heading over to investigate, the main team, including geologist William Dyer, found the expeditionary group—most of the pieces, anyway. The team—both men and dogs—were slaughtered. One team member, Gedney, as well as one of the dogs, was missing. So were several Elder Thing fossils—the ones that were not partially dissected.

Dyer and a graduate student, Danforth hopped in a plane and headed over those enormous, mystifying mountains. And discovered the expeditionary team's fictional ancient city was real.

### MYTHOS SURVIVAL TIP:
### STAY FROSTY

Don't thaw Mythos creatures. If it's cold, keep it cold. Don't warm up strange, alien corpses to room temperature. Don't try to cut into them. Terrible things occur when you thaw supposedly dead beasts from another planet.

## INSIDE THE ANCIENT RUINS

Inside the city, giant sculptures conveniently illustrated the entire story of the Elder Things. Many millions of years ago, the creatures inhabited the city. They created biological creatures to do their bidding called shoggoths.

The shoggoths didn't take well to the "do your bidding" way of life. So they staged a revolt. It didn't go well. The Elder Things subdued them again . . . or so the Elder Things thought.

Dyer and Danforth advanced deeper into the city. They discovered one of the campsite sleds, as well as the headless remains of the Elder Things from camp. And now it all made sense. Well, except for the headless part.

The aliens awakened in the humans' camp, only to find they were being dissected. Naturally, this got on their nerves, so they killed everyone. Then the freshly-awakened creatures headed home to decompress, and get a little R&R.

But before they could sit down, relax, and kick up their Elder Thing feet (or whatever those things were), something attacked the aliens, severing their heads. Just what attacked the Elder Things, Dyer and Danforth couldn't tell. But the shoggoth sloshing around the corner, heading straight toward them, seemed like a good bet.

The two men tore out of the city (of the choices available to you when encountering a shoggoth, running is *always* best. Although poking it with a stick would have been more entertaining). And although they escaped without physical harm, Danforth mistakenly looked back as they fled. And *something* he spotted, something worse than his slaughtered friends in camp, the Elder Thing aliens, or the burbling shoggoth, drove poor Dyer to the point of complete insanity.

As for Danforth, well, he devoted his energies to thwarting future Antarctic expeditions, trying to convince folks that they really should try someplace warmer and quieter instead. Maybe Florida . . . or Tahiti?

## WHAT TO DO IF YOU'RE INVITED ON AN EXPEDITION

There's an easy answer: *don't go.* But, since you are likely to go anyway, lured by exciting tales of treasure or tomes, ask the following questions:

1. What is the expedition looking for? If anything involves the word *curse* or *doom* maybe you should sit this one out.

2. Is the expedition funded by Miskatonic University? If so, then pass on it.

3. Will any Miskatonic University professors be joining you? (Not a good sign.)

4. Will you be going to a remote place, such as Antarctica, with little means of communication or rescue? (Think about it. Regardless of who sponsored the expedition and who's going, does it sound like a good idea?)

5. Are there any ancient cities, or tombs involved?

6. What is the SBP (Slaughter Breakover Point)? In other words, what is the living-to-dead ratio for the expedition, at which point team leaders will consider the mission a failure, and will return home?

7. If an ancient alien corpse is discovered frozen in the ice, will the expedition be thawing it? If so, why? (Feel free to provide them with a copy of the film *The Thing* at this point.)

8. Will the expedition be exploring newly discovered caverns or ancient cities? (Unless they are known to have been occupied by humans, nothing good will come of the expedition.)

9. Has anyone in the expedition team ever suffered amnesia?

10. Did the idea of the expedition come from a passage in the *Necronomicon*?

## What to Do When You Encounter a Shoggoth

Shoggoths are great, gurgling masses that appear throughout Lovecraft's fiction. Initially created by the Elder Things as servants, they pop up in different times and places, causing trouble. The creatures are large, amorphous masses—like a bubbly, oily black trash heap with eyes. It is well documented that they are not very communicative, nor friendly. Here are several tips, should you encounter one:

1. Try talking to the massive, amorphous blob. This won't do any good, but it will give you a sense of accomplishment before you die.

2. Run.

3. If you have a friend with you, trip him, then run.

4. This one's a bit tricky—shoggoths have eyes anywhere they want. But you could try saying, "Hey, what's that over there?" This may or may not distract them. Most likely not. But there's that whole sense of accomplishment thing.

5. Try speaking to them in the language of the Elder Things. This will promptly get you killed, as shoggoths loathe their enslavers, and will obviously mistake you for one of them. But you won't have all that anxiety of wondering if you can outrun them. And, that's an accomplishment in itself.

6. Poke it with a stick. This is absolutely pointless, and extremely dangerous. Before doing so, make sure you have a friend there to witness it. At least he'll be able to recount the tale of your spectacular stupidity and futile efforts.

7. Ask your friend to poke it with a stick. This will distract the shoggoth long enough for you to flee, and will give you a tale of spectacular stupidity about how your friend actually followed your instructions. It's important to always have friends you can rely upon.

CONTINUED . . .

## WHAT TO DO WHEN YOU ENCOUNTER A SHOGGOTH (CONTINUED)

8. Don't move. Ever.

9. Sing it a song—shoggoths are not known for their fondness of music. But you never know. It might lull the creature to sleep.

10. Try stomping on it. Just a single, slimy corner. It may distract it. More likely it will anger the creature, and it will kill you instantly. But you never really had any true chance to escape. So just go with the moment.

# Dunwich

One dreads to trust the tenebrous tunnel of the bridge, yet there is no way to avoid it. Once across, it is hard to prevent the impression of a faint, malign odour about the village street, as of the massed mould and decay of centuries. It is always a relief to get clear of the place, and to follow the narrow road around the base of the hills and across the level country beyond till it rejoins the Aylesbury pike. Afterwards one sometimes learns that one has been through Dunwich.

—H.P. Lovecraft, "The Dunwich Horror"

In comparison to Arkham, the rustic town of Dunwich is underdeveloped and downtrodden, fraught with hard times and economic woes. The lonely landscape is overrun with wildlife, and the human population is sparse. Buildings are run down, few, and far between.

The small score of inhabitants are unintelligent, superstitious folk, and the population dwindled further after the *The Dunwich Horror* arrived for a visit.

## THE DUNWICH HORROR

In "The Dunwich Horror," H.P. Lovecraft describes the exact type of small town no one ever wants to visit. Dunwich, which is a neighbor of Arkham, makes the backwaters in the film *Deliverance* look like a thriving, intellectual college town. While occasionally the random traveler finds his way to Dunwich, everyone else tries to avoid it. The town is known for its insane wizards, and strange breeding of Cthulhu Mythos deities and humans. And most of this Dunwich's fame is centered around a person named Wilbur Whateley.

### ABOUT WILBUR

It all began with a very ugly child, Wilbur Whateley, who was born to the albino Lavinia Whateley in 1913. The family resided in the house of Lavinia's father, Old Whateley—a man clearly off his rocker. Wilbur was described as a chinless and goat-faced child who aged at a disturbingly fast rate—by the age of three, he resembled a ten-year old (albeit a goat-faced ten-year-old). At four and a half, with his smattering of facial hair and cracking voice, he easily looked like a teenager. In addition to his freaky fast aging, there was something *wrong* about Wilbur. The townsfolk weren't fond of him. Nor were the dogs around town.

In fact, the dogs pestered him so much that he carried a gun for protection. He ended up shooting a dog or two (fear not, dog lovers . . . the canines get the last laugh . . . or bark in this tale).

### THE WHATELEYS GET WEIRDER

Old Whateley swelled with pride for his peculiar grandson. Running about town, the old man rambled on about how wonderful Wilbur's father was. Sometimes he let slip a few words here or there about something called *Yog-Sothoth*. The Whateleys were known to be odd, so Old Whateley's idiosyncrasies weren't much of a surprise.

For some reason, one day the Whateleys decided to remodel their house. They added doors on the second floor. Ramps leading to the new doors (clearly not adhereing to local codes). And, when the old man started buying scores of extra cattle (though the size of his herd never grew), people in town *really* started to talk.

Old Whateley died when Wilbur reached his teenage years (his actual teenage years, not age four-and-a-half). As the old man expelled his final breath, Old Whateley mumbled to Wilbur about opening the gates to Yog-Sothoth, and procuring a copy of the *Necronomicon* for some strange ceremony.

Lavinia disappeared a couple years after Old Whateley's death. Suddenly, Wilbur was on his own.

## MYTHOS SURVIVAL TIP: SAY WHAT?

Throughout Mythos tales, you will hear of weird folks muttering strange words you've never heard before: Yog-Sothoth. Azathoth. Cthulhu.

Here's a guideline to follow: if you can't figure out how to spell it, it's not good for you (which is why I never learned how to spell *grean beens*). And, anyone chanting a litany of barely-pronouncable, un-spellable names is not to be trusted.

If you've just heard someone spew out a bunch of spooky-sounding names, and you're not sure whether to run, consult the *Cthulhu Quick Reference* chapter in this book. If you find any of the names in the quick reference, run away, as fast as you can. If you don't find them in this book, run anyway.

## CALL THE LOCKSMITH

Sometimes referred to as "the key and the guardian of the gate," Yog-Sothoth is an *Other God* (also commonly referred to as *Outer God*, although this was not Lovecraft's term). The Other Gods are monstrous and unfathomable Cthulhu Mythos deities. Most of the Other Gods wish to ignore humanity entirely, but when backwoods families and crazy cults set about summoning them, sometimes it's not an option.

Yog-Sothoth, in its vastness, transcends time, and is believed to be the guardian between this universe, and that of the Other Gods. This prevents pesky deities from descending into our world and causing further chaos, and it keeps us out of their homes—mostly. So, technically Yog-Sothoth has kept humanity safe from the rest of the Other Gods . . . so far. Thanks a bunch, Yog-Sothoth.

## DOG SNACK

Like most irrational people, Wilbur devoted his efforts to procuring a copy of the *Necronomicon*. He attempted to convince Dr. Henry Armitage, head librarian at Miskatonic, to loan out the university copy. Just for a little while, of course. When this idea didn't go over with Armitage, who knows how dangerous the tome was, Wilbur tried another approach: whining. Well, to be fair, Wilbur added in some cajoling and bribing the staff of various libraries and universities housing the *Necronomicon* (yes, there are a few others). Finally, like all people who really are in need of a book, Wilbur resorted to breaking into the Miskatonic University rare archives collection. But, apparently he hadn't received the memo about the guard dog.

The shredded remains of Wilbur Whateley were found upon the library floor, the morning after Wilbur's break-in attempt (this is what he gets for disliking dogs—word clearly got around). But the gruesome discovery wasn't the terrifying part—it was the body of Whateley itself. Instead of blood, he leaked a disgusting, stinky greenish-yellow ichor across the rug. Fur peeked from underneath his clothes, along with disgusting tentacles with sucking mouths.

Clearly, Wilbur was a terrible monster, intent upon wreaking havoc upon Dunwich with arcane spells from the *Necronomicon*. With the fiend dead and his plans thwarted, the town must be safe.

Not quite.

## THE HORROR IN DUNWICH

Around Dunwich, a great, horrific beast began terrorizing the countryside. And it seemed to have an appetite for cattle. Naturally, the townsfolk locked up the cattle. This forced the beast to upgrade its diet to people. The townsfolk realized a few gobbled-up cattle, in comparison, weren't so bad.

Meanwhile, Dr. Armitage had been conducting some research on his own, having received a cryptic copy of Wilbur Whateley's diary for translation. His studies, along with translation of the journal, led to disturbing findings about the Whateley family. So the professor, with two of his colleagues, traveled to Dunwich to verify his findings—and hopefully save the small town.

During his tenure as head librarian at Miskatonic University, the professor amassed a wealth of arcane knowledge and magic. And with the help of his companions, he conjured a powerful spell, dispatching the rampaging monster as the townspeople gazed on in horror and wonder.

Afterward, Armitage explained what he had learned—the beast was Wilbur's twin brother (yes, Wilbur had the good looks in the family—who'd have guessed). The twins were both sons of the great deity Yog-Sothoth. So poor Wilbur was simply trying to make a very long distance call, and contact his long-lost father. Sure, Wilbur's father would likely destroy the world, and then invite all of his deity brothers to come through the gate, and party. Still, it's touching tale.

## WHERE TO STAY IN DUNWICH

Nowhere. Why would you want to visit Dunwich? Move on to Kingsport or Innsmouth. You'll love the tourist attractions in these towns.

### HORROR AND WONDER IN H.P. LOVECRAFT'S UNIVERSE

Like most writers, Lovecraft had a literary agenda. He wasn't simply writing tales of uncanny and unimaginable horror for the pure entertainment of readers—although some level of entertainment was probably hoped for. However, one of his main objectives was to raise "horror" to the sublime, or, put another way, create "sublime horror."

Today the concept of the sublime is mostly lost on us, but dating back to the Romantic Period of literature, many writers have attempted to produce the sensation of the sublime in a reader. Now you might be wondering: Just what is this "sublime?" Well, like so many things in Lovecraft's writing, it can't be described—at least accurately. The sublime is more of an experience, a moment when a person sees or understands something so far beyond the human condition that it fills him or her with wonder and amazement—pure awe. And in Lovecraft's case, it brought pure horror with it as well.

So in the end, H.P. Lovecraft wasn't trying to skip the descriptions of the monstrous creatures and events in his writing; rather, he was working to get the reader to experience a sublime horror by letting the reader's imagination fill in the blanks. After all, we always imagine something far worse than what is before us. And like the Romantic writers, Lovecraft let the power of the human imagination do its work whenever he could.

DUNWICH

## What to Do If You Meet a Whateley

1. Is he attractive? Or is he the ugly one? (This is a loaded question because you can't trust either; in the end, there is no hope for a solid, long term relationship, so the best thing to do is run).

2. If a Whateley asks you for a copy of the *Necronomicon*, tell them you've never heard of the book. (Obviously you have heard of it by now, but lie. No matter how much they flatter you or even bribe you, a Whateley with this book pretty much means the end of everything—in which case, not even running will help.)

3. Don't go to dinner with a Whateley. (There's no telling what you'll be eating, or if you are on the menu.)

4. Avoid Old Man Whateley at all costs. That goes for his daughter, Lavinia, too.

5. To some, Lavinia Whateley has her charms, but overall one should avoid dating her. Like most Whateleys, she has a plan. (And she spends far too much time talking about her children).

6. Hide your cattle.

7. Introduce your unwitting best friend to the Whateleys, and then while he or she is busy, skip town. (Make sure to find a new friend after this. As you know, they are indispensable in the Cthulhu Mythos.)

8. Try poking the Whateley with a stick. (This accomplishes nothing, except maybe a brief moment of confusion, but given everything you know the Whateleys are up to, it somehow seems rewarding.)

9. Ask, "did you say, Yog-Sothoth, or Yog-Shoggoth?" (This mix-up is more common than you probably realize, and it is quite embarrassing when pointed out.

CONTINUED . . .

## WHAT TO DO IF YOU
## MEET A WHATELEY (CONTINUED)

Considering that the Whateleys are not very bright, it's bound to keep one of them confused for hours. Once the Whateley is properly befuddled, take your leave promptly.)

10. Whistle for a dog. (Remember, the canine network knows about the Whateleys, but the Whateleys don't know about them.)

# Kingsport

*Then beyond the hill's crest I saw Kingsport outspread frostily in the gloaming; snowy Kingsport with its ancient vanes and steeples, ridgepoles and chimney-pots, wharves and small bridges, willow-trees and graveyards; endless labyrinths of steep, narrow, crooked streets, and dizzy church-crowned central peak that time durst not touch; ceaseless mazes of colonial houses piled and scattered at all angles and levels like a child's disordered blocks; antiquity hovering on grey wings over winter-whitened gables and gambrel roofs; fanlights and small-paned windows one by one gleaming out in the cold dusk to join Orion and the archaic stars. And against the rotting wharves the sea pounded; the secretive, immemorial sea out of which the people had come in the elder time.*

—H.P. Lovecraft, "The Festival"

Southeast of Arkham, the town of Kingsport is nestled amongst craggy cliffs. Kingsport is a bustling seaport town dating back to the seventeenth century. It's known for its friendly inhabitants, great seafood, and as might be expected, unusual happenings.

## Where to Stay in Kingsport

Should you choose to visit Kingsport, the best rooms in town can be found at The Cottages at Water Street (ocean views cost extra).

And, should you wish to try your hand at a bit of knowledge-hunting, and don't mind the risk of possibly getting chopped up into little pieces, your best bet for finding excitement will come from wandering down Water Street and visiting The Terrible Old Man (pretending you're a lost traveler always works).

According to "The Terrible Old Man" penned by H. P. Lovecraft, the fellow sporting the same name as the title of the short story is steeped in trouble and mysterious events.

"The Terrible Old Man," the person, not the story, is legendary throughout Kingsport (something in the name gives it away). According to legend, he stashed a tremendous fortune inside his house—hidden somewhere. The rumor is naturally reinforced by his spending habits, which involve his paying for everything with Spanish gold (perhaps acquired during his alleged stint, back in the day, as a captain of East Indian clipper ships). And come on, if you're spending Spanish gold anywhere in the last one-hundred years, that's just plain suspicious. You know he's not getting the best value for his gold, not to mention the historical worth.

He's also well known for keeping strange, temple-like creations in his front yard to scare away the local children (not talking garden gnomes here). And then there's his freaky bottle collection, each bottle containing a piece of lead, somehow suspended inside. Some people claim they've witnessed the Terrible Old Man speaking to the bottles. And the lead trinkets inside the bottles vibrate, as if speaking back.

But The Terrible Old Man is probably best known for the robbers he allegedly murdered when they attempted to beat him out of his fortune.

## WHAT TO DO WHEN YOU DECIDE TO ROB THE TERRIBLE OLD MAN

Greed is a great motivator, and few can ignore the allure of a Spanish treasure. Should you decide to rob the Terrible Old Man of his hidden fortune, don't try the direct approach:

When a team of robbers—Angelo Ricci, Joe Czanek, and Manuel Silva—heard rumors of The Terrible Old Man's money, they decided he was easy pickings. So they set up an appointment to have a "talk" with him.

The plan was as follows: Ricci and Silva would visit the house and rough him up—just a little—while Czanek waited in the car for the fast getaway. Czanek insisted Ricci and Silva go easy on the old guy, after all, he was old and feeble. No need to add a murder rap to a simple robbery. Besides, the Terrible Old Man had a tough life, being an outcast due to his eccentricities (really, who *doesn't* talk to bottles with lead suspended in them . . . every once in awhile).

Not long after Ricci and Silva entered the house, horrific screaming echoed through the air, to Czanek's dismay. Clearly the two men decided not to follow the plan. Czanek became even more dismayed when the door flew open, and instead of Ricci and Silva, the Terrible Old Man emerged, flashing a wicked smile.

Later, townsfolk discovered Ricci and Silva on the beach—most of them, anyway. Their bodies were mauled and mangled. No one knows what actually happened, but if you're feeling brave, you could knock on The Terrible Old Man's front door and ask about it.

In the end, Ricci, Silva, and Czanek's plan turned out to be a bad idea. This is speculation, but speaking to The Terrible Old Man about his secret riches is probably a risky proposition. If you really need Spanish gold, perhaps finding an old Spanish galleon beneath the ocean is easier. Obviously, The Terrible Old Man has such an ominous name for a reason.

KINGSPORT

Due to his eccentricities (and probably the whole murder thing), the Terrible Old Man is mostly shunned in Kingsport. Few visitors drop by. Those who do get spooked by his long conversations with those glass bottles. But in addition to antique gold coins, the Terrible Old Man possesses a wealth of Mythos lore. Anyone brave enough to stick around for a chat (and not attempt to steal his loot) will be rewarded with invaluable nuggets of Cthulhu Mythos knowledge.

## Season's Greetings

If you're in town around the Christmas holiday, you don't want to check out Kingsport's yearly Yule Festival. According to Lovecraft's story, "The Festival," many of the townspeople don cloaks around eleven in the evening, spilling into the streets. The crowd heads up to the white church in the center of town, where they proceed inside and play lovely flute music. Sounds nice enough . . ..

Then again, maybe not. At least if we are to believe the patient who awakened in Kingsport hospital, screaming about the Yule Festival rituals.

### Flutes and the Cthulhu Mythos

In general, the whistling of flutes in relation to anything in the Cthulhu Mythos is bad. If you're in a forest, or a town, or lost in an ancient, underground cavern, the sound of flutes is the last thing you want to hear. While it is possible the sound is coming from an unwary, practicing flutist, most likely it is the call of a very vicious Mythos creature—or the warning of the sudden appearance of one. In any case, if you're in a location where things just don't seem right, and there's an uncanny, unexplainable feeling that has overcome you, and it is punctuated by the sound of flutes, run . . ..

Apparently, the pleasant-sounding flutes are actually used to summon loping, winged creatures that bear the riders further into deep caverns—leading them across a wide river, flowing underneath the church. Dark rituals are surely practiced there, but no one knows for certain—the patient didn't hang around long enough to find out.

He had been guided to the festival by an older, creepy-looking relative, whose bland, lifeless face resembled a waxen mask (certainly it wasn't a cheap disguise). The elderly man tried everything in hopes of convincing the younger fellow to stay for the popular, annual ritual. Using a tablet and stylus (he wasn't much of a talker), the old fellow scrawled convincing arguments about the younger man's obligation to his family. Who knows, the old man might have made his point eventually. If he hadn't gotten jostled, causing his waxen mask to fall off his face, revealing the total absence of a human face, or any face for that matter.

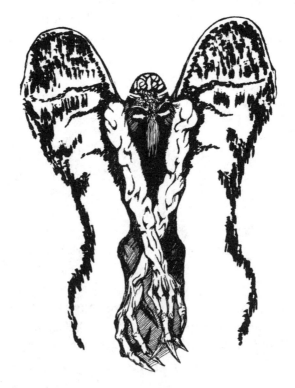

The younger man promptly jumped into the river. Later, he awakened in the Kingsport hospital. After being transferred to St. Mary's Hospital in Arkham, the attendants decided that reading a nice book would settle his addled nerves. So they loaned him a copy of the *Necronomicon*. (Alas, if only poor Wibur Whateley had simply gone to the hospital in Arkham for reading material, he'd be alive and destroying the world this very moment). In case you're wondering how the young man is doing, just flip back to the section on the *Necronomicon*. Nothing good ever comes from reading that book.

## THE STRANGE HIGH HOUSE IN THE MIST

In his writings about Kingsport, Lovecraft describes one of the town's most recognized sites in his story, "The Strange High House in the Mist." Oddly, this site is named: The Strange High House in the Mist. The legendary house is situated at the top of high cliffs to the north of Kingsport. It is rumored to contain a solitary resident. But the occupant is never seen about town . . . even for a quick trip to the grocery.

As the cliffs are nearly inaccessible, no one is quite sure how the house's inhabitant travels about. When the philosopher Thomas Olney moved to town, this puzzle taunted him, and he yearned to know more about the Strange High House in the Mist. Being a philosopher, Olney didn't see much adventure. As a result, he craved thrills and mystery—probably why he moved to Kingsport to begin with. So, with an itch that could only be scratched by exploring the cliffs, he set out for the house in the mist.

Olney used a circuitous, backward route that nearly led him to Arkham and back—he was a philosopher, not an adventurer. Eventually he managed to find a path into the cliffs. Unfortunately, the house was clearly designed by a dropout from Miskatonic University's short-lived and highly unsuccessful architecture program. The cottage's only door faced the sheer wall of the cliff. So it was a stroke of luck when an elderly, bearded fellow popped over to the window, pulling Olney inside.

Yes, everything in Kingsport has to do with a strange old man, in some way or another. There are a lot of strange, old men lurking about the city. Maybe it's something in the water.

Despite his hermit-like behavior, the house's sole inhabitant was actually quite friendly. Olney and his host were soon deep in conversation—speaking of Kingsport's ancient legends, discussing the city's long history, chatting about the warm weather streak Kingsport was having. Then, unexpectedly, a knock came at the unreachable door. This even spooked the elderly fellow (rightfully so, his door being inaccessible and all, not to mention the huge *No Solicitors* sign tacked outside).

Knowing nothing good would come of it, the old man refused to answer the door. In time, the unwelcome visitor seemingly left, and the two men merrily resumed their discussion.

But it wasn't long before *another* knock sounded. Sure, The Strange High House in the Mist may have been the hardest place to reach in the town's history. Perhaps in *any* town's history. But that didn't make it any less popular.

This time, the elderly inhabitant didn't blink. Striding to the door, he flung it open and in marched a tide of guests, right out of the misty sea—including Nodens and Neptune. And they were all ready to party.

Olney got caught up in the festivities—he didn't stumble back to town until morning. And Olney must have had a very good time, because as he wandered back to Kingsport proper, he didn't remember a single thing from the night before.

People say Olney wasn't the same after his trek up the craggy slope. He lost his sense of adventure, and became content with the mundane (umm, he was already a philosopher). Olney and his family moved out of town shortly thereafter, but during the brief remainder of his stay in Kingsport, he no longer stared up at the Strange House in the Mist with wistful imaginings. He didn't get lost in daydreams. In time, rumors swirled around Kingsport that Olney left his soul in that little cottage up in the mist. But those were probably rumors started by people with overactive imaginations.

## WHAT TO DO WHEN YOU HAVE AN EXTENDED STAY IN KINGSPORT

Sure, Olney's overnight visit at the house in the mist ended well, but Olney was lucky. What if he had gotten lost, or stuck on the cliff? Always remember to take the following on any hike to unreachable locations in Kingsport:

1. Water (always bring more than you think you need; you never know, the god of the ocean might drop by with an unquenchable thirst).

2. A bedroll or comfy sleeping bag.

3. Protein bars—enough to share with unexpected, but very determined visitors.

4. Rope (Climbing and descending cliffs usually require this).

5. A first aid kit.

6. Supportive hiking shoes.

7. Light sticks, flashlights, flares, pretty much anything that generates light.

8. A friend. Friends are very handy on extended journeys. You'll have someone to talk to, and someone who can locate help, in case of emergency. And you'll also have someone to offer up as sacrifice, if you run into nasty creatures or cultists.

9. A copy of Plato's *Republic* (this aids in sleeping, but also might help you regain your senses about visiting impossible locations).

10. A map (this way you don't walk to the neighboring town to find a path to the town in which you started).

# innsmouth

*It was a town of wide extent and dense construction, yet one with a portentous dearth of visible life. From the tangle of chimney-pots scarcely a wisp of smoke came, and the three tall steeples loomed stark and unpainted against the seaward horizon. One of them was crumbling down at the top, and in that and another there were only black gaping holes where clock-dials should have been. The vast huddle of sagging gambrel roofs and peaked gables conveyed with offensive clearness the idea of wormy decay, and as we approached along the now descending road I could see that many roofs had wholly caved in.*

—H.P. Lovecraft, "The Shadow Over Innsmouth"

Another seaside locale anchored in Mythos legends is the town of Innsmouth. Founded by Jebediah Marsh in 1643, Innsmouth rests on the mouth of the Manuxet River. The town thrived as a shipbuilding site and seaport prior to the Revolutionary War. Its success continued into the early nineteenth century, as factories sprung up, harnessing the great power of the Manuxet. But after the war of 1812, Innsmouth's prosperity waned. Eventually, the town fell into a state of decay. And by the early 1900s, little of Innsmouth's great industry remains, except for the Marsh Refinery, and the ever-abundant fishing industry.

To be quite honest, there is no need to visit Innsmouth. Avoid it if you can . . . the native population is far from friendly to outsiders. However, if you've recently noticed certain changes in your appearance, or your personality/demeanor, it may be time to visit the secluded seaside town (remember in the Cthulhu Mythos, *always* keep a sharp eye for changes in appearance and demeanor).

## TRAVELING TO INNSMOUTH

Little is known about Innsmouth—the residents live in seclusion, shunning the outside world. These days, there is minimal travel to the seaport. However, a daily bus route runs from Hammond's Drug Store in Newburyport, stopping in both Innsmouth and Arkham. Don't stare too hard at Joe Sargent, the bulging-eyed, greasy driver. Sure he looks unusual, well. at least for someone outside of Innsmouth, but gazing at him for too long won't bode well.

## WHERE TO STAY

"The Shadow Over Innsmouth" is one of Lovecraft's most popular tales. In the story, he describes the sleepy seaside town, and the woes of visiting it. Of course, if you're insistent, and find yourself venturing to Innsmouth, then be sure to stay at the Gilman house.

Sure, it's dingy, dirty, and shabby, but it is slightly better than sleeping on the street. At least, once you get past the dust, the permanent moldy smell, the cranky attendants, and the strange, creaking sounds in the middle of the night.

Also, security is light at the Gilman House (the door bolts keep disappearing). Make sure you bring a set of tools and padlocks for your door, ensuring a restful night of undisturbed sleep.

## WHERE TO DINE

Not much can be said for the local Innsmouth diner, which doesn't even serve a decent plate of fish and chips. However, you can rest assured that the First National Grocery chain has a store in Arkham, stocked with all manner of necessities that will get you through your visit. For a special treat, try their cheese crackers. For the most part, visiting Innsmouth means coming prepared.

## INVESTIGATIONS IN INNSMOUTH

There's not much to see in the decrepit, old town, except rickety factories and crumbling houses. The mystery of Innsmouth rests with the town's inhabitants. Just remember—you're best not staring at any of them for too long. Doing so is not only ill mannered, it might get you killed at the hands of an angry, suspicious mob. One might say, "What happens in Innsmouth stays in Innsmouth."

Over the years, the town's population has dwindled down to a mere 300-400 "people." And in general, all of the locals look alike. No, this isn't some sort of racist statement on my behalf (although some argue it was an idea Lovecraft had). Seriously, the folks in Innsmouth do look alike. It is termed the "Innsmouth look." And it's kind of hard to miss. We're talking about oddly bulging eyes, webbed feet and hands, and flabby lips. There's also some issues with scaly skin, but maybe that can be attributed to the salty air.

Although Innsmouth is a very closed-mouth town, rumors still stir about. And outside of Innsmouth, tales continually circulate about the town's residents, and how they came to acquire "The Innsmouth look." This has led several non-residents to conducting investigations. Robert Olmstead, antiquarian, traveled to the

Miskatonic Valley from his native Ohio, in order to learn more of his genealogy. When the trail led to Innsmouth, he ventured upon a fateful side trip. (Someone in his past must have changed his last name; or there was a grave mistake made in Innsmouth).

## THE SWAMPY MARSHES

With stern fish-eyed gazes of distrust, the residents of Innsmouth offered Olmstead little help. But the town drunkard, Zadok Allen, who decidedly lacked the signature "Innsmouth Look," was his usual chatty, helpful self. Not that Olmstead much minded the residents' "Innsmouth Look"—people always commented upon Olmstead's slightly enlarged eyes, too, so he didn't consider it a big deal.

But Olmstead wanted to glean more about the mysterious town. With a bit of whiskey for lubrication, tales freely flowed from Zadok's mouth.

## HOW TO TELL IF YOU'RE ACTUALLY FROM INNSMOUTH

1. People often tell you, "My, what big eyes you have."
2. Constant, insistent cravings for seafood platters (not necessarily to eat them, but to frolic in them).
3. You find a drink of salt water refreshing.
4. You spend more time in the water than out of it.
5. A visit to the beach is the most exciting part of your year.
6. When you speak, it always sounds like you have a frog caught in your throat.
7. Your last name is Marsh.
8. Your last name is Gilman
9. Your last name can somehow be related to fish or water (see 7 & 8 for reference).
10. They don't make glasses large enough for your eyes.

The elderly drunkard elaborated upon the history of Innsmouth's most famous family. Particularly, Captain Obed Marsh, descendent of town founder Jebediah Marsh. During his sea travels, Obed stumbled across a peculiar Polynesian island. It sported an unusually high abundance of fish. Regardless of the season, or the scarcity of fish in the area, the natives' fishing prospered. And the island's inhabitants strutted about wearing loads of gold trinkets—bracelets and amulets—the glint of gold promptly catching Obed Marsh's eye.

Sensing his interest, the local chief explained how these great fortunes could belong to Obed's as well. That's right, gold trinkets and abundant fish for everyone. And all Obed had to do was perform a few human sacrifices—a meager two times a year—to the frog-fish creatures, known as "Deep Ones," that dwelled in the depths of the sea.

Obed contented himself with trading instead. Much less messy than sacrifices. After returning home, Obed sold the islanders' strange, gold trinkets to the folks of Innsmouth—at a hefty profit. Business prospered, until one day when Obed returned to the island to find the natives had been mysteriously wiped out. But Innsmouth's demand for gaudy gold trinkets never abated. Forced to keep up with demand, Obed had few options. He stealthily rowed out to Devil's Reef twice a year, offering sacrifices to the greedy Deep Ones. And again, Innsmouth prospered. Fish practically leapt from the sea and onto the residents' plates—not that they cared to eat them. Eventually, Obed founded a new religion to worship the great sea deity, Dagon. Some might call it a "club" more than a cult, but either way, it was named "The Esoteric Order of Dagon."

## Something's Fishy

Residents eventually connected Obed's sea ventures with the periodic disappearances of young people around town. Decidedly angry, the townspeople tossed Obed and his cohorts into jail, to the great dismay of the local, watery Deep Ones. The frog-fish folk, fat and happy due to Innsmouth's supply of human sacrifices, decided to lend Obed a webbed hand.

## DAGON

There have been only a handful (webbed and otherwise) of people who have reported sightings of the sea-god, Dagon. Really, Dagon is the sort of omnipowerful critter you don't want to lay eyes on. One of the few known accounts is a suicide note found in the residence of a morphine-addicted soldier of the Great War, described in Lovecraft's story "Dagon."

In the soldier's note, he told of an unfortunate adventure at sea when his ship was overtaken by a German sea-raider, and he, along with others, was taken prisoner. He managed to escape on a small boat with some provisions, drifting aimlessly. But when he fell asleep for the night, he later awakened to find his boat beached, stuck in a sticky black mire.

The soldier traveled on foot, finally reaching a great canyon. On the opposite side, a huge monolith rose from the ground, covered with inscriptions and crude sculptures of humans—or half-humans—with those same, flabby lips, webbed feet, and bulging eyes as the inhabitants of Innsmouth. As the soldier watched, a gigantic creature—with enormous, scaled arms—wrapped itself around the monolith.

At this point, the soldier, naturally, went a bit crazy. Seeing Dagon, and many other Mythos creatures, has this affect on people. Singing and laughing, he traipsed back to his boat. Next thing he remembered, he awakened in San Francisco. Wow.

Forever tortured by his brief glimpse of Dagon, the soldier tried morphine to ease his anxiety. No luck. Instead, he thought he'd have better luck with suicide. This really comes down to how one defines "luck."

Whether he was lucky is difficult to say, since all news of the event was submerged beneath paperwork and cover-ups.

But the last tortured words of the suicide note offered the best indication as to what had happened—"God, that hand! The window! The window!"

Okay, maybe it wasn't the *best* indication, but it was better than nothing.

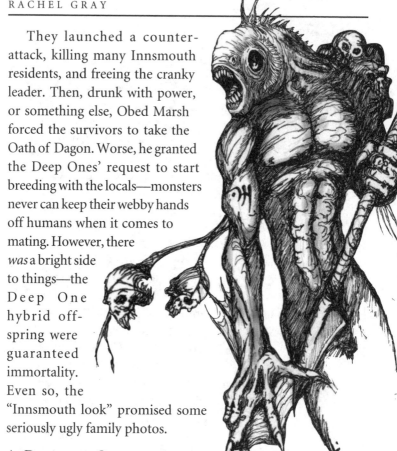

They launched a counter-attack, killing many Innsmouth residents, and freeing the cranky leader. Then, drunk with power, or something else, Obed Marsh forced the survivors to take the Oath of Dagon. Worse, he granted the Deep Ones' request to start breeding with the locals—monsters never can keep their webby hands off humans when it comes to mating. However, there *was* a bright side to things—the Deep One hybrid off-spring were guaranteed immortality. Even so, the "Innsmouth look" promised some seriously ugly family photos.

## A DUBIOUS OLMSTEAD

But all of that was in the past, a tipsy Zadok explained to Olmstead. Now the Marsh family ruled over the town. Barnabas Marsh—aka Old Man Marsh—oversaw the Marsh refinery. But his time above water was dwindling—his increasingly bulgy eyes (not to mention the horrid fishy smell) guaranteed Barnabas would soon take to the water. It was the fate of all hybrid Deep Ones.

Not being familiar with the Cthulhu Mythos, and being engaged in a conversation with a drunk, and not having a name in any way related to water or fish, Olmstead was skeptical. But when the bus to Arkham mysteriously broke down, forcing Olmstead to stay overnight at the Gilman House, he quickly had a change of heart.

In the middle of the night, a crowd converged upon the Gilman House. But before they could seize Olmstead, he escaped through a window. The terrified man fled his pursuers, and found his way out of town, but not before witnessing the backup search party—slimy, gray-green creatures with white bellies, croaking as they flopped their way toward town.

Olmstead's escape likely would have ended the matter—if Olmstead hadn't been so nosy. But Olmstead had originally trekked to the Miskatonic Valley to learn of his genealogy. So he couldn't let sleeping fish lie.

Inquiries at the Arkham Historical Society, and his continuing research back in Ohio, eventually unearthed the truth—there was a reason why everyone commented on his large, bulbous eyes. He was a descendant of the great Obed Marsh (I knew it, I was right about the name change).

Olmstead took it rather well. He decided being a Deep One hybrid wasn't so terrible—what with the immortality and all. So he set off for the great, underwater metropolis of Y'ha-nthlei, right next to Devil's Reef. Y'ha-nthlei was Deep One hybrid friendly. And, being underwater, the real estate prices were a steal.

## WHAT TO DO IF YOU'VE GOT THE INNSMOUTH LOOK

So, based on your new Mythos knowledge, you may suspect you're a Deep One hybrid. Perhaps you're not quite ready to take the plunge and move underwater. Or even move back to Innsmouth (although the place hasn't been the same since the government raid). So here are a few tips to hide your creepy "Innsmouth Look":

1. Try oversized glasses. If you don't need glasses, use plain lenses (this is optimal, since people will assume your larger eyes are due to lens magnification).

2. If you're looking a little green, try tanning spray.

3. Flabby lip problem? No worries—these days, people

CONTINUED . . .

## WHAT TO DO IF YOU'VE GOT THE INNSMOUTH LOOK (CONTINUED)

will just assume you've had Botox injections.

4. A good hairdo can hide almost any flaw in your appearance! Talk to your stylist about the best way to hide fish-like features.

5. Webbed hands and feet are harder to conceal. Keep poolside trips to a minimum. Wear gloves as much as you can, but only when it makes sense (for example, fluffy winter mittens at the beach, in the middle of summer, are not recommended).

6. Once again, friends always come in handy. Recruit ugly friends. If your friends are weirder-looking than you, no one will notice your frog-like face.

7. Be wary of snoopy people. If someone says, "Say, how do you pronounce, "Y'ha-nthlei," don't blurt it out. Instead, do what you *should* be doing right now—sound out the word and ask who the heck came up with that spelling (if you're expecting me to provide a pronunciation table for this word, re-read this paragraph; you're not going to catch me).

8. Don't hang around aquariums with your new hairdo and gloves, whispering to the fish that "you'll get them their freedom and revenge."

9. Many Deep Ones also worship Cthulhu. This means you need a good explanation if you're reading this book and you have the Innsmouth look.

10. Keep the bling to a minimum. Okay, if you're a hybrid or a Deep One, there is no shortage of gold trinkets for you. But wearing too much gold is bound to set off alarms.

INNSMOUTH

# Providence

*Old Providence! It was this place and the mysterious forces of its long, continuous history which had brought him into being, and which had drawn him back toward marvels and secrets whose boundaries no prophet might fix. Here lay the arcana, wondrous or dreadful as the case may be, for which all his years of travel and application had been preparing him.*

*—H.P. Lovecraft, "The Case of Charles Dexter Ward"*

## A History of Providence

When it comes to the Mythos, Lovecraft's hometown of Providence, Rhode Island, has a complicated history. "The Case of Charles Dexter Ward" offers details of Providence's infamous resident, Joseph Curwen.

In the early 1700s, Joseph Curwen settled in Providence. He quickly grew powerful in the shipping business, involving himself in numerous town activities and civic improvements. By the mid-1700s, everyone in town knew of Curwen. But not because of his great wealth and community service. Rather, people noticed strange, coffin-shaped boxes, appearing at Curwen's home. They chattered in town about the way he never appeared to age. He was obsessed with occult matters and rituals. And rumors swirled about stinky alchemical experiments performed in the lean-to on his Pawtuxet Village farm.

When Curwen realized he had an image problem, he decided to fix it—by permanently weaseling his way into the society's upper crust. He married eighteen-year-old Eliza Tillinghast, daughter of the well-known Captain Dutee Tillinghast. Much to the annoyance of her current fiancé, Ezra Weeden.

### The Investigative Team of Weeden and Smith

After being cast aside, the estranged fiancé, Ezra Weeden, swore vengeance upon the man who stole his bride. Weeden vowed to unearth the scandalous details behind the strange stories surrounding Curwen. With the help of Elezear Smith, Weeden sneaked about and spied upon Curwen at his residence in Olney Court, and at Curwen's farm in Pawtuxet.

Soon, Weeden's investigations bore results—the young man discovered a series of catacombs, snaking beneath the farm. One night, Weeden and Smith staked-out the farm, hearing screams, chants, and mumblings, rising up from the ground. Tortured wails also echoed from Curwen's lean-to laboratory. Clearly, Curwen was planning something most nefarious.

With an arsenal of detailed notes, Weeden approached the prominent residents of Providence with his findings. It didn't take much. Marrying Eliza hadn't altered Curwen's creepy status around town. The town elders decided to organize a raid on the Pawtuxet farm.

The raiding party consisted of three teams, converging silently and quickly upon the Pawtuxet farm. It conveniently worked out that Curwen was in the middle of a particularly nasty experiment when the teams arrived. Later, the raiders refused to speak of the events of that night and what they'd discovered. But rumors abound of inhuman creatures, seemingly made of flame, witnessed at the Pawtuxet farm.

Curwen died in the raid, and the matter was laid to rest along with his body. At least for one-hundred years or so.

## The Case of Charles Dexter Ward

When young antiquarian Charles Dexter Ward stumbled across town records, indicating the enigmatic Curwen was his great-great grandfather, he was keenly interested in discovering more about his most notorious relative. A visit to Curwen's house uncovered a portrait of Curwen—painted directly on the wall paneling. The resemblance to Ward was uncanny, and the young antiquarian decided to bring it back to the Ward family home. But hidden behind the wooden paneling, Ward discovered the secret diary of Joseph Curwen.

Ward, fascinated by all things historical, dove into the journal. But as his interest in the diary grew, his personality and demeanor changed (please refer to *What to Do if Family/Friends Exhibit Changes in Personality or Demeanor* in the Arkham chapter). Ward grew increasingly quiet and secretive. The long, exploratory walks around Providence, for which he was well known, halted. He obsessed upon his long-lost relative, eventually dropping out of school so he could travel abroad, hunting down additional clues about Curwen.

The Ward family, and their physician, Dr. Marinus Willet, fretted over Charles' mental state, hoping the travel would help the young man work some weirdness out of his system. Instead, Charles grew worse, conducting mysterious alchemical experiments in his study, and stinking-up the Ward house for weeks on end. From his isolated room, the Ward family heard bizarre chanting in an unknown language, at all hours of the day and night. And whenever Ward began his strange recitations, dogs all over town howled loudly.

Eventually Ward realized his experiments were causing concern. Moving to a bungalow in Pawtuxet, he enlisted the help of a scraggly-looking, scholarly stranger named Dr. Allen.

Ward's arrival didn't improve Pawtuxet's real estate value. Suddenly, an epidemic of grave-robbing plagued the area. A series of vampiristic attacks and murders horrified the sleepy village. Not to mention there was a new dog-howling problem. And when a truckload of corpses—addressed to Ward—arrived in Pawtuxet, village-folk cast terrified and suspicious gazes toward Ward's bungalow.

## A Change of Heart . . . and Demeanor

Just when it seemed things weren't working out so well, Dr. Willet received a frantic letter from Ward. In the letter, the young man swore off all of this research nonsense, and planned to move away from the bungalow. He arranged a meeting with Dr. Willet to explain everything. Oh, and if Dr. Willet happened to see Dr. Allen anywhere about, would Willet please kidnap Allen, and dunk him in an acid bath for good measure.

Dr. Willet agreed to meet the young man (although he was noncommittal on the acid-dunking of Dr. Allen). Unfortunately, Ward was a no-show. Of course, this made everyone wonder where he was, and start searching for him. By the time the family tracked him down, Ward had suffered a change of heart—he insisted all was well, and everyone should forget his prior fussing in regard to Dr. Allen—the strange looking doctor was actually a bang-up guy.

But Charles Dexter Ward had difficulty speaking. His language was archaic, unfamiliar, and forced. His actions strained. Clearly Ward suffered from *yet another* change in personality and demeanor.

By now, Dr. Willet and the Ward family had reached their strangeness limit. They trucked Charles Dexter Ward off to the sanitarium, where he lived happily ever after . . . albeit a very brief ever after. Shortly following his admittance to the sanitarium, Charles Dexter Ward disappeared from the asylum, never to be heard from again.

But Pawtuxet rejoiced—the vampirism attacks ended, as well as the grave-robbing. Even the dogs were happy. Everyone considered the strange case of Charles Dexter Ward to be closed.

## What Really Happened

As Ward had descended further into the depths of madness, Willet began conducting his own research into Curwen's history. His investigations suggested Curwen had figured out how to reanimate

---

### How to Conduct Dangerous Experimental Research Without Getting Caught

In your attempt to prepare yourself for the world's inevitable doom, you may find yourself needing to partake in an alchemical experiment of your own (I'm referring to the "legal" kind). So it is useful to learn from the mistakes of Charles Dexter Ward and his predecessors:

1. If you need corpses for your experiment, don't dig locally! Get your corpses from a neighboring town's cemetery.

2. If you need even *more* corpses, don't have them shipped straight to the house in coffin-shaped boxes.

3. Keep it down! Believe it or not, it's possible to keep all of that chanting to a minimal mumble. Or try sound proofing your room.

4. If your concoctions smell particularly putrid, consider stocking up on air fresheners, or using an outdoor laboratory (like a lean-to).

5. If you're having a problem with howling dogs, visit a few dog hot-spots prior to any spell recitations. Dog biscuits laced with tranquilizers work wonders.

CONTINUED . . .

---

the dead (poor Herbert West, he never did get a break). This explained Curwen's need for those coffin-shaped boxes—they contained dead bodies for his reanimation experiments.

When weak-willed Ward developed an interest in his family history, Curwen manipulated the young man into doing his bidding, from beyond the grave. In Ward's travels abroad, he found and reanimated Curwen himself. Returning to Providence under the guise of Dr. Allen, Curwen used his scraggly beard-and-glasses disguise to hide his resemblance to Ward. Eventually Ward panicked, deciding to abandon Allen and his Pawtuxet experiments. So Allen killed him and took his place. (Stick with it. Events get easier to follow.)

---

### How to Conduct Dangerous Experimental Research Without Getting Caught (Continued)

6. Consider renting a cottage—you know, one that is far away from everyone else.

7. If you're suffering from changes in personality and/or demeanor, make sure you put some time in between any bouts of depression and inability to cope with other people *before* you start dabbling in the arcane.

8. Re-read any diaries you have; check the newspaper accounts about your ancestors; follow-up on rumors about previous members of your family. If you're thorough, you'll likely find the negatives outweigh the positives, which means you can avoid the experiments altogether.

9. Venting is important. If you don't go with an isolated lab, have fans installed in your secret laboratory.

10. Make sure to keep the door locked to your "secret place." Most clandestine experiments are foiled by overzealous experimenters who forget to lock the doors.

---

Eventually, Dr. Willet confronted Ward, aka Allen, aka Curwen, in the sanitarium. Curwen, realizing the jig was up, commenced chanting an incantation, in an attempt to bring down some serious pain upon Dr. Willet, in the form of none

## KEEPING IT IN THE FAMILY

It doesn't take long to notice that in H.P. Lovecraft's writings, there is a common theme about family and relatives. Heredity is a "hot topic" in the Mythos, because your ancestors can screw-up things for you long after they are gone. Some people believe that Lovecraft's seeming fixation on heredity was connected to his father (he'd had some troubles, and spent some time in an asylum). And while this is probably true, it is also true that the entire world in Lovecraft's day was pre-occupied with heredity. Without any understanding of genetics, the world was on fire with the desire to improve the human breeding stock. After all, humans had been improving animals through breeding, so why not humans? This notion eventually led to the Eugenics Programs of several countries—including the United States. And as Lovecraft did rely upon contemporary science and scientific theory for many of his stories, it's not surprising he'd repeatedly return to one of the hottest topics of the day: heredity.

Of course, the early eugenics programs turned out to be bad ideas (reference World War II and the Aryan "super race" for one powerful example). So, the facts about eugenics and heredity faded away in the depths of history, leaving what appears to be Lovecraft's and the Cthuhlu Mythos's seemingly strange obsession with family history and genealogy.

In the end, all of this works out to be a strong reminder of the real human horrors of the past, and it serves as a warning about the future—in case history repeats itself. Again, we see the power of Lovecraft and the Cthulhu Mythos serving the world—or its demise.

other than Yog-Sothoth. But Willet prepared ahead of time, and unleashed some nasty counter-chanting of his own. Joseph Curwen disintegrated into dust, dying for the second time—and presumably the last.

## More Experiments in Providence

Some people think that H.P. Lovecraft's famous story, "From Beyond," serves as a warning about technology beyond mankind's control, and the horrors it can unleash. But more importantly, it demonstrates what can happen if you aren't supportive enough of your best friend, particularly if that best friend happens to be a total jerk.

Crawford Tillinghast, self-important scientist, had been working on a new experiment—a machine capable of creating a powerful resonance wave. This resonance wave stimulated the pineal gland. In such a stimulated state, a person could see other worlds—other dimensions, and also the creatures from those other dimensions. Basically, the things *from beyond* (cue dramatic music).

Naturally, Tillinghast revealed all of this to his best friend, with great, dramatic flourish, as the two stood in Tillinghast's attic laboratory. But instead of receiving the admiration and support Tillinghast expected, his best friend expressed dubiousness as to whether this whole *beyond* thing was a good idea.

If there's one thing you don't do, it's question a potentally insane, obsessed scientist about his ideas. Not surprisingly, Tillinghast was enraged, and booted the skeptic from his house, and out of his life . . . for at least two and a half months.

Eventually, the separation compelled Tillinghast to invite the friend back. The fact that Tillinghast wanted to show off his creation probably had nothing to do with the invitation. Besides, Tillinghast really had no other friends, especially the sort who would appreciate his resonance wave machine. Having spent many weeks toiling over the device, Tillinghast now prepared to gloat about his amazing success. And then kill his unsupportive best friend.

With glee, Tillinghast activated the machine. It glowed and

whined—and probably popped and buzzed. After a few moments, ghastly flopping, floating creatures drifted across the attic. These creatures, Tillinghast revealed to his friend, could also see *them*. And these smaller beasts were nothing compared to the larger, slimier, nastier monster, just like the one that killed all of the house servants, floating just behind Tillinghast's now decidedly ex-best friend.

And *that's* what Tillinghast's ex-best friend got for not being supportive.

So Tillinghast's ex-best friend whipped out a gun and shot the machine (bad idea). Later, when the police arrived, they found Tillinghast dead of apoplexy, and the ex-best friend lying unconscious upon the floor (this is why you need to follow the steps about conducting secret experiments; it turns out, all of Tillinghast's neighbors were suspicious).

However, being Mythos savvy, Tillinghast's former best friend likely went on the market for a new best friend. They are truly indispensable—at least until you need to dispense of them.

## Is Everyone in the Cthulhu Mythos Related in Some Fashion?

By this point, you might have noticed the reoccurences of a few last names. Popular ones are Marsh, Tillinghast, Gilman. But just because a smattering of people across a handful of stories have similar surnames doesn't mean all of these folk are related. Actually, they're not. They just have popular names. Oh, and the names that resemble modern, living or dead people are merely coincidence as well. Such is the power of the Cthulhu Mythos.

## WHAT TO DO WHEN YOU STIMULATE YOUR PINEAL GLAND

The pineal gland is located in the center of the brain, and is reported to exist primarily for the manufacture of melatonin. However, the pineal gland, known as the "third eye," is also believed to be connected to psychic ability, allowing a trained psychic to see beyond space and time.

To this end, always ensure your pineal gland gets plenty of exercise, and is stimulated properly:

1. Daily, try *reaching out* to others using your pineal gland. Think nice thoughts about them, and see if they respond in kind. If they respond rudely, attempt to hurt them using your pineal gland (while it's still in your body).

2. With the aid of meditation, try expanding your awareness—to extend your vision beyond the realm of normal sight—using only your pineal gland.

3. If you have access to a resonance wave machine, you can use it to stimulate your pineal gland—but *limit usage!* Overstimulation of your pineal gland may result in you being dinner for an otherworldly beastie.

4. Invite a friend to help. First say, "pineal gland," and ask your friend what he or she thinks it's used for. The answer can be quite enlightening, and may result in some activity completely different from what you set out to do.

5. If you're the type of person who doesn't like playing with your pineal gland, then consider some other sort of disastrous experiment. There are plenty to choose from. No need to compromise your integrity just for a few minutes of fun with a pineal gland.

6. Some people have sensitive pineal glands. This means you may already be seeing long, serpentine creatures drifting around your bedroom or other places. In these

CONTINUED . . .

## WHAT TO DO WHEN YOU STIMULATE YOUR PINEAL GLAND (CONTINUED)

cases, it is best to avoid overstimulation. Just let things be. All will work out in the end.

7. It is not uncommon to find yourself with an undersized pineal gland. While this doesn't limit the amount of fun to be had, or the number of dimensions you can explore, it does tend to produce insecurity. To offset this, a person with this condition should chant every morning: *I'm proud of my pineal gland; it is as big as it needs to be, and it makes me happy.*

8. Be careful when venturing into other people's heads— using your third eye, or pineal gland. Exploring the psychic landscape of others is considered rude in many cultures. It's best to ask permission first—even if the other person participating is a best friend.

9. If you're inexperienced at using your third eye, start slowly. Unless you're conducting insane experiments in your attic, or longing for revenge upon your best friend, you have all of the time in the world to explore your pineal gland. Take baby steps, and make sure you engage in other activities. Obsessive behavior always leads to greater troubles.

10. Don't show off your pineal gland in public. It's fine to reveal how powerful your psychic sense is when you're with friends, but flaunting it simply makes enemies.

## THE CHURCH OF STARRY WISDOM

While in Providence, you might feel inclined to visit the infamous Church of Starry Wisdom, at the top of Federal Hill. If you do feel inclined, then don't do it. It's not a good idea. Lovecraft's tale "The Haunter in the Dark" explains why.

The Starry Wisdom sect, dating back at least as far as the 1800s, has long since abandoned the church. But its dark influences remains. Locals won't speak of the church. When asked about it, don't be surprised if they recoil in fear, or make a strange sign with their right hand (either they're hoping to ward off spirits, or it might be that they're "shooing" you to go away).

The diary of Robert Blake, whose room overlooked Federal Hill, really tells us all we need to know about the church. Each day, while toiling away on his supernatural fiction novel about cults (he would have been better off staying at the Witch House in Arkham), he peered at the dark, crumbling church on the hill. Eventually, curiosity won. He decided to check out the Church of Starry Wisdom, and plodded up the hill in search of mystery.

## WHAT'S UP WITH ALL THESE NON-EUCLIDEAN ANGLES?

Inside the church, Blake found typical stuff you'd find in an old, abandoned, rotting church—cobwebs, dust, broken furniture. A copy of the *Necronomicon*. A few other insanity-inspiring tomes. A mysterious cryptogram, housed inside a leather-bound volume. A set of notes that apparently once had belonged to the dead guy on the floor. Yes, the dead guy on the floor.

Oh, and there was also a large box, containing a strange, shimmering Shining Trapezohedron.

Just ordinary church stuff.

Upon closer inspection, the notes revealed how the Starry Wisdom sect liked to gaze into the strangely alluring trapezohedron (its decidedly non-Euclidean angles would have delighted poor Walter Gilman). When the church-goers stared into the device, a mysterious creature stared right back at them. This creature, known as the Haunter of the Dark, revealed knowledge and secrets. In return, it demanded human sacrifice. Good deal.

Blake returned to his room with the leather-bound volume, containing the cryptogram. Instead of working on his fiction book like a dutiful writer, he slogged over the cryptogram, eventually cracking it. And boy-howdy did he learn quite a bit.

The trapezohedron initially resided in Egypt. Functioning as a sort of window into other dimensions and times, the trapezohe-

## WHAT TO DO WHEN YOU ENCOUNTER A SHINING TRAPOZOHEDRON

1. Don't look at it. Maybe before reading this book you had an excuse, but now you don't—unless you skipped this section.

2. Avoid the slightest glance in its general direction. The more you flirt with peeking at it, the greater the compulsion becomes to give it a good, hard stare.

3. Poke yourself with a stick. Or have a close friend do it. A poke in the eye is probably the best bet. This will likely keep you preoccupied, and perhaps even produce a slight aversion toward the thing you should not be gazing at.

4. When you do eventually look at it (and let's face it, you know you will), try not to stare at it for very long. Maybe set an egg timer.

5. After you've stared at it for awhile (obviously ignoring the chime of the egg timer), you will notice a Haunter of the Dark staring back at you. At this point, you really need to stop looking at it.

CONTINUED . . .

dron had been the toy of pharaoh Nephren-Ka (who, by the way, was rumored to be a toy of the mischievous deity, Nyarlathotep). The creature inside the traphezoderon, The Haunter of the Dark ,despised light—hence the creature's name. It mostly kept to the non-Providence side of the trapezohedron, thanks to an ample supply of streetlamps in the town.

### FEELING POWERLESS

You probably saw this one coming. Yes, the streetlamps proved useless during unexpected power outages. And then suddenly,

## WHAT TO DO WHEN YOU ENCOUNTER A SHINING TRAPOZOHEDRON

6. Once you've stared at the Hunter in the Dark long enough to learn its secrets, offer up your friend as the sacrifice (after all, he did poke you in the eye with a stick).

7. Try as you might, you can't trick the Haunter of the Dark. Using your pineal gland and its third eye abilities won't work.

8. Speaking of tricks, while no one has tried, you could set-up a series of mirrors, and gaze at the shining trapozohedron indirectly. If this one works, send me a note. Or have your friend send me a note, because if it *did* work, you're about to lose your mind.

9. Re-gift it. Find that unspecial someone, and hand him or her a box with the shining trapozohedron. Make sure to mention it requires close scrutiny to grasp its full beauty.

10. Run. Simple, but effective.

Providence was plagued with them—power outages that is. During one extended outage, a few people spotted a black, wispy shape, shooting from Federal Hill toward the east. Not long after, Blake was found, staring out his window, up at the hill, eyes bulging with terror. He was indeed dead. Apparently, he'd died of fear.

The local coroner, being one not to ask too many questions, attributed Blake's death to "natural" causes. If you consider being frightened to death by an all-knowing supernatural creature, living in a realm accessible only by a Shining Trepozohedron to be *natural*, well, then, sure, the coroner hit the nail on the head.

# New York

*In the spring of 1923 I had secured some dreary and unprofitable magazine work in the city of New York; and being unable to pay any substantial rent, began drifting from one cheap boarding establishment to another in search of a room which might combine the qualities of decent cleanliness, endurable furnishings, and very reasonable price. It soon developed that I had only a choice between different evils, but after a time I came upon a house in West Fourteenth Street which disgusted me much less than the others I had sampled.*

—H.P. Lovecraft, "Cool Air"

There were plenty of things in the Cthulhu Mythos that Lovecraft could have—*should* have—disliked. Consciousness-swapping aliens, mad scientists and their crazy experiments, frog-fish people, human sacrifice . . .. But, according to Lovecraft's personal writings, he reserved most of his hatred for New York City. And rightfully so—it was crowded, dirty, and chock full of unsightly things. Furthermore, unbeknownst to most of its residents, the city was teeming with nasty Mythos creatures and cults—and also a few mad scientists. Alas, if you must live in New York City for any reason, keep to yourself. Don't join any cults. Make sure you pay your air conditioning bill, and avoid Greenwich Village and Brooklyn, and things should be just fine.

## RED HOOK

It appears from Lovecraft's tale, "The Horror at Red Hook" that he wasn't particularly fond of this neighborhood in Brooklyn. And if we are to believe what he wrote about it, it's best to avoid taking up residence in Red Hook.

After a series of strange crimes, Inspector Thomas Malone was sent to investigate the events. During his time in New York City, Malone had witnessed plenty of murder and mayhem (it was the early 1900s after all). Yet nothing matched the horror he uncovered during his stint on the streets in Red Hook—but that wasn't what really got Thomas Malone all worked up.

Thomas Malone had a terrible fear of buildings.

Okay, maybe that's a slight exaggeration. Malone wasn't afraid of *all* buildings, just certain types of large buildings, and mostly if they appeared to be tumbling down upon him. And to be fair, the building phobia was a relatively recent affliction, mainly due to the events at Red Hook.

### THE STRANGE CASE OF ROBERT SUYDAM

Malone first arrived in Red Hook to investigate Robert Suydam. The crotchety recluse hailed from Flatbush, but spent a great deal of time in shady Red Hook—enough to attract the attention of the federal authorities. Apparently, Suydam had developed a bad habit of hanging out with evil, gangster types, possibly organizing some sort of crime ring. Worse (at least from his family's perspective), Suydam's heirs feared he was spending his way through their rightful inheritance. The eccentric old man spent ridiculous sums of cash fixing up his Red Hook flat, and buying occult tomes from overseas. Those international shipment costs really added up.

Hoping to prevent Suydam from burning through all of the cash, the family sought legal action against him. But the court didn't favor the family. It seems Suydam had won the judge's favor by confessing to the fact that he was definitely scruffy, scraggly, and weird. But he attributed his fascination with unconventional occult tomes to his studies of certain European traditions. And, he pointed out, Red Hook's ethnic population allowed Suydam to study these traditions in closer detail.

The judge let him off with a scowl, but the feds and Malone, continued their investigations—it seems his plea of "cultural education" didn't go far with anyone else. After a quick raid on Suydam's home, even the FBI and Malone were at a loss. The unexpected visit revealed little, other than Suydam's bizarre occult painting collection (only proving his extremely bad taste in artwork). The feds also raided a dance hall in Red Hook—several children had gone missing in the area, and when neighbors spotted a young child in the dance hall window, it gave them cause. Besides, the dance hall was reputed to be a hangout for Suydam's sinister gangster friends. But as with Suydam's house, the search revealed nothing.

## Mid-Life Crisis

And then, something very *strange* (or very common, if you're getting a feel for the Cthulhu Mythos) happened. Suydam exhibited a sudden change in personality and demeanor. The shabby old man cleaned up his appearance. He shaved his scraggly beard and donned new threads. He whipped about town, behaving in a socially acceptable manner, throwing swank parties, acting generally less cranky.

Suydam attributed his "second youth" to lifestyle/diet changes. True, this reasoning is not original to the Mythos, but people tend to buy into it every time.

In time, folks around town started to like the "new" Suydam. Before long, he was engaged to the socially appropriate Cornelia Gerritsen of Bayside. Life looked good for the once crotchety old man. Until Suydam and his new bride left for their honeymoon on a ship out of Cunard Pier.

Once the honeymoon cruise was underway, the crew were abruptly summoned by a horrific scream to Suydam's cabin. There they discovered the grisly bodies of both bride and groom in the Suydam stateroom. Claw marks sliced Mrs. Suydam's neck—scratches decidedly not from a human hand.

Immediately a tramp steamer pulled alongside the ship. The tramp steamer's crew bore a note from the deceased Suydam. Written in Suydam's hand, it conveniently spelled out what to do in the event of Suydam's (apparently very likely) death: His body must be turned over to the suspicious crew of the tramp steamer.

Though puzzled, the ship's crew allowed the strange seamen to depart with Suydam's body. Only afterward did the flustered crewmates realize the tramp steamer crew had departed with most of Mrs. Suydam's drained blood, as well.

## THE CRUMBLING MALONE

Back in Red Hook, Malone investigated Suydam's Red Hook flat. In the basement, a suspicious-looking locked door caught his attention. As Malone attempted to break through the door, it mysteriously gave way from the inside. Unexpectedly, Malone was sucked into the next room—a room crawling with monstrous horrors, strange, elemental creatures, and great, evil gods, cavorting and dancing. Clearly there was a celebration underway. And standing at the center of everything, surrounded by the dark, chanting figures of the tramp steamer crew, was Robert Suydam—looking a bit worse for wear.

You'd think Suydam might have been delighted to escape death. Not so. Instead, the grumpy, newly reanimated man tore away from his circle of chanting friends, heading toward an auspicious-looking golden altar, promptly toppling it.

Or at least, this is how Malone recounted it afterward—remembering little else. The building, and several neighboring structures, crumbled—likely due to the unstable network of tunnels, running from Suydam's flat to the dance hall (the tunnels were once used for smuggling goods into Brooklyn, and goodies out of Brooklyn).

In the end, everyone except for Malone died in the cave-in. Though Malone had no proof, he suspected Suydam and the tramp steamer crew was involved in some sort of sinister cult—the dancing monstrosities probably gave him the idea. As to the child kidnappings in Red Hook, the purpose was never discovered, but fortunately the kidnappings ceased when the "cult" members perished.

As for Malone, he agreed to go on indefinite leave traveling to Rhode Island for some quiet recuperation time. After all, nothing ever happens in Rhode Island.

NEW YORK

## WHAT TO DO WHEN YOU GET INVOLVED IN THE OCCULT

Although the exact nature of the ritual described in "The Horror at Red Hook" remains a mystery, as well as why Suydam had a change of heart, Suydam was clearly deeply involved in cult activities, and the practice of occult magic. This is pretty much a given in Mythos stories. And remember, Lovecraft liked "open" endings because it required the reader to use imagination, generating a much more profound horror than being told what was going on.

Not surpringly, cults crop up often in the Cthulhu Mythos. Often, they worship powerful, extra-dimensional deities, practice supernatural rituals, and attempt dangerous summonings. They live on the edge.

But, occult magic isn't limited to just cults. Charles Dexter Ward often dabbled with alchemical experiments, as did Asenath Waite.

And given the fact that Cthulhu is sleeping, but will someday awaken, you might find it useful to join a cult (other options are explored later in this book). At the very least, to have any sort of advantage, you'll need to understand occult magic in order to survive what the Mythos throws at you. Remember the following tips to stay out of trouble:

1. This should be obvious by now, but please remember: avoid sudden changes in appearance, language and demeanor. It's a guaranteed indicator to the neighbors and family that you're up to *something*.

2. Take a lesson from Herbert West—think *fresh!* The fresher your spell ingredients, the better.

3. Whether it be for experiments or sacrifice, don't go local. You're performing occult rituals, not opening

CONTINUED . . .

## What to Do When You Get Involved in the Occult (Continued)

a restaurant. Local ingredients should *not* be on the menu. Bodies, live humans, dogs, whatever you need—make sure you acquire your spell ingredients from remote locales.

4. If you find yourself inadvertently wrapped up in cult happenings, all is not lost—you might not end up like the unfortunate Robert Suydam. Win over your fellow cult members. Put some charm and wit to use (or at least an inclination of "charming"). If that fails, spread vicious rumors about the current cult leader to get yourself elected in his place. While this can be risky, so is life in a cult. Once you're in, be in it to win. Shoot for the top.

5. If your fellow cult members ask you to write a note, explaining what happens to your body *when* you die, consider another cult.

6. Avoid government and local police investigations. Honestly, there will be enough people investigating you already—friends, strangers, philosophers, lost travelers. There's no need to get any government officials involved.

7. Don't wear cult icons in public. Sure, the cult of the Bloody Tongue likes to show off their sign. Deep Ones can't help it. And members of the Esoteric Order of Dagon need the cult "look" to get admitted. But if you settle for a more relaxed cult, then dress normally in public, and save the black robes and silver dagger for weekly ritual nights.

8. At first glance, it might seem wise to take over an abandoned church and turn it into a cult's headquarters. However, in the long run, this never works out.

CONTINUED . . .

NEW YORK

## WHAT TO DO WHEN YOU GET INVOLVED IN THE OCCULT (CONTINUED)

It attracts attention, and folks begin to wonder what all the ruckus is about every ritual night. This leads to rumors spreading, dogs dying, and eventually, the burning or collapse of the vacated church. Consider a remote cabin, or abandoned cave. Far less local traffic, and the ambience is just as good if not better.

9. Sure, you're a cult member, but most likely you're there more in name than spirit. Leave the dirty work to others. And when the night comes to summon the mind-shattering god the cult worships, don't look. Keep your eyes closed, wear sunglasses, put on eye patches and claim you have an eye infection. Peering at Cthulhu Mythos deities always ends badly—usually with insanity, and possibly a long stay at the local asylum.

10. Never tell the cult, "I quit." Cults don't take to this sort of behavior. It's a secret society, and having former members strolling about blabbering on arcane topics is very risky. Instead, when you're ready to leave a cult, burn down your apartment or house. Make sure you leave a rambling note (this makes the cult think you were very devoted as you were clearly insane). And then move to another place—preferably not Rhode Island.

## A CHILLING TALE

Summertime in New York means the stinky smell of sewers and rotten trash in the hot, muggy air. And if you don't have air conditioning, the heat is intolerable. In Lovecraft's story "Cool Air," he dabbles with the latest craze: air conditioning (remember these stories were written in the 1920s and 1930s). In this yarn, New York resident, Dr. Muñoz, suffers from an ailment requiring him to stay cool. So he created a home-made air conditioner. Utilizing an ammonia-based cooling system and gasoline engines,

Muñoz kept his apartment a comfy fifty-four degrees Fahrenheit. Nevermind the leaking ammonia, seeping through the floor and into his neighbor's flat below.

Lucky for Muñoz, he built up good karma with said neighbor, after one of Muñoz's odd medical concoctions saved the man from a heart attack. The two became friends (good approach). The neighbor visited Muñoz 's apartment regularly, never once commenting on how pale and clammy Dr. Muñoz looked. Clearly the friend was quite polite.

### SWEATER WEATHER

As things always turn for the worse when involved in the Mythos, Muñoz's illness worsened. He grew even more pale and sickly. But he kept his poor health at bay by cooling the apartment further—now he kept it at an icy thirty degrees. And, at a most inconvenient time in the middle of the night, one of the air conditioning pumps failed.

> ## MYTHOS SURVIVAL TIP:
> ## IT'S A *WHAT*, NOW?
>
> So, you've heard rumors about a strange device in your neighbor's attic laboratory. Or your new roommate is trying out some unconventional, home-brewed air conditioning system, aimed at saving a dime.
>
> If the machine glows, drips, emanates eerie, unnatural, pulsing lights, or otherwise exhibits odd behavior, stay away from it. Strange devices in the Mythos are rarely designed for the purpose of *good*. Even if they are, they rarely end up *doing* good, anyway.
>
> And if you're not sure if the device is uncanny, measure the owner's explanation: "See into other dimension," "bring the dead back to life," "contains the secrets of the universe," or "I'm sick and I need to stay nearly frozen" are all explanations that point to trouble. Running away is the best option when confronted with such strange devices.

NEW YORK

Desperate, Muñoz called upon his neighbor to ferret out replacement parts. But finding parts for a home-made air-conditioning system, in the late hours of the night, is a daunting task. To keep Muñoz cool in the meantime, the neighbor enlisted a local loafer to make runs to the grocery store, delivering a steady supply of ice to the apartment.

## ICY DEAD PEOPLE

After searching the city through and through, the neighbor hunted down the appropriate parts, and the necessary mechanics. He returned to Muñoz's apartment, but it was too late. The grocery delivery boy neglected to deliver enough ice—typical. And in place of his friend Dr. Muñoz, the devoted neighbor only found a disgusting pile of mushy remains in the apartment, along with a polite (although slimy) note.

The note explained Muñoz had actually been dead for eighteen-some years. A combination of medical cocktails and the extreme cold allowed Muñoz to retain his current, not so active, and somewhat lifeless lifestyle. And although it was most unfortunate, Muñoz realized he must eventually succumb to death.

In the end, this left one devoted neighbor without a friend, a couple mechanics with nothing to do, a grocery boy with no tip, and an abundance of parts to rebuild an air conditioning unit powerful enough to keep the dead alive. Everyone agreed to go home instead.

# Other Places, Other Times

After he went to Ireland, Barry wrote me often, and told me how under his care the gray castle was rising tower by tower to its ancient splendor, how the ivy was climbing slowly over the restored walls as it had climbed so many centuries ago, and how the peasants blessed him for bringing back the old days with his gold from over the sea. But in time there came troubles, and the peasants ceased to bless him, and fled away instead as from a doom.

—H.P. Lovecraft, "The Moon-Bog"

As you leave the domain of sleepy New England villages, tales of the Cthulhu Mythos written by H.P. Lovecraft tend to diminish. Not because the rest of the world suffers a dearth of Mythos activity. But Lovecraft couldn't be everywhere at once, documenting every weird Mythos event in the world. So he primarily stuck to the East Coast of the United States. Yet, even with that said, the occasional account of Mythos history crawled out of different parts of the globe.

## Something's Up at the Priory

Lovecraft's "The Rats in the Walls" takes us on a visit to Anchester, England. The great de la Poer family lived in Exham Priory, just outside Anchester, for hundreds of years—until Walter de la Poer decided to murder his entire family, flee to Virginia, and change his name to Delapore.

It wasn't like the de la Poer family had a great reputation prior to the murders—the de la Poer history was tainted with disappearances and murders. So when one of the younger Delapore descendants decided to buy Exham Prioriy and renovate it, he shouldn't have been so surprised when the local village residents hated him.

Undeterred, Delapore moved his seven servants and nine cats to his swanky new English residence. All was going quite well until he started to hear the scurrying of rats from within the walls. The scampering sound echoed throughout the house, driving both Delapore and his oversized cat collection crazy. His servants claimed not to be able to hear the sounds, maddening Delapore further. Determined to find the source, Delapore followed the noise into the sub-cellar, where he discovered a massive vault, apparently of Roman origin. With the assistance of a family friend (lucky Delapore), Edward Norrys, he convinced a team of scientists in London to travel to the priory, and assist him in further investigation of the vault's depths.

### It Runs in the Family

Underneath the priory, the team discovered a subterranean grotto filled with Roman ruins, and an unimaginable heap of bones. The scientists determined the bones were human—or near human. The creatures had been kept in pens, like cattle, eventually devolving into quadrupedal beings. They were farmed, and eaten, by the residents above, until hungry hordes of rats finished off the wretched critters.

To his horror, Delapore found a seal ring in one of the buildings, with the de la Poer coat-of-arms. Suddenly, Delapore understood why Walter de la Poer had killed his cannibalistic family (seems pretty obvious when you put it that way).

Not surprisingly, all of this was too much for Delapore to handle. He suffered a fit, and screaming wildly, he scurried off into the tunnels' depths. The scientists went looking for Delapore. Eventually, they discovered him in the darkness, snacking on the half-eaten remains of Edward Norrys—Norrys was a good friend, and tasty. The scientific team quickly determined that Delapore took after the *wrong* side of the family. And once again, it comes down to a person's anscestors. If Delapore had studied his family tree, he might have avoided a great deal of embarrassment, and maintained a friendship with Norrys.

## THE BOG MUST GO

If the last tale didn't put you off the idea of buying and/or renovating a newly-discovered ancestral manor in the Great Britain countryside, the story of "The Moon Bog" might. When Denys Barrys decided to settle into his ancestral home in Kilderry, Ireland, he set about renovating the old castle. He just wanted to relax, enjoy the pastoral countryside, and spend the wealth he'd accumulated over the years. Oh, and maybe drain the stinky old bog, wasting perfectly good space on his land. (If Barrys knew more about the Cthulhu

### MYTHOS SURVIVAL TIP: ANCESTRAL FAMILY HOMES

In general, it's not a good idea to renovate the ancestral family home in Great Britain and move into it. This is all the more true if you have a shady family history. Instead, consider a condo or an apartment in a large urban setting that is not on the East Coast of the United States.

OTHER PLACES, OTHER TIMES

Mythos, like you, dear reader, he'd know that draining the bog at his ancestral home was a bad idea.)

For some reason—ahem—the bog-draining idea didn't sit well with the locals. They believed a curse rested upon the bog, and the curse extended to anyone who attempted to drain its murky waters. Allegedly, a guardian spirit kept watch from an islet over the bog. Tales had it that the ruins of a great, stone city lay beneath its surface. Therefore, the bog, and the city beneath, was not to be disturbed.

But Barrys didn't give in to such superstition—he was a modern, educated man. Undaunted, he continued with his plan to drain the bog—even as the local peasants fled for less cursed pastures. Unperturbed, he hired new servants and laborers from the north. The kind of people who were unfamiliar with ancient bog-cities or crazy curses.

---

## WHAT TO DO WHEN YOU ENCOUNTER A CURSE

During your adventures, you'll likely stumble across a curse or two. Perhaps it will be related to an ancient artifact, a forgotten tome. Or an entire moon-bog. Curses are easy to avoid, as long as you are careful:

1. If you discover an item, or location, rumored to be cursed, odds are good it is *cursed*. Err on the side of caution. Leave it alone.

2. Do your homework! Research the item, location, or spooky tome. Ensure it's not cursed prior to using, visiting or reading it.

3. Strange lights, dancing creatures, or the word "DOOM" scrawled upon *anything* likely means the item, or place, is *cursed* in some fashion. In this case, refer to tip #1.

4. Remember the primary key to Mythos survival: reliable friends. If you think a book is cursed, have your friend read it first.

CONTINUED . . .

---

**OTHER PLACES, OTHER TIMES**

## WHAT TO DO WHEN YOU ENCOUNTER A CURSE (CONTINUED)

5. Okay, let's say you find a cryptogram hidden in a book titled *Necronomicon.* Sure, the cryptogram might not be cursed, but the rest probably is. Keep your eyes on the big picture. If you need to solve a puzzle, give the local newspaper's crossword a shot.

6. If you relocate for work and find yourself in a town where all of the residents say you resemble a dead tyrant or sorcerer, assume you're probably related to the person. *Do not* start excavating beneath your house in hopes of finding some treasure or long lost relative. Just move. In the end, things will turn out for the better.

7. You say it's not cursed. The locals say it is. Go with the locals.

8. Curses can be difficult to detect. "Am I cursed? Am I not cursed?" The answer doesn't always come easily. Don't bother with fortune tellers or local gypsies. If you're cursed, they probably had something to do with it. It's best to buddy-up with someone and wait for the curse to reveal itself. If you're clever, you'll finagle a way to transfer the curse to your friend, and then split town.

9. You've probably heard not all curses are bad. This isn't true. Sure, at first being cursed with immortality sounds great. But there's always a catch. It's a *curse!* Even if the curse sounds good, don't try to make the best of it. You'll only end up dead—usually through some horrid, painful process. The best action is to find a cure.

10. On occasion, you may find yourself in the position of being able to curse someone. Don't do it. Most likely the intended victim has read these tips and probably has made you his or her best friend. Trying to pull off cursing someone almost always results in it backfiring.

## But the Bog-Wraiths say no

A night or two before the impending bog-drainage enterprise commenced, a great light-show appeared over the water's surface. It was quite dazzling, and both unexpected and unexplainable. But here's where it gets good. Accompanying the eerie lights was the sound of reedy, piping flutes and pounding drums (you were warned about this type of stuff). Then, seemingly out of nowhere, strange creatures—bog-wraiths, clad all in white—appeared, dancing and waving their translucent arms about.

Totally entranced (but not in the good way), the servants stumbled out of the house, following the bog-wraiths. The laborers did as well. Everyone trailed the bog-creatures in an apparent drunken stupor. When the bog-wraiths descended beneath the water, the column of humans blithely followed.

Of course, being a man of substance, Denys Barrys did not join the cavorting throng into the marshy depths. Well, actually, no one saw Barrys ever again. But if the screams heard from the castle were any indication, he would have fared better with a boggy demise.

As for the bog, it seems as though it might be a great place for a water park—fireworks, music, dancers. Sometimes one can make lemonade out of lemons. And sometimes one can't.

OTHER PLACES, OTHER TIMES

# The Art of the Mythos

*Any magazine-cover hack can splash paint around wildly and call it a nightmare or a Witches' Sabbath or a portrait of the devil, but only a great painter can make such a thing really scare or ring true. That's because only a real artist knows the actual anatomy of the terrible or the physiology of fear—the exact sort of lines and proportions that connect up with latent instincts or hereditary memories of fright, and the proper colour contrasts and lighting effects to stir the dormant sense of strangeness.*

—H.P. Lovecraft, "Pickman's Model"

ong before Richard Dreyfuss was sculpting his potatoes in the film *Close Encounters of the Third Kind,* the Great Cthulhu was sharing dreams with humans. Perhaps the dream sharing wasn't intentional, but regardless, Cthulhu's dreams influenced those who were sensitive—particularly artists. In fact, in the popular Lovecraft tale, "The Call of Cthulhu," it caused the artist Henry Anthony Wilcox to sculpt a miniature version of the sleeping Great One—just like the potatoes were used in the aforementioned film. We might say that Cthulhu is a fan of the arts—in a manner of speaking.

And of course, most every form of art plays an important role in the Cthulhu Mythos, whether it be painting, writing, sculpting, or music. It might be that many artists unwittingly find their muse in the turbulent dreams of great Mythos deities. And sometimes, the arts are utilized for good—or for great evil.

## Boston Ghoul Party

Sure, Boston is a town steeped in rich tradition and history. Anyone new to the Boston area will immediately marvel at the quaint old buildings and unbeatable collection of pubs. However, any true Bostonian knows the city's most treasured heirloom is not an idyllic landmark or set of historic documents. It's the collection of ghoulish artwork by Boston's own, Richard Upton Pickman.

Okay, maybe not. But many cults and sorcerers think as much.

In 1926, H.P. Lovecraft penned a tale titled "Pickman's Model." And from the first reading to the present, it has been a favorite among Mythos fans. For the most part, the story is about an artist named Pickman, and of course his close friend Thurber—can't leave the friend out. One day, Thurber noticed his other painter-friend types steered clear of the peculiar Pickman. Maybe they had their reasons, but it didn't stop Thurber—he'd always thought of himself as an open-minded guy. So it follows that he didn't mind Pickman's eccentric and nightmarish paintings of ghastly, canine-humanoid creatures, which were sometimes depicted gnawing on human bones. After all, true art pushes boundaries.

THE ART OF THE MYTHOS

THE ART OF THE MYTHOS

## CLOSE ENCOUNTERS OF THE CTHULHU KIND

It is said that the Great Old One, Cthulhu, communicates with humanity through dreams. Since these dreams of strange, alien landscapes are often difficult to interpret, they often inspire painters and musicians to create fabulous works. The Great Cthulhu often shares (probably unintentionally) powerful visions with people susceptible to his influence—or maybe they have highly sensitive pineal glands which are attuned to Cthulhu's dream frequency. In any case, artists are often compelled to repeatedly paint alien vistas that haunt their dreams. Or score musical compositions, playing ceaselessly inside the composer's mind.

For good or bad, the visions imparted by Cthulhu tend to be anything but mundane. Cthulhu won't have you making mountains out of mashed potatoes. Instead, you'll feel compelled to chant rhythmically, while painting a picture—using the fresh blood of a recently-sacrificed goat. Or human. It seems much of it depends upon Cthulhu's mood.

Luckily, if you're not an artistic type, you're probably not susceptible to Cthulhu's unearthly influence. But for those who are, seldom can they resist the mighty call of Cthulhu. Unfortunately, there is no way to turn off Cthulhu's dream-time broadcasts, so if you happen to see one in your dreams, then, just go with the flow. Maybe find a friend to bring along for the ride. There is a good chance your eldritch art will bring you fame—followed by death shortly thereafter. Such is the price for great art.

Nor was Thurber bothered when Pickman brought him to his creepy Newbury Street studio. Pickman created his finest (and most nightmarish) work there. The studio was located in the cellar, because any artist knows that there's no better place to produce works of great art than in a poorly-lit, dank, dusty, stinky cellar of a two hundred year old building. I mean, who was Thurber to judge the source of Pickman's gruesome inspiration?

As might be expected, or not, the walls were splattered with more pictures of the strange dog-like creatures. Eventually, even the unspookable Thurber started feeling a little uncomfortable. Just when Thurber was about to reconsider just how open minded he should be, Pickman suddenly dashed from the room—with a revolver in hand. Right after this unexpected vanishing act, the report of six shots followed.

Moments passed. Had he been thinking clearly, Thurber probably would have left. But then, Pickman returned, offering a feeble excuse about a rat problem. Clearly, a serious rat problem. If anything, Pickman was decisive. Of course, the situation was a bit awkward. Friend or not, if a rodent problem is so bad you need to use six revolver shots, it's time to consider departing. And that's just what Thurber did. But after he'd left, Thurber realized he'd accidentally pocketed a photograph from Pickman's studio—obviously the commotion caused him to forget. When he examined the photograph, Thurber was surprised to see that the fearsome, ghoulish creatures were not products of Pickman's imagination after all. The monsters—one of which was depicted in the photograph—were real.

The more he gazed at the horrifying photograph, the more likely he understood why the rest of the cliquey artist circle had dumped Pickman.

# APRIL IN PARIS

As any good college student knows, when traveling, it's best to find the cheapest lodging available. Even if that lodging is the strangest, most distant lodging you encounter. In "The Music of Erich Zann," a metaphysics student does just that. He secures lodging *so* distant and so seemingly bizarre that he permanently loses track of where it was located (there goes his security deposit).

When the student found a cheap room on the Rue d'Aueseil, he didn't think twice about the peculiar abode offered to him. Without a care in the world, he quickly moved in. Even though he was kept up all night by the incessant, unearthly music from the apartment upstairs, he didn't complain. A great deal is a great deal. The music was a mere minor hindrance, and a bit uncanny.

As it turned out, a man named Erich Zann occupied the top flat of the building. He was a German viola player who had intentionally taken the top floor so that he could play his strange nightly concerts without bothering anyone. And he was incapable of speaking as he was dumb—although his hearing was remarkable.

In time, the student gained a liking for the haunting music. In fact, he became so infatuated with it that one day he crept up to Zann's flat and asked the musician to play a composition. Reluctantly, Zann agreed, but he didn't play any of the strange music which normally drifted downstairs in the wee hours of the morning. Hearing mudane music didn't satisfy the student. To satisfy his thirst for the unusual, the student requested one of the unordinary tunes. This request agitated Zann.

While maintaining his calm, Zann explained by penning a quick note that the music was not meant to be heard—in fact, Zann indicated that he'd appreciate it if the student kept his ears to himself, and restricted his listening to Zann-approved tunes only. To ensure compliance, Zann had the student moved to a lower flat—and it was a bit nicer (Zann generously covered the extra expenses).This thrilled the student. His swanky new pad would be great for parties. Plus, he could always sneak upstairs and listen to Zann's bizarre musical tunes whenever he liked.

## A CRAZED CONCERT

It seems that even a hip apartment isn't enough to get friends to visit if it is in a weird part of town. With little hope of tossing a roaring party, the student resorted to sneaking upstairs and listening at Zann's door. He was very hard-up for entertainment. Then, just as he'd settled in, the student heard a strange commotion, accompanied by extremely loud and frantic viol-playing. As the noise bolstered inside Zann's flat, the student banged on the door. In moments, Zann opened the door and eagerly admitted the student.

With frequent, frightened glances toward the window, Zann sat down at his tiny desk, and began writing. Apparently, it was time to share the secret behind his haunting music. But as the student awaited enlightenment, Zann dropped his pencil mid-story. He snatched his viol, and began playing with alarming intensity. The wind banged tumultuously against the window-shutters while Zann's music grew to a feverish pitch. And as luck would have it, the sheaf of papers explaining *everything* (this is why a copy of this book should always be handy) swirled about in a gust of wind, flying out the widow before the student could snatch them out of the air.

Upon second glance, it was clear the window was no ordinary window. With great horror, the student realized the window did

### MYTHOS SURVIVAL TIP: STAY OUT OF TUNE

It's likely you've received a chill feeling running up your spine at some point in your life, hearing a haunting strain of music, or eerily addictive tune. Don't believe it when people tell you the shivers come from the music's inherent *beauty*. More likely, the music is *dangerous*. It can lull you into a trance. It can brainwash you. The best action is to clamp those ears shut, and get out of hearing range, as quickly as possible. If possible, run from the room screaming to clearly demonstrate the danger of the music.

THE ART OF THE MYTHOS

not look out upon a serene cityscape with twinkling lights. Rather, before him was a strange, black abyss. And still Zann frantically played his viol, using magic music only he knew, attempting to force *something*, outside in the abyss, to remain outside (in restropect, maybe we should cut Nero some slack for "fiddling while Rome burned").

The student begged Zann to leave the room, and abandon the viol. But his pleas went unheard, or ignored. Finally, after considering his options, the student ran from the house. And he didn't stop until he was miles from the low cost flat, Zann, and even the Rue d'Aueseil itself. Sometimes running is the best option. Of course, later, when the student wanted to gather-up his belongings, he was unable to find the apartment, or even the Rue d'Aueseil. In fact, everyone he spoke to claimed they'd never even heard of such a place. Very strange. Next time, he'll probably go for a slightly higher costing dorm room on campus. At least the parties would be better.

## YELLOW IS NOT YOUR COLOR

Originally envisioned by Robert Chambers, the tales of the King in Yellow, and of the mysterious Yellow Sign, became an integral element of the Mythos canon. As H.P. Lovecraft was a fan of the writings of Robert Chambers, it's not a surprise that the two authors should overlap in areas.

On the surface, spotting The King in Yellow might seem easy. And sometimes it is; although on other occasions there are only oblique references in several Chambers stories—for instance, a play, titled "The King in Yellow" that drove any and all readers insane.

For most people, the famous play, "The King in Yellow" has an innocuous first act. But anyone foolish enough to eyeball the opening phrases of the second act might as well book a one way trip to Arkham Sanitarium.

For example, the events transcribed in "The Yellow Sign" describe a painter, Mr. Scott, who took a break from his canvas, and decided to peer out the window. There he caught a glimpse of a pale, dough-like man, standing. Then this doughy man rather unexpectedly returned Scott's gaze. Unnerved, Scott hurried away from the window—clearly this pale figure's stare was very unsettling.

Later, when he returned to painting, he couldn't get his colors right. No matter how brightly he tried to paint his lovely model, Tessie Reardon, the colors always turned out sickly and dead.

Somewhat defeated, he gave up painting for the day. With time on their hands, Tessie and Scott enagaged in a discussion about the pallid man. It didn't take long before a shocked Tessie realized she'd dreamed of the unusual man before. In those dreams, Scott lay in a coffin, inside of a hearse.

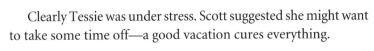

Clearly Tessie was under stress. Scott suggested she might want to take some time off—a good vacation cures everything.

## THE YELLOW SIGN

However, Scott was still not satisfied with what he knew about the elusive figure standing outside his window. So, he asked about town, discovering the pale, clammy fellow worked as a night watchman for the nearby church. No one knew much about him, but it was generally agreed he was creepy.

After some tiresome legwork, Scott encountered a bellboy, Thomas, who reluctantly confessed to his gruesome experience with the dough-man. It seems Thomas had a dispute with the man because the freaky fellow was always leering at him, and this terribly annoyed the bellboy. Push came to shove, and the argument nearly came to fisticuffs. But when the dough-man grabbed Thomas, the bellboy managed to pull away. And to Thomas's disgust, one of the dough-man's soft, mushy fingers came along as well.

Upon hearing this tale, Scott decided it would be best if he simply steered clear of the dough-man. And mostly, he was successful— except for one night when the dough-man was hanging about, mumbling repeatedly, "Have you found the Yellow Sign?"

## DON'T LOOK IN THE BOOK

Completely refreshed, unlike Scott, Tessie arrived at her next modeling session with light feet. Scott, however, hadn't been resting, and he was something of a downer—although oddly cheerful. Scott related, laughingly, his dream from the night before—a dream identical to Tess's dream. It involved the dough-man, and the hearse. But knowing better, he dismissed it as imagination. Tessie didn't brush it aside so easily. She grew quite upset. She confessed to worrying about something happening to Scott. Worried because she liked him. You know, liked him in *that* way.

This revelation brought on a bout of fevered kissing.

Once Scott and Tessie became an item (jeez), the next modeling session was a bit awkward. However, being a caring gentleman, Scott solved the problem by allowing Tessie to wear a costume instead of stripping down to bare skin (sounds like things were much better for Scott now). And to further defuse the situation, he presented her with a gift of a necklace. Excited, Tessie returned the favor with a gift of her own—a black onyx clasp with a curious symbol. She had discovered the clasp last winter—the same day she started having the terrible dreams about Scott and the dough-man. Lucky for Scott, Tessie didn't believe in coincidence—or maybe she did.

With all of the excitement and jubilation, Scott wasn't himself and while moving a canvas, he fell and sprained both wrists. That put an end to painting for awhile. Being his livelihood and hobby was working with brushes and paints, not surprisingly, Scott quickly became bored. To occupy his time, he began prowling the vast book collection in his library. And there it was! High upon a shelf rested a strange, yellow tome he did not recognize. The book was a stand-out among the others. It didn't take long for Tessie to climb up and retrieve the volume for him. And then he was hit with another surprise. The book was an actually copy of the infamous and dreaded play, "The King in Yellow."

Having never read the play, even purchased the book, Scott was at a loss as to how it ended up in his library. Disturbed by its unexpected presence, and the rumors that it caused insanity, he implored Tessie to return the volume to the shelf. But, as friends in uncanny situations are wont to do, Tessie thought the matter to be a great game. Instead of returning the book, she skipped away with it, laughing and dancing about the house (do read the information box titled *More About Friends, Partners, and Loved Ones in the Mythos* a few times).

For those of us who are fans of books, we know that dancing, laughing, and skipping with a book in hand is of limited entertainment. Tessie soon discovered this as well, and decided to peek inside the mysterious volume.

## Told You Not to Look in the Book

By the time Scott hunted down Tessie, she was in a dazed trance. Hurriedly, Scott settled her upon the sofa, hoping to help her condition. And as he sat there, waiting, it occurred to him

## More on Friends, Partners, and Loved Ones in the Mythos

As previously stated, it is always good to have a dedicated friend nearby when dealing with entities or Mythos related events. While these friends are trusted, and liked, close and loyal, they are nonetheless dispensable. And a true friend understands this. After all, the whole point of having a pal or a chum when exploring the Mythos is to toss them into the fire while you flee.

But when you make a girlfriend or spouse your friend, this adds some wrinkles to the matter. Odds are you're overly emotionally attached to the "friend," and probably not as willing to let harm befall them. If this is the case, then it spells trouble. Just like this: T-R-O-U-B-L-E. In the end, if you're truly devoted to this type of friend, you're more likely to sacrifice yourself than your "friend." This benefits you little because in the Cthulhu Mythos universe, you are not judged in terms of "good and evil." Such a universe doesn't have space for petty philosophies. Survival is the most important element, and getting involved in an emotional, lovey-dovey relationship is simply going to end badly for all involved.

If this happens, do yourself a favor. Make sure you're first to throw your "friend" into the trouble—before it happens to you. Or, better yet, avoid the situation entirely. Become a bitter old man or woman, lock yourself away, and enjoy life as it was meant to be—alone, but with expendable friends.

that passing the time would be easier with a little reading. So, he read the play in its entirety. Later, when Tessie awoke, she and Scott discussed the play endlessly, in a sort of monotonous trance. Now they knew that the strange, onyx clasp she'd gifted to Scott bore the Yellow Sign. They also understood they must dispose of the accursed item. Yet, knowing and doing are different things. Although he understood why he should, Scott couldn't bring himself to part with it. With their newfound knowledge, there was no shock when the crunching of wheels upon gravel sounded from outside—it was a hearse, approaching. At long last, the dough-shaped man had arrived to claim his Yellow Sign.

While the strange events unfolding were completely comprehensible to the couple, the reality was more difficult to deal with. After only a brief glimpse of the dough-man's face, Tessie fell over dead from fright. But she was the lucky one—poor, crazed Mr. Scott hung on for some time afterward.

## THE KING IN YELLOW

It's not clear as to whether the pasty-faced, dough-man visiting Scott and Tessie was actually the King in Yellow (maybe he was just really ugly and pasty). Many speculate the King in Yellow is an avatar of the supernatural creature *Hastur* (also known as *The Unspeakable One*, so it's best if you don't say the name Hastur very often).

When all was over, neighbors rushed to the flat, discovering Tessie's body and the dying Scott—and they also found the crumpled, decomposing form of the night watchman. It was obvious the watchman had perished months before, so how he

### MYTHOS SURVIVAL TIP:
### BOOKS ARE BAD

This warning has been offered before, but it's worth repeating. Other than this book, and a small handful of others, remain wary when reading a Mythos tome. Sure, they are excellent sources of knowledge, but with great knowledge comes great responsibility. And also great pain and suffering.

Just remember—every morsel of Mythos knowledge comes at a price. The price is normally an equally-sized morsel of your sanity.

continued to shamble about was a mystery to all. Likely the King in Yellow inhabited his form to regain his precious Yellow Sign (though it's surprising no one ever commented upon the watchman's sudden change in personality and demeanor . . .)

## WHAT TO DO WHEN YOU'RE AFFECTED BY A MYSTERIOUS ITEM

1. If you start having strange dreams, hallucinations, or health issues, after having acquired a unique piece of jewelry or peculiar bauble, it's best to get rid of the item. Most people won't connect the two, but that's why most people won't survive an encounter with something from the Cthulhu Mythos.

2. Only re-gift the item if you truly despise the intended victim. If you want a relationship, or are otherwise involved with the person, avoid offering it to them as a gift. Do, however, consider giving it away at your employer's annual *White Elephant* Christmas party. Nothing but fun and delight can come from this.

3. If it glows, pulses, shimmers, makes strange sounds, or talks to you, as a rule, dump it. Sure, you're likely to doubt your sanity, and want to share it with a friend to verify its unusual qualities. Only do this if you have an abundant supply of close friends and are willing to lose one.

4. If a bizarre-looking, unsettling person suddenly enters your life, or appears on your doorstep, dispose of the item as soon as possible, and redirect the mysterious stranger to a neighbor's house, or friend (again, only if you currently have a full supply of friends).

5. The less you know, the better off you are. If you find yourself daydreaming, and your attention is captured by a figure outside your window, don't rush down to learn why the strange person gives you the chills. Close

CONTINUED . . .

## WHAT TO DO WHEN YOU'RE AFFECTED BY A MYSTERIOUS ITEM (CONTINUED)

the window instead. Don't research the person; don't read books he suggests; and take extra precautions to avoid personal injury. You'll need to be in top form to flee later.

6. Don't let love and emotions cloud the matter. You're unsettled by something you can't put a finger on. Then your partner reveals he or she has had a horrible dream about your death. At this point, end the relationship to avoid a matching dream. If you move on to a new person, then there's a chance the new partner won't have the same portentous dream. If he/she does, move along again.

7. Even if you're bored, don't read the mysterious book that suddenly appeared on your bookshelf. No one expects you to be able to remember every book you've purchased, but you can avoid the ones that unnerve you. Basically, when events in your life start to feel unnatural, avoid books altogether.

8. If you decide to ignore the advice in the previous guideline, at least try to refrain from telling your partner about the book you spotted—but shouldn't have spotted to begin with. All this does is generate unnecessary interest, and most likely results in a very silly game of dancing-with-the book. Of course, no one can dance with a book for long without taking a little peek inside. But in this case, the results can be disastrous.

9. Cover your windows with well known, sanity safe landscapes. A large variety can be just as entertaining as gazing out a window, and with a regular rotation schedule, you'll have far more visual variety.

10. Visit a friend's house and drop any mysterious item you've found into his cereal box. He will likely think it to be a prize. After all, everyone loves a free prize (cursed or not).

# Crypts and Cemeteries

*The vault to which I refer is of ancient granite, weathered and discolored by the mists and dampness of generations. Excavated back into the hillside, the structure is visible only at the entrance. The door, a ponderous and forbidding slab of stone, hangs upon rusted iron hinges, and is fastened ajar in a queerly sinister way by means of heavy iron chains and padlocks, according to a gruesome fashion of half a century ago.*

—H.P. Lovecraft, "The Tomb"

In genre fiction, tombs and cemeteries are terrible places to hang out, unless you're dead (or Herbert West). Bad things happen in cemeteries. But sometimes a late-night trip to the crypt visit is inevitable. Here are a few tales, tips, and tricks to keep you above ground.

## RANDOLPH CARTER GOES TO THE CEMETERY

Randolph Carter appears throughout Lovecraft's fiction. Hailing from Arkham, Carter is a weird fiction writer with prophetic abilities. He's also known to have strange, vivid dreams that often crept into his writing. Sound like any other weird fiction writers mentioned in this book?

In Carter's adventures, he's journeyed across the chasm of space and time, and traveled to distant planets. He's also visited the bizarre, alternate dimension of our dreams, known as the Dreamlands. And not to mention, he's tangled with dangerous, otherworldly creatures, and embarked upon lengthy quests to find magical cities.

And when he isn't involved in those things, odds are he's in some sort of trouble in the cemetery.

In "The Statement of Randolph Carter," the adventuresome Mr. Carter offers a great yarn to authorities in an attempt to explain the unexplainable. Naturally, he'd sojourned to a cemetery, after which Carter was found wandering aimlessly around Big Cypress Swamp.

Carter's colleague, and somewhat friend, Harley Warren, had made a strange and startling discovery in a book recently procured from India. But Warren was stingy with his research, not willing to share much of anything with anyone. Instead, he asked Carter to accompany him to an ancient cemetery for field research, offering little else in way of explanation. And since it was a cemetery, Carter naturally couldn't resist.

The two arrived at the cemetery at night (this is a trend with researchers; why go in the day, when the darkness of night adds a level of difficulty). Warren headed to a tomb covered by a heavy black slab. The two men moved the block out of the way, revealing stone steps descending downward.

## MYTHOS SURVIVAL TIP:
## STAY INFORMED

Don't go on field trips without knowing why. If you have to go, do a bit of research on your own. As a general rule of thumb, if your professor-friend has been busy doing research in a strange book procured from foreign lands, and he won't share his findings, this might be the trip to skip—even if it is in a graveyard.

## INTO THE DARK

Warren left poor Carter on the surface and descended into the tomb alone. He insisted Carter was nothing but a frail bundle of nerves, offering little or no assistance (especially since all the heavy lifting was done). Reluctantly, Carter eventually agreed to allow Warren continue the journey alone. After all, that's what friends are for.

The two communicated via telephone line, as Warren descended into the depths of the tomb. And all went well, for awhile. At least until Warren started screaming.

He shrieked about terrible, monstrous things inside the tomb. Apparently Warren had been expecting some bad things down there. But not *this* bad. Warren insisted Carter should return the slab, and get the heck out of the cemetery.

Carter, not getting the hint, and clearly not understanding the purpose of friends, contemplated descending the steps, causing Warren to scream all the more. There came a final, agonized cry. And then the sound from the tomb vanished completely.

Still unsure, Carter shouted for his friend, receiving no response. Finally, whatever horrible, gruesome beast awaited inside the tomb got sick of hearing Carter's yelling, and responded with a disembodied voice, which floated up from the depths of the tomb stating: "You fool, Warren is DEAD."

Finally seeing the big picture, and probably remembering why friends bring friends on Mythos explorations, Carter returned to the surface.

## THE UNNAMABLE

You would think at first glance that the title says it all. In other words, nothing. And if there was a tale named "The Unnamable," you'd think there was little to say about it—as you can't really describe what it is you're talking about. But that would never stop Randolph Carter. In Lovecraft's story, "The Unnamable," Carter argued with his good friend, Joel Manton, about Carter's over-use of the word "unnamable," in fiction, and just in general (remember, Carter is a writer of weird fiction). Manton believed Carter's fiction was far from sensible, and had no qualms with telling him so.

This discussion unfolded as the two were seated upon an old, spooky, seventeenth-century tomb in the cemetery. That's right, another *cemetery*. Apparently Carter didn't learn the obvious lessons from his last cemetery experience. Instead, he chilled with his friend and argued about words like "unnamable" (amazingly, this is what writers really do). As they debated in the yard of the dead, nearby them stood an old, spooky, abandoned house. Also not a great place to hang out.

With his feathers ruffled by Manton's criticisms (writers are sensitive critters), Carter decided to let loose with a tale of an "unnamable" monster. This abomination was rumored to have ravaged the area many years ago. And because Manton had cited one of Carter's stories, "The Attic Window," as one of those "trashy" tales Manton couldn't get his head around, Carter revealed that very tale was based on notes found in an ancestor's diary. It pretty much seemed like a slam-dunk case for Carter, at least to Carter. To Manton, it seemed like a slam-dunk case for him.

Carter went on, revealing that the diary chronicled several attacks of a great, eldritch beast. Many years ago, the beast stalked the nearby town. Carter's ancestor himself had been mauled, clawed—even stomped on a little—by the creature. And Carter's distant relative was one of the luckier ones—several people were killed by the monster.

CRYPTS AND CEMETERIES

## What to Do When You Have Lead Feet

The first time you encounter a Mythos creature, you're going to get scared. You can't do anything about it. Prepare yourself now, and you might learn how to deal with it. Here are a number of common Mythos tropes which offer the greatest threat to you. In this instance, you will more often than not be the "narrator" or "hero," as you're the one stuck in the situation. Or, you might be the narrator's unfortunate friend. In any case, study them, memorize them, and learn from them:

1. The narrator runs away.

2. The narrator goes insane.

3. The narrator runs away, but in the process of running away, witnesses something horrible, and goes insane.

4. The narrator discovers an unimaginable horror, and his friend goes insane.

5. An unimaginable horror discovers the narrator, but the nearby friend attempts to fend off the monstrosity. In the process, the friend dies, and the narrator barely escapes alive.

6. The narrator's friend asks for assistance in an investigation, but it is the narrator who becomes obsessed with the research and eventually ends up in an asylum.

7. The narrator offers the reader a story that seems unbelievable. During the recounting of the tale, few details are offered about what is occurring, but the reader is re-assured that everything is terribly frightful. In the end, the reader learns the narrator has killed himself, or is institutionalized. So maybe the story was true. Maybe not. Things are up in the air.

8. The main character, which is often the narrator, decides to undertake some crazy task. His good friend seems

CONTINUED . . .

## WHAT TO DO WHEN YOU HAVE
## LEAD FEET (CONTINUED)

dubious, and as events unfold, the friend realizes that the hero/narrator has truly lost it, and in an attempt of self preservation, flees.

9. After the hero/narrator researches his family history, his life becomes a shambles. Try as he might, whatever haunted his ancestors, now haunts him. The hero/narrator calls upon a friend, who usually ends up exploring some dreadfully dangerous location, after which the friend is dead. Thinking all has been set right, the narrator returns to his daily routine, only to learn that the ancient ancestral horror is still present. All that remains for the hero/narrator is insanity or death. Sometmes both.

10. Knowing better, the narrator ventures off into some eldritch location, exploring and hoping to learn some mystery about the universe. The exploration is a success, but the narrator dies of fright just as he finishes penning his account of the entire event.

Overall, being prepared will help prevent having "lead feet" at critical moments. If you're able to predict how events might unfold, you're already one or more steps ahead of the danger.

But it didn't stop at that. There were also tales of a curious young boy who decided to visit the house where the monster supposedly hung out, in the attic. No one knew what the boy found, for he returned from the house screaming mad.

None of this convinced Manton. At least not entirely. But he *was* intrigued enough to want to visit the house for himself—certainly he felt safe with a close friend such as Carter nearby.

Delighted at Manton's interest, Carter cleverly, and extravagantly, revealed that the house in question was the spooky abandoned place right next to them.

As if on cue, a great rustling and crashing sounded from the attic. A tremendous creature swooped from the house, attacking Carter and Manton. The beast must have been in a particularly pleasant mood—both men survived. They awoke later to find themselves in the hospital, Manton raving about a slimy creature with a "thousand shapes of horror." The only word he could find to accurately describe the monster was "unnamable."

All of this ended Manton's career of literary criticism. Meanwhile, it spurred Carter upward to even more uncanny adventures.

## Mythos Survival Tip: Keep Out!

Randolph Carter's expeditions to the cemetery were completely unnecessary, and fraught with peril. If you can avoid it, don't hang out in cemeteries, or around spooky, abandoned houses.

## Why Buy a New Mattress When You Can Have a Cozy Tomb

While it's best to stay out of cemeteries whenever possible, sometimes you just can't help yourself. Lovecraft's story "The Tomb" describes the unfortunate adventures of Jervas Dudley, a young man compelled to frolic about in crypts and cemeteries.

Jervas had always been a bit strange—a self-confessed daydreamer and something of a loner. At a young age, Jervas stumbled across the tomb of the Hyde family. The Hydes lived in their giant mansion on top of the hill, until their mansion inconveniently burned down. Instead of rebuilding, the family decided to return to their native land. Still, it was a shame to put a perfectly good cemetery to waste, so whenever a loved one passed away, they'd ship an ash-filled urn back to the United States.

## I Like My Horror With a Dash of Sublime

All right, maybe the first time you encountered the explanation of Lovecraft and the sublime you didn't get it. As a result, maybe you shrugged it off as one of those things that wasn't really important. Well, it is *that* important, so here is another approach to understanding Lovecraft and the sublime:

Perhaps you've noticed by now that may of the creatures in Lovecraft's fiction are never described directly. Lovecraft's fiction illustrates the notion of *sublime horror*—the idea that the terrible monster *not* seen, lurking forever beyond the next door, is far worse than any monster you ever *could* see.

You know, like that horror movie you just watched recently. A man is running down the hall, terrified. He keeps glancing over his shoulder, eyes wide with a panic. Trying to escape . . . *something.* The *something* lurking right behind him. A *something* so awful, it can't be revealed yet, because your mind will implode upon the sight of it.

He reaches a door, but it's locked. Nowhere to go.

The man turns around slowly, to face his monstrous nemesis, back pressed against the door. Close-up of the horrified man's face. He's screaming. Eyes bulging, filled with terror. The *something* looms closer, is nearly upon him.

Pan out to reveal the terrible monster . . .. The most horrifying monster imaginable . . ..

. . . and there, in front of the guy, is a "zombie" in a cheap rubber mask. Fake blood is plastered to his face, and splattered over his shabby, alternative grunge outfit. He waves his arms about, grunting "Uhhhh" sounds. Suddenly, it's not so scary.

In Lovecraft's fiction, it's clear he believes less is better—what we imagine will always be worse than the reality.

155

As children are often attracted to the very thing they shouldn't be, young Jervas developed an unhealthy obsession with the new-found tomb—he would often travel to visit it; once he even attempted to break into it, and to make matters worse, he occasionally slept next to it. It seems Jervas was in dire need of other friends. Or any living friend for that matter.

Unfortunately, his tomb-fancy turned out not to be some passing fad. As Jervas grew older, his interest in the creepy crypt increased. And one day, upon waking from a nice, comfy nap next to his favorite hangout, Jervas was certain he'd heard voices, and saw a light inside the tomb, which had been quickly extinguished.

## INTO THE TOMB

One day Jervas discovered a key to the tomb. It was, in fact, hidden in his own attic. Joy overcame him, so he didn't ask the obvious question about why the key was in his attic. Instead, he was filled with electric elation—as the best part of a tomb is really the inside.

Without a second thought, he rushed to the crypt, eager to cavort about the dank interior to his heart's content. Sure enough, the key turned in the rusty lock. And soon, Jervas spent every evening romping through the inside of the tomb, exploring its depths, sleeping inside it, and just generally hanging out. Really, when one is young, what else is there to do?

However, it was only a matter of time before Jervas suffered from the inevitable change in personality and demeanor that comes to most in the Cthulhu Mythos. His

CRYPTS AND CEMETERIES

diction changed. So did his knowledge and interests. He spooked people in town by relating stories he shouldn't know anything about. And he developed an extreme, irrational fear of both fire and thunderstorms.

Not surprisingly, his parents grew concerned. They enlisted friends to clandestinely spy upon Jervas. One morning, Jervas was spotted emerging from his tomb-bedroom. Jervas detected the spy watching him from the bushes, but he breathed a sigh of relief when the spy reported to his parents that the youth spent his nights sleeping *next to* the tomb, and not *inside* of it.

## POSESSION IS NINE-TENTHS OF THE LAW

Although the family found his behavior a little weird, they decided not to curtail his visits to the tomb—it kept him out of trouble . . . mostly. But to all good things there comes an end. One evening while walking back to the tomb, Jervas discovered the once burned-down mansion was now intact—seemingly rebuilt. He wandered into the house and discovered a party in full swing.

But before he could join in the festivities, a crash of lightning speared the mansion, sending flames shooting into the air. Guests ran for exits, screaming. Jervas followed their example, but he wasn't fast enough. Embraced by the flames, he wailed as his flesh burned.

And as the last thoughts were passing through his head, he found himself put off by the fact that he would not be buried in the family tomb. He was a *Hyde*. And furthermore, being burned to a crisp inside his family mansion destroyed his ability to sleep eternally inside the tomb. Sure, maybe Jervas wasn't thinking clearly. But then again, he was being roasted alive.

After the tumult faded, neighbors and Jervas's father discovered the young man squirming and screaming at the long-incinerated site of the Hyde mansion. Jervas demanded to be buried in the tomb of his ancestors. Nearby, a box, uncovered when lightning struck a spot of rubble, deepened the mystery. Inside, neighbors discovered a porcelain miniature of a young man who was the spitting image of Jervas Dudley. The box sported the initials "J.H."

Jervas revealed he entered the tomb every night, sleeping in it.

CRYPTS AND CEMETERIES

But his father sadly shook his head, explaining the tomb's padlock remained in place. It appeared the crazy Jervas, who now fancied himself to be a member of the Hyde family, had only been visiting the tomb in his dreams.

As to be expected, the young man was carted away to the asylum. After a bit of coaxing, Jervas convinced his assistant, Hiram, to check out the tomb. Hiram did as much, and reported back to his insane friend, reenforcing Jervas' suspicions. For inside the tomb, an empty coffin awaited him, bearing the name "Jervas." And from that moment, Jervas knew that one day, his wish would be fulfilled. He'd resume his rightful place in the tomb of his ancestors.

## A Little Grave-Robbing Never Hurt Anyone

No matter what your friends and peculiar relatives tell you, grave robbing is never a good idea. Think about how many stories and films you've read or seen. How many times do things turn out well for the grave robbers? Sure, they might survive—well, some of them might survive—but there is always a great cost. This alone should steer you away from grave robbing. But some people are determined, regardless of the consequences. In Lovecraft's story, "The Hound," one English fellow, along with his companion St. John, discovered this the hard way. The two men had developed a nasty habit of looting local cemeteries. They even set up a macabre museum in their basement. In addition to standard tomb loot, the displays overflowed with disgusting souvenirs from their night-time cemetery visits—skulls, preserved heads, mummies. These two were just begging for trouble to find them.

Eventually, the two men traveled to Holland, hearing rumors of a ghoul buried in a churchyard. This particular ghoul also happened to be a grave-robber—when he was alive. Five hundred years prior, the ghoul allegedly nabbed a powerful item from a sephulcer. The two men concluded it must have been buried with the ghoul (one can only wonder why they believed such a thing; after all, Holland has a few grave-robbers as well).

## MYTHOS SURVIVAL TIP:
### SLEEP ELSEWHERE

If you ever find yourself compelled to perform strange acts, or do socially unacceptable things (such as sleeping inside a tomb), consider whether or not you may be *possessed*. Possession is sometimes a gradual thing. You may start feeling strange urges, or compulsions. In most cases, you won't even realize these new thoughts are not your own—as you are possessed.

Don't consider professional help. More likely than not, a psychiatrist will toss you in the loony bin. An exorcist *may* help, but it really depends on the type of possession.

In general, the best option is to remain wary of unfamiliar thoughts and behaviors. Learn to suppress such thoughts, through sheer will. For example, if you find yourself overwhelmed with the desire to sleep in a tomb, force yourself to sleep in your own bed. Buy one of those new-fangled adjustable air mattresses—they're supposed to be quite comfy. Find friends, any friends, and reveal to them your desires. If they think tomb-napping sounds fun, then find new friends. At some point, someone is going to mock you—and really, the mocking can help suppress the compulsive urges. Of course, there is a risk to this. It might be that you later seek revenge upon those who've mocked you, but that's another story.

Digging up the alleged ghoul's grave, the two men found the corpse. Amazingly it was intact, despite five hundred years of resting beneath the ground. On closer examination, the body appeared to have been mauled by an animal. But what really caught the grave-robbers' eyes was the exquisite green jade amulet inside the coffin, depicting a winged hound (this is when the first internal alarm should sound for most people).

Not giving it a second thought, they absconded the item, and returned to England with their newfound treasure. But after a few days at home in their manor house the morbid pair suspected they had uninvited company. They heard strange fumblings echoing inside the house. Knocks at the door at late hours of the night. A shrill cackling. Chatter, in a language that sounded like Dutch. And often, the eerie sound of a hound, baying in the distance.

And then things turned bad. One night, as St. John headed home from the railway station, a creature descended upon him, shredding poor St. John into pieces. With his last, croaking

## MYTHOS SURVIVAL TIP: GUARD YOUR ITEMS

Sometimes a book or a trinket comes with a powerful curse. Naturally, you'll want to rid yourself of the supernatural punishment that accompanies ownership of such an item. Most likely, in a moment of greed or blind ignorance, you picked-up the item, thinking you'd be wealthy, and instead your backlog of close friends started dying—assuming you've prepared your friends properly.

This means you'll most likely find yourself wishing to rid yourself of the accursed thing. Returning it to its owner or resting place is always a good start. But regardless of how you remove the curse, it is essential to keep close track of what has become of the most important item in your life—your fate rests with it. This requires you to keep the item locked away until it is safely returned to its proper place. And like most powerful Mythos items, it attracts other greedy or blindly ignorant people (think of how it was acquired in the first place). The absolute worst option is leaving it in plain sight, in your hotel room, just before you are about to return it. Be assured if this happens, it will vanish. This is because curses, like most stage plays, enjoy irony. Keep it safe, keep it hidden.

whisper, he blamed the cursed amulet. His friend, fearing a similar if not worse fate—as he *was* a friend, after all—decided it was time to leave town. Furthermore, to insure his safety, he was determined to return the jade trinket to its burial place. He hurriedly journeyed to Holland, but he made the unfortunate mistake of leaving the amulet unattended, in his Rotterdam hotel.

Unexpectedly, a gang of thieves looted the Englishman's room, taking with them the amulet. But this time, the joke was on them. The following day, the paper reported a den of thieves was attacked by a strange creature, and everyone was torn to shreds. Witnesses spoke of hearing the baying of a hound.

Desperately, the Englishman returned to the gravesite, exhuming the ghoulish creature (possibly to ask for advice). But he recoiled in horror when he saw jade amulet, clasped within the ghoul's gnarled and decomposing hand. Clearly, returning the amulet would not allow him to escape his fate. He, too, would be ripped to shreds by the eldritch hound, which now reminded him of his eventual death, baying incessantly in the distance.

# Not Dead, But Dreaming

Three times Randolph Carter dreamed of the marvelous city, and three times was he snatched away while still he paused on the high terrace above it. All golden and lovely it blazed in the sunset, with walls, temples, colonnades and arched bridges of veined marble, silver-basined fountains of prismatic spray in broad squares and perfumed gardens, and wide streets marching between delicate trees and blossom-laden urns and ivory statues in gleaming rows; while on steep northward slopes climbed tiers of red roofs and old peaked gables harbouring little lanes of grassy cobbles.

—H.P. Lovecraft, "The Dream-Quest of Unknown Kadath"

Dreams are an essential facet of the Mythos. Not only did many of Lovecraft's stories originate from his dreams (or nightmares), but he returned to the subject of dreaming repeatedly. Dreams, hallucinations, even drug-induced stupors, can lead to divine insight and artistic illumination in the Cthulhu Mythos (and so claim many Romantic writers from the 18th century).

In some of his writings, Lovecraft brought to life a strange, alternate dimension known as the Dreamlands—a reality existing on top of our own. The Dreamlands are resplendent with magical vistas, mysterious inhabitants, and dangerous creatures—some of which can travel to the waking realm. As your Mythos knowledge grows, you will learn how to harness the tamer creatures—and avoid the rest.

## THE CRAWLING CHAOS

Often, in the Cthulhu Mythos, drugs are utilized to harness the power of dreams—or hallucinations. Sometimes, such power is discovered inadvertently. For example, in the story, "The Crawling Chaos," a plague patient, receiving an accidental overdose of opium to treat his symptoms, learns that the drug helped to ease his headache, but also induced frightening visions. This begs the question: Is the treatment worth the cost of the side effects?

During his overdose, the patient found himself inside an elaborate room—decorated with fancy vases, ottomans, and the like. While he rather liked the fancy surroundings, an incessant pounding in the background disturbed him dreadfully.

The patient searched for the source of the noise. He checked the window, and noticed a tumultuous storm brewing. Seething waves lurched forward from the angry sea in the vista before him. And each surge threatened to submerge the house entirely. Completely spooked by what he saw, he ran for it, heading inland, eventually finding a safe spot underneath a palm tree where he rested.

He didn't get much rest because a young child promptly dropped from the tree, and floated toward him. Solemnly, the child explained what the waves were about—the world was coming to an end. But no worries, the boy, along with two more floating godlike friends, would gladly escort the man to the blissful land of Teloe, and there he would dwell happily ever after.

On the surface, the decision was easy. But that's the trick of the Mythos—things always seem simple and evident, until you get involved in them. But having no close friends to scout the way, and having not read this book, the man floated upward with the child-like entities. As they climbed, the crowd increased, until eventually it was a total party—people dancing about, singing, and playing lutes. Floating ever upward, the patient realized this Teloe place must be pretty darn cool. And all he had to do, the child whispered in his ear, was keep looking forward, and never look back down, at Earth (obviously this was a sinister child-like thing). To no one's surprise (including you and me), the patient looked.

Below, he saw the surface of Earth being consumed by monstrous waves. Eventually, a great rift opened across the flooded planet, swallowing the water and spitting it out as steam. The rift widened, and with much cracking and hissing, the planet finally exploded in a fiery blast. This was enough to wake the patient (tells you a little about him—child-like entities partying isn't disturbing, but a good planet crunch is worrisome).

Of course, it's possible the patient simply experienced the results of an opium overdose—but then no one would be writing about it. It's also possible he witnessed the destruction of the entire world. Either way, a lesson can be learned from the patient's experience (who obviously spent the rest of his days kicking himself over the whole "don't look back" mistake).

Umm, here is where the "lesson learned" should go. But as this tale was akin to Lovecraft's Dreamland stories, it's a bit open ended. You see, Lovecraft did admire the writers of the Romantic Period, and they bought into the power of imagination and the sublime (remember the sublime?). And a number of Romantic writers dabbled in the supernatural, and drugs, or recounted dreams, occasionally leaving their works open to reader interpretation. That's to say, it's best to let the reader's imagination explore and find its own meaning. What this means to you the reader is that while a "lesson" can be offered for the previous story, it would be one person's interpretation. In the end, the best "lesson" comes

## WHAT TO DO WHEN YOU HAVE APOCALYPTIC VISIONS

1. Consider cutting back on the opium. Maybe it doesn't help, but it certainly doesn't hurt.

2. If you *do* take opium, and find yourself being guided to a paradise in the sky named Teloe, and are told not to look back, *don't look back*. It's pretty simple.

3. Keep a record of how often apocalyptic visions occur. For the most part, everyone agrees as the level of danger increases, so does the frequency of the visions. If the number is low, keep gathering friends. If the number is high, start brainstorming a means of escape—this varies depending on the content of the visions you're having.

4. Consider taking a few classes in literature. At first blush, this might seem pointless. But closer inspection reveals that most apocalyptic visions are laden with heavy metaphors. Learning how to interpret these elusive metaphors can mean the difference between living and dying. In other words, *yes*, an English class can save your life, and the lives of others.

5. Just how apocalyptic is the vision? Consider it carefully. If the destruction and horror seems isolated to a particular part of the globe, then maybe just avoid that area. While most people view these horrifying visions as the "end of the world," this isn't always the case. Sometimes it's just the end of a specific place—take Atlantis for example. Sure, it was apocalyptic for the denizens of Atlantis, but it didn't bother most other people.

6. If you're not using drugs or alcohol while having apocalyptic visions, maybe consider adding them into the mix. See what comes up. If things get better, then maybe the issue was stress related. If things get worse, then cut back on the booze and dope. Regardless, this is not a long term solution. It is more of a means of determining the type of visions you're having.

7. Are there zombies or masses of undead in your visions? If so, then it's most likely not related to the Cthulhu Mythos. Horrific, all-powerful creatures are the foundation of a Mythos apocalyptic vision, as is the prompt and concise destruction of the world. Aimless, wandering dead is an entirely different book.

CONTINUED . . .

NOT DEAD, BUT DREAMING

> ## WHAT TO DO WHEN YOU HAVE APOCALYPTIC VISIONS (CONTINUED)
>
> 8. This may sound silly, but are the dreams yours? Before taking any action, make sure you don't have a revengeful *former* friend (who survived) using his pineal gland to induce nightmares into your otherwise peaceful sleep. The easiest way to uncover this one is to change your sleep schedule, but don't let anyone know.
>
> 9. Have you read a Mythos book recently? The *Necronomicon* is one that pops to the top of the list, but any of the other tomes mentioned in this book are likely candidates. If you have read one of these, the good news is the world is probably not coming to an end . . . yet. The bad news is you're insane from reading one of those tomes.
>
> 10. Examine your diet. While it might not be apocalyptic, it still could be unhealthy. And eating before sleeping, or consuming foods which disagree with you—or produce allergic affects—can result in apocalyptic visions. Actually, in a wide variety of visions. But given the fact you're reading this book, most likely the visions will be of the end of the world. Maybe a simple allergy test can resolve the entire "end of time" visions, and you'll be all the healthier for it.

from the reader—assuming the reader can come up with a lesson. If one is needed in a pinch, try the used, but proven, "don't look back" lesson. Honestly, the man was told not to do it, but he just couldn't resist temptation. Now most everyone has read that type of story before. But no one seems to learn.

## HOW DID THAT DREAM MAKE YOU FEEL?

Perhaps you're already experiencing unusual dreams (even before embarking upon your studies of the Cthulhu Mythos). If you are, tread carefully when it comes to having them analyzed. Take the case of Joe Slater, an institution asylum inmate from the Catskills, whose case was documented in "Beyond the Wall of Sleep."

Slater had always been a little odd, but one day he suffered a screaming, shrieking fit, after waking from a dream. His neighbors made the mistake of attempting to restrain him. This left several neighbors with bumps and bruises.

Being generous, the neighbors decided not to complain, especially after they saw what happened to the *other* guy. Or at least the pulpy mess that once had been the "other guy." It seems, in a fit of delirium, Slater pulverized one of the neighbors, which did earn him a quick trip to the sanitarium.

After spending some time institutionalized, one of the interns developed a special interest in Slater. The intern was intrigued when Slater suffered a series of bizarre attacks. During the fits, Slater rambled about fantastic, gorgeous vistas, straight out of a fantasy novel. This struck the intern as odd, since Slater was a seriously backwoods kind of guy, with little exposure to supernatural fiction (or any fiction for that matter).

But despite the awe-inspiring vistas of Slater's dreams, the wretched man spent most of his time during the attacks ranting about a malevolent being. The malign entity held Slater in contempt, mocking and tormenting him. Slater swore revenge against the creature, proclaiming he'd find and destroy it, even if he had to venture across the chasm of space to do so. If anything, Slater clearly had ambition.

## LET ME JUST ATTACH THIS WIRE HERE . . .

With each passing day, Slater's health declined, and he grew feebler. The intern decided to reconstruct a "cosmic radio" device he invented in college (what luck!)—hoping to telepathically get inside Slater's addled brain.

He connected the device to Slater's head, and to his own. Nothing happened. As most people are wont to do when an uncomfortable telepathic head-rig is attached, the intern became bored and drifted into slumber. Then things became exciting. He found himself inside Slater's fantasy dream-land, and it was even cooler than Slater had described. Great, shadowy mountains and valleys. Haunting music. And an ethereal light-being, who dropped by to have a chat with the intern.

NOT DEAD, BUT DREAMING

The light-being explained he was Joe Slater's "other" self—the cosmic version of Slater's planet-bound soul. Unlike planet versions, cosmic souls transcend time—a light-being is just as likely to end up in the mind of an Egyptian pharaoh, as in a bumbling idiot such as Joe Slater.

## MYTHOS SURVIVAL TIP: YOU WON'T BELIEVE ME, BUT . . .

So, you experienced something. A supernatural event, or Mythos experience that should have left you gibbering like a mad person. Maybe it did, for awhile. Regardless, the event has left you marred for life, and shaken, but with no substantive evidence—not even a prize like: *I Just Saw Nyarlathotep and All I Got Was This Crazy T-Shirt* tee.

After you've weighed all sides and ruled out whether you really *are* crazy, you'll probably start thinking about telling someone. Anyone. Your parents. Your teacher. Your best friend.

Don't. Telling people you trust inevitably leads them to the conclusion that you've gone insane. Sure, it seems odd. After all, where did the "trust" go? Sadly, that's just the way things are. People you trust believe you are crazy if you reveal crazy-sounding things. Drunks and strangers are more apt to believe you, by the way.

So instead of blathering about the weirdness going on inside your head, sit back, relax. Keep your mouth shut. Take your time, and try to gather proof to support your mad tale. If you're never able to do so, no worries—when your best friend is eaten by the tentacled, winged creature you've been dreaming about every night, you'll find it to be much easier to run away when you're not inside the sanitarium. And you'll know, just before your friend died, that he or she truly understood what it was that was bothering you—but which you wouldn't reveal.

So the light-being was feeling like he'd been short changed, due to his forty-two years of "Joe" time. With Slater's death, the light-being could escape for awhile and get down to business. Particularly the business of slaying his tormenting, mocking, long-time foe, which dwelled near the star of Algol (light-beings lead a confusing life it seems). And, finally finding his freedom through Slater's death, the light-being sped away, traveling across the stars, to slay his enemy—leaving poor Slater as the first casualty of the event.

Of course, when fellow hospital employees found the intern, snoring and drooling, on top of dead Joe Slater, the intern couldn't tell them anything. These were trusted friends, and the intern understood the risk of telling them such a crazy story—he did work in a sanitarium. But the intern did take a small amount of comfort, at least, upon hearing of the new star discovered not far from Algol—it blazed brightly in the night sky for a few weeks before fading away.

## THE DREAMLANDS

One of the more unique realms of the Cthulhu Mythos is the Dreamlands. It resides in a dimension beyond this one. You can't book a flight there, or travel by rail. For the most part, dreams are about the only means of access. Or if you're really good at it, willpower alone can transport you there.

Initially, the concept of the Dreamlands is tough to wrestle with. The best way to think of it is as a reality superimposed over our own—complete with its own geography, and its own moon. As you might guess from the name, the place is pretty dreamy. And sometimes nightmarish.

With all of that said, according to Lovecraft's writings, there are a few ways to sneak into the Dreamlands. Some people, like Randolph Carter, easily cross into the Dreamlands during slumber. Others utilize drugs to reach the appropriate level of unconsciousness (not to mention a wicked buzz—but this maybe still counts as a dream of sorts). Other folk claim to be able to visit the Dreamlands through a more direct physical means.

NOT DEAD, BUT DREAMING

As might be expected, there are many things that are different in the Dreamlands. For instance, time passes differently there as opposed to the waking world—a six month trip around the ocean may occur in a single night's of slumber in our dimension.

Of course, none of this actually describes what the Dreamlands are. One approach is to say the Dreamlands is a place of light and dark fantasy—perhaps more dark. A land where great kingdoms vie for dominance over one another. In the Dreamlands, men and creatures launch wars against each other. This might sound like a dangerous place to visit, and it can be for the unwary traveler, or if you step on the tail of a cat.

## An Order of Terror With a Side of DOOM

One of the greatest cities of the Dreamlands exists now only in legend. This place was dubbed Sarnath, and in Lovecraft's tale "The Doom that Came to Sarnath," its history is revealed.

It was some ten thousand years ago, when the city of Ib overlooked a vast lake, in the land of Mnar. The sagging, lizard-like residents of Ib were beings that were soft like jelly, with bulging eyes and big, floppy mouths. They lived contently until one day, a group of tribesmen arrived upon the lake, and built the city of Sarnath. These new tribesmen distrusted the strange, lizard-like inhabitants of Ib, and frowned upon their worship of the water-lizard Bokrug.

Deciding to protect themselves against a possible future threat (proactive defense), the warriors of Sarnath promptly marched to Ib and killed every denizen within the city. The invaders also sacked the place and razed it for good measure. The only remnant of Ib remaining was a sea-green stone idol, chiseled in the likeness of Bokrug, which the warriors brought back to their temple in Sarnath. Some things are too good to destroy, even if they should be destroyed.

And then things started to go wrong. The next morning, the high priest, Taran-Ish, was found dead in the temple. Apparently he'd died of fright. And to make things worse, the sea-green idol was missing.

NOT DEAD, BUT DREAMING

But there was a clue. Scrawled shakily upon the altar, probably the handwriting of Taran-Ish, was a single word: "DOOM." No matter how you spell it, the word wasn't a good omen.

## NICE PLACE TO VISIT, BUT . . .

But even a bad omen can't keep a city from flourishing. Sarnath established trade routes with nearby cities. Its warriors conquered neighboring territories in Mnar, and eventually Sarnath's control spread over the land.

For those visiting the great city of Sarnath, it was a sight to behold. It sported huge walls of polished marble, streets of onyx, and its palaces and gardens were legendary.

To make sure no irony was lost when the promised "doom" arrived, the residents of Sarnath celebrated every year with a festival dedicated to the destruction of the city Ib. Given that the battle was a lopsided victory, and the attack was predicated on nothing other than Sarnath's prejudice against Ib's jelly-bellied residents, the celebration might have seemed unusal to outsiders (but they didn't understand the need for dramatic irony in Sarnath). Undaunted, the townspeople of Sarnath held a feast, danced, and sang—all in celebration of the destruction of non-threatening Ib. Things were shaping up to be grand.

The best traditions are those which span centuries, and this was a spectacular tradition—it lasted nearly one thousand years. And as the big one thousand year party approached, the inhabitants of Sarnath decided to crank up the energy, and host the largest gala ever. This grandest of grand events was ten years in the planning, and Sarnath residents were certain the party would be the talk of all the land. The party to end all parties. After all, no one partied like the people of Sarnath.

With all of the excitement of the party, no one noticed the strange, green mist settling over the city. Or the weird lights upon the rapidly rising water. Given these are the sort of things that are difficult to ignore for long, eventually some folk did take notice. This transformed into a vague fear which spread throughout the city. The out-of-towners, mostly royalty from distant lands, decided not to stick around, heading out to find less misty venues.

NOT DEAD, BUT DREAMING

Most likely, they'd learned about dramatic irony from their scholars and saw the writing on the wall—so to speak.

But all of this strangeness didn't perturb the citizens of Sarnath. At least most of them. They continued undaunted, undisturbed, and found they were in for quite a show.

## This Party's Over

Around midnight, screams filled the night air as the celebrants fled the festival. Terror roiled over the city. Folks poured through the gate, citizens and visitors alike. Later, the few surviving guests (none of the citizens of Sarnarth were to be found) spoke of the horrific sight they beheld. Horrifying vast hordes of flabby, lizard-like creatures filled the banquet hall, and stood in the very spots where the royalty of Sarnath danced moments before.

For many years following, travelers avoided Sarnath. But eventually, a few worked up the nerve to visit the city—or at least its location. Those who arrived found that the once glorious city of Sarnath had disappeared—a bit like Ib had vanished. Sitting in the sand was the sea-green idol of Bokrug, the water-lizard.

## Mythos Survival Tip: Pick Your Battles

When encountering a Mythos creature, don't make assumptions. The creature may not be stronger, smarter, or swifter, but through literary tropes, it might be able to best you.

Sure, a harmless, flabby, jelly-like lizard creature may be easy to kill—okay, they are. But they wield the power of irony, or the anger of their god. The last laugh belongs to them. However, if you feel compelled to destroy every last one of them, and burn their city to the ground, *don't* take the statue of their god. It's clearly a set-up, and the deities of the Cthulhu Mythos have plenty of time to exact revenge.

Although it took nearly one thousand years, it appeared that like vengeance, doom is a dish best served cold.

## When the Cat's Away

Perhaps you're familiar with some of the writings of H.P. Lovecraft and you're reading this book just to reassure yourself that you are familiar with his writings. If so, that means you already have read another one of Lovecraft's famous Dreamlands tales, "The Cats of Ulthar." For those unfamiliar, yes, the title has "cats" in it. If you're clever, you'll notice that "cats" is occupying the normal spot where words such as "thing," "doom," "shadow," "terror," and other such dread-filled words appear. This could serve as a useful tidbit of information. It might even give you something to ponder. Did Lovecraft equate "cats" with these other dark words? Even for those familiar with Lovecraft's writings, it's still worth pondering for a few moments.

If there is a golden rule in Ulthar, it would be: Don't kill any cats. Actually, that's a law in Ulthar. Prior to this unusual ordinance, a nasty cotter and his wife would kill any cat unfortunate enough to stray onto their property. Judging by the tortured sounds wafting from their cottage at night, the couple enjoyed the activity.

No one in Ulthar knew what to do about the frightful couple, and there wasn't anyone in town who dared confront them. Residents simply kept their cats as far away from the mad cotters as possible.

As might be expected in a land of mystical fantasy, one day, a caravan arrived. With it came many travelers, and among them was a small boy named Menes. Young Menes had a tiny, black kitten that he loved to play with. The unfortunate boy had lost his family to a plague, and this tiny kitten was all he had left in the world (you can see this one coming).

### Oh, No, Not the Little Orphan Boy's Cute Little Kitten!

That's right, unable to restrain themselves, the monstrous cat-killing couple sank their evil claws into Menes' poor, innocent, tiny black kitten. No doubt it mewed longingly as the vicious abductors nabbed it. Sadly, the kitten was never seen again—by anyone else.

Suffice to say, young Menes was put off by all of this. And for reasons unknown, the boy set about chanting in a strange tongue. As he did, the clouds floating overhead swirled into shadowy, nebulous forms (storms are literary metaphors for "bad things").

This chanting continued for quite some time. But eventually Menes wrapped it up, and seemingly with no apparent effect. The wanderers left town the next day. But it didn't take long for the residents to notice that every cat in town had vanished.

Quickly, tales from snooping people came to light. Rumors spread of the cats being seen pacing around the old cotter's house. Yet, now the cats were nowhere to be found. There seemed only one conclusion: The cotter and his wife had killed all of the cats. Every last one, probably in some horrid, painful manner.

## Nine Lives

It turns out, there was more than one possible conclusion. It seems a misuse of logic simply led to the incorrect conclusion,

### Mythos Survival Tip: Become a Cat Person

Have you been a dog-lover all of your life? Well, if you find yourself trapped in the Dreamlands, it's time to change sides. Cats are the animal of choice in the land of deep slumber.

The cats of the Dreamlands are sentient beings, often willing to help out a kind human. Cats follow a *scratch my back and I'll scratch yours* philosophy (or scratching post, whichever is most convenient). Do a cat some good in the Dreamlands, and it will return the favor.

Always go out of your way to pet a cat, and make sure you're carrying an ample supply of catnip.

because the cats all returned. The residents of Ulthar were delighted, and even the cats were fat and sassy. With no worries, and the sun shining brightly, the cats did nothing but lay about for days on end, content to do nothing than doze and purr. Pretty typical cat stuff.

Although the people of Ulthar weren't quite as fast to pick-up on the absence of the cotter and his wife—when compared to the missing cats. The people eventually did notice. After careful consideration, a group of villagers worked up the nerve to visit the cranky cotter. No one answered the door, so they let themselves inside. And there, they found two skeletons upon the floor, picked clean.

The news traveled quickly, and Ulthar residents immediately put the "no killing cats" law into effect.

## Wrap it Up in Celephaïs

It's not clear how the Dreamlands came to be, and who created them. But the tale "Celephaïs" offers a clue. The story tells of a great city, Celephaïs, bursting into existence when King Kuranes dreamed it up.

Kuranes hadn't been a king in England, back when he still had a body. But in the land of dreams, he ruled the city of Celephaïs (which seems fair, after all, he created it). When Kuranes initially began dreaming about Celephaïs, he couldn't get enough of it. He had the placed decked out with marble walls and great bronze statues. But in time, journeying there became more difficult. It seemed the harder he tried, the harder it was to return to the magical city.

### A Drug Trip to the Dreamlands

Desperate, Kuranes ingested every drug he could find. Admittedly, this wasn't a brilliant idea, and as it turns out, did little to actually help. Not even a vast array of herbal and manmade pharmaceuticals promised a return to his dream-city. Eventually he ran out of drugs and money. Being broke, he was kicked out of his home (landlords are tough about not paying the rent, future king of a Dreamland city or not). All Kuranes could do was wander the streets aimlessly. Or so it seemed.

On the streets, Kuranes encountered a friendly contingent of knights. And these dedicated fellows were ready to escort him to the city of Celephaïs. Delighted, Kuranes followed as the armored knights politely led him down the road, and over the side of a cliff.

The next day the townsfolk found Kuranes' body floating along the shore. Naturally, they assumed he was dead—having no pulse and being very pale. As it turns out, they couldn't have been further from the truth. Kuranes and his loyal knight contingent floated gracefully downward, off the cliff, and into the grand city of his dreams.

One would think Kuranes was completely satisfied. But irony runs rampant in the Dreamlands, and after a while the man found himself homesick—for England. He longed for the simple boyhood life in the countryside. It turns out, being a king isn't all that easy. Or to turn an old phrase, the grass is always greener in another reality.

But this time, there wasn't anything left for Kuranes to do. Certainly no knights from England would show up and escort him home—after all, he was a pauper back in England.

## It's All About Randolph Carter

You probably recall the plucky weird fiction writer named Randolph Carter. He was mentioned a few times in previous chapters. That's right—the guy who can't stay out of cemeteries. Well, Randolph Carter also had an affinity for dreaming—in fact, he had quite a talent for it. And this proved exceedingly handy on Carter's multiple ventures within the Dreamlands.

Carter's most famous adventure is described in "The Dream-Quest of Unknown Kadath." The tale chronicles his attempts to find Kadath, the place where the gods live, in order to ask them a few questions.

Several times, Carter dreamed of a fantastic city that blazed golden in the sunset, full of perfumed gardens, silver fountains, and streets made of marble (marble is abundant in the Dreamlands). But he only received brief glimpses of his dream-city, and was pulled away before he could wander its wide streets or frolic in the fountains.

Taking matters into his own hands, Carter decided it was time to consult with the gods. The gods of the Dreamlands lived in the dream-city of Kadath. Though weaker than the powerful Outer Gods, the gods of the Dreamlands had to, at the very least, know how to get to Carter's amazing city. But gods being gods, they weren't in the mood to be found. Carter found it very difficult to locate gods who were not returning calls. He tried praying to them. No luck there. Carter suspected they were hanging around their city of Kadath, and just ignoring him. Not the type to give up, Carter embarked upon his quest to find Kadath. And once he was there, he fully intended to ask those reclusive gods a question or two.

## How Many Steps, Now?

For Carter and his quest, it turns out there are two phases to entering the Dreamlands. In light slumber, the dreamer descends seventy steps, down to the cavern of flame. But it is seven hundred more steps to reach the Gate of Deeper Slumber, and the Enchanted Wood beyond. All in all, this was easier than counting sheep because there was a definite number offered for success.

The Enchanted Wood is the home of small, rat-like creatures known as the zoogs. For a bunch of rodents, the zoogs are very intelligent and inquisitive—and in some circles known to be quite fast. When Carter entered the Enchanted Wood, a contingent of zoogs decided to follow him upon his quest. While zoogs can be dangerous to humans, Carter cleverly forged a pact with the creatures. He even spoke a bit of their weird, fluttering language. So they didn't bother him (and the creatures even shared some of their awesome moon-wine, offering him a bottle for the road).

When asked, even the zoogs didn't know how to find Kadath. The best they offered was that he should visit Ulthar and check out the informative Pnakotic Manuscripts. He could also consult with the priest Atal, who had his own history with the gods.

## Of Drunk Priests and Other Things

As it turned out, the Pnakotic Manuscripts were of little use. And Atal wasn't very forthcoming, either. He knew nothing of Carter's "city of dreams," and grew tight-lipped on the subject

NOT DEAD, BUT DREAMING

## MYTHOS SURVIVAL TIP:
## AVOID ZOOGS

Zoogs are small, brown creatures that primarily hang out in the Enchanted Wood, although they've been known to venture further to satisfy their inquisitive nature The zoogs' primary diet is a fungi growing in the wood. But they've also been known to partake of the occasional human-snack.

Your best bet to avoid zoog attacks is to stay out of the Enchanted Wood entirely, or traverse through it as quickly as possible. Though the creatures are small, a good-sized swarm of zoogs can easily bring a human down. Luckily, if you die in the Dreamlands, odds are *pretty* good you won't die in real life. Pretty good.

If you absolutely *must* travel though the Enchanted Wood, bring a cat, if you can. Zoogs and cats get along smashingly.

of visiting the gods. Atal and his companion had tried to do so, once, and his companion died for it. Such is the fate of friends even in the Dreamlands.

Disappointed, Carter tried another approach—he offered Atal some of the moon-wine, which resulted in the priest becoming stinking drunk. Carter was a writer, and he clearly understood the many uses of alcohol. The two go hand-in-hand (writers and booze that is).

With no inhibitions to hinder him, the priest babbled about an image depicting the likeness of the gods. It was carved into the mountain of Ngranek, on the Oriab Isle. Allegedly, there were mortals in the Dreamlands who lived close to the gods' great city of Kadath, and these mortals resembled the gods. So all Carter had to do was climb this mountain, check out the carving, and then scour the Dreamlands for mortals that resembled the carving. After that Kadath had to be nearby.

Remember, this is drunk logic, so it doesn't follow the rules of Aristotelian logic.

## OFF TO ORIAB

Carter ditched his inquisitive zoog-escort in Ulthar, thanks to the cats (the cats gobbled up the zoogs when a young zoog started making "Mmm, tasty" sounds at one of the black kittens). Heading to the port town of Dylath-Leen, Carter hoped to catch the ship to Oriab.

In Dylath-Leen, Carter questioned the locals about Ngranek. But they had little to say as they were all fretting over the dread black galleys docked in town. Sure, the galleys were stuffed full of rubies upon arrival. This made their existence more tolerable. But townspeople continued to whisper about their strange crews, with their odd-shaped shoes and strangely pointed turbans. Not unlike the citizens of Sarnath, the people of Dylath-Leen seemed a little intolerant of different cultures.

Unperturbed by all of the locals gazing, one of the merchants from a black galley approached Carter, smugly claiming to have information regarding Carter's quest for Kadath. Being a master of booze, Carter tried his moon-wine trick again. However, it seems that moon-wine doesn't affect everyone the same way. Instead, the merchant smirked and offered Carter some wine from *his* bottle. Sadly, Carter wasn't smart enough to recognize his own trick, or perhaps the writer in him couldn't resist a quick nip. All it took was one sip, and he was unconscious (in a manner of speaking when referring to the Dreamlands).

Carter awakened on a black galley, sailing straight to the moon (yes, the moon), and over to the dark side (yes, the dark side of the moon), where no human had ever tread before (if you know some songs from the album, start humming them now).

## NEVER FEAR, THE CATS ARE HERE

Upon his lunar arrival, Carter was escorted to a very unpleasant city. While there, he spotted inhuman figures, moving about on the wharves. They were large, gray-white creatures, called *moonbeasts*, and they were the ones running the show. It just so happens the unfortunate crews of the black galleys were actually slaves to

NOT DEAD, BUT DREAMING

the moon-beasts. And the slaves were not human, either—the turbans and funny shoes disguised their non-human features. It didn't take long for the hangover-headed Carter to comprehend that the moon-beasts planned to trade Carter for a variety of goodies, to the deity Nyarlathotep (yes, he's everywhere).

Being the prepared sort of person, Carter had always been a cat-person. And in addition, during his visit he'd treated the cats of Ulthar well. The cats heard whispers of Carter's plight, and called upon their Cat Army to descend en masse upon the moon-beast city. They rescued Carter, and then cuddled up all around him, creating a snuggly, furry cat-transport used to whisk him back to Dreamlands-Earth (don't laugh at it until you've tried it).

### . . . Oh No, Not Again

Even though he was a writer, somehow Carter managed to overlook the abundant use of irony in the Dreamlands. So after finally boarding a ship in Dylath-Leen, Carter arrived at Oriab Isle. Once there, he dutifully climbed the mountain of Ngranek. And to his surprise, although it shouldn't have been, the gods in the carving resembled sailors Carter had seen before—in the port of Celephaïs.

But before Carter could start back down the mountain, he was kidnapped—again—by a giant, winged creature called a night-gaunt. This particular critter was guarding Ngranek. The fearsome creature tickled Carter into submission (yes, tickled; this is the night-gaunt's preferred method of attack). Clearly having defeated Carter, the night-gaunt carried Carter away from Ngranek and dropped him at the vast vale of Pnoth. The only company he found there were bones.

But Carter had another *friend* card yet to play. Many ghouls dwelled in the vale of Pnoth, and Carter shared a mutual acquaintance with the ghouls—none other than the eccentric artist, Robert Pickman. Out of friendship, the ghouls indicated they might help Carter find his way back—unless the creepy, worm-like dholes inhabiting the vale gobbled him up first.

## Ghouls, Gugs, and Ghasts . . . Oh My!

The ghouls were happy to help, and escorted him to his old friend, Robert Pickman, who now dwelled in the Dreamlands—permanently as a ghoul. In his new, gibbering manner of speech, Pickman advised Carter to reconsider this quest idea (it sure wasn't going well so far). Being determined, Carter would have none of it. Reluctantly the ghouls agreed to help Carter escape, though the escape led them through the terrifying city of the enormous, hairy gugs. Fortunately, it was the safest time to sojourn into the gugs' town—they were all snoring after a hearty meal. Besides, gugs were oddly afraid of ghouls anyway. But the ghoul-crew needed to stay sharp in case they were assaulted by ghasts—equally terrifying creatures that often crept into the city for the occasional gug snack.

Carter and his ghoul companions tiptoed through the city, dodging the occasional gug sentry, and lurking ghast. They headed into the Tower of Koth, up the stairway inside . . .

. . . and out into the Enchanted Wood beyond.

That's right, Carter was back where he started, and back to the literary tropes.

## CAT FIGHT!

As Carter traipsed yet again through the delightful Enchanted Wood, he heard the zoogs whispering feverishly about retaliation plans against the cats, due to the now infamous *black-kitten-zoog-eating* incident. Apparently, the zoogs were planning a stealthy counter-strike upon Carter's feline friends of Ulthar, and hadn't

---

### MYTHOS SURVIVAL TIP:
### SURVIVING A NIGHT-GAUNT KIDNAPPING

Night-gaunts are large, black, slippery creatures with wings, claws, horns, and a long tail. And they are intimidating to gaze upon. If you find yourself in the clutches of a night-gaunt, try not to struggle. If you do, they will tickle you incessantly.

The best defense against a night-gaunt is to stay away from the areas guarded by night-gaunts, such as Ngranek. If that's not possible, or if you encounter a night-gaunt somewhere other than the great mountain, you'll fare best if you happen to not be ticklish (layering garments may offer additional defense). If you are ticklish, well, a GPS or other navigation device may help for when you are inevitably dropped in the vale of Pnoth (sorry, cats are of no help this time, except perhaps for company).

If you ever manage to learn the ghoul language, it's helpful when dealing with night-gaunts. Although Carter didn't know it yet, night-gaunts work extensively with the ghouls, and respond to commands in their language.

This means it might be worth having a friend or two who is a ghoul.

---

NOT DEAD, BUT DREAMING

realized that in order to be stealthy, maybe they should stop whispering about their plans so loudly.

Carter, loyal to the cats, decided a little *kit* for *kat* would be in his best interest. He sent a message to the cats by cat-telegram (the cats traveled from one to the next relaying messages all the way back to Ulthar). Soon the Cat Army arrived, unleashing some serious hurt on the entirely unprepared zoogs.

After teaching the zoogs who's the boss, the cats settled down with them and negotiated peace terms. This mainly consisted of the promise of no more cat-disappearances on the border to zoog territory. As a guarantee, a few zoog nobles would be kept as hostages in Ulthar, and lastly, the zoogs had to pay a poultry fee to the cats—that is, provide poultry for free. While things went swimmingly well for the cats, Carter didn't fare as well. Since he was clearly involved in the entire escapade, his treaty with the zoog was revoked. And there would be no more moon-wine doled out to him.

## ON TO CELEPHAÏS

Once this entire cat-zoog-human political mess was behind him, Carter traveled to the city of Thran. There he booked passage on a galleon traveling to Celephaïs. During the journey, he inquired about the sailors he'd seen in Celephaïs, the ones who resembled the gods. From his inquiries, he discovered the sailors hailed from Inquanok, a land well known for its impressive onyx mines. So as to avoid capture yet again, Carter decided after Celephaïs, he'd make straight for Inquanok, but *in disguise*—pretending to be an old onyx miner. After making port in Celephaïs, Carter consulted the city's high priest, hoping for some tips on locating Kadath. Regrettably, the priest simply reiterated a common theme: stop looking for the gods and *go home*. The gods didn't want to be found.

Not content with the priest's answer, Carter decided to visit his old friend, King Kuranes (Carter was well connected if anything). It turns out Kuranes and Carter were friends in the "real" world, before Kuranes dreamed his sorry self out of existence. And because the king had grown quite homesick for his native

Cornwall, he'd dreamed up some pastoral English countryside outside of town, spending all his time there.

Carter spoke with Kuranes about finding Kadath, to which Kuranes responded: Stop looking for the gods and *go home*. The gods don't want to be found. But this time, the king was speaking from experience. Once upon a time, Kuranes, quested for a magical city. Yes, it was the great city of Celephaïs. And now he was trapped in the Dreamlands—king or not.

## AND TO INQUANOK

Of course, Carter ignored all of the advice. He ventured to Inquanok, using his ingenious *old onyx miner* disguise. On several occasions during his travels, he noticed a shifty merchant. The man was apparently traveling in the same direction as Carter. And rumors abounded about the merchant trading with the people from the dreaded Plateau of Leng. Carter made a mental note of this.

Upon arriving at Inquanok, Carter marched farther inland, using a variety of paltry excuses about finding the ultimate onyx-mining experience. Once he was out of sight, or so he thought, he rented a yak and headed northward. It didn't take long for the strange merchant to quickly catch up and kidnap Carter.

So, for the third time during his trip, Carter had been captured. And once again, it appeared he'd find his way to Nyarlathotep. The sneaky merchant had decided to summon an elephant-sized, winged creature known as a shantak-bird. It was this creature's task to deliver Carter to a monastery, located upon the Plateau of Leng. Once there, the wily writer was brought before a strange priest wearing a silken robe and mask. The priest, known as the "High Priest Not to Be Described," was . . . well, the name says it all.

Things seemed at an end for Carter—until we take into account that the shifty merchant wasn't too bright. He'd also come along for the trip, and as he led Carter toward the priest, he was momentarily distracted. Being quite familiar with this literary trope—having used it a few times in his writing—Carter took advantage of the moment and pushed the merchant into a well. Without delay, the stalwart writer fled. He hurriedly stumbled through the monastery's labyrinthine corridors, and eventually

## WHAT TO DO WHEN YOU GO ON A DREAM-QUEST

You've likely noticed a common theme in the Dreamlands. There are some pretty fabulous cities. Often, these cities compel dreamers to do some pretty stupid things, attempting to find them. While upon a city-quest, please remember:

1. When searching for information about lost cities, don't blabber around town about your quest. This will surely get you into trouble if the city is not supposed to be found.

2. Be careful not to spend too much time in the Dreamlands, hunting for your city (unless you want to end up a permanent resident like good old King Kuranes).

3. Make plenty of friends in the Dreamlands! Cats, ghouls, even zoogs. A well-placed ally will help you when you inevitably get captured or kidnapped.

4. Some people like epic quests, such as looking for lost gods. If you are such a person, carefully reconsider the matter. Gods, lost or hiding, along with someone looking for them, is most likely a formula for disaster.

5. Learn the local languages. Sure, speaking ghoul is handy, but knowing how to chat with cats and carouse with zoogs is equally useful, if not more so. And while you're at it, learn a few of the languages of the local sailors. This makes plotting behind your back much more difficult.

6. Bring booze. All right, it can't be carried directly from the waking world, but once you're in the Dreamlands, start loading up on the alcoholic beverages. Drink is a universal lubricant in worlds of fantasy. Never be caught without something to offer an unexpected guest or kidnapper.

CONTINUED . . .

NOT DEAD, BUT DREAMING

## WHAT TO DO WHEN YOU
## GO ON A DREAM-QUEST (CONTINUED)

7. Remember that not everyone is affected by alcohol the same way. What gets a priest drunk in one town might have no affect on a sailor in the next town. Size up the target, ask a few questions about their preferred drink, and then select your poison.

8. Go easy on the booze. If someone offers you a drink, most likely it's because he or she is attempting to get you drunk. While the imagination runs wild with the thrills of being drunk and being at the mercy of a pirate of your favorite gender, in all likelihood, you'll just end up being sold into slavery—the hard labor type of slave.

9. Buy a map. Even in a universe where the landscape sometimes changes, it is useful to have a map. This makes it easier to find a safe place should you be dropped off in some remote location by a night-gaunt.

10. Have a friend call you. Let's face it, too much of anything can be bad. If you're questing in the Dreamlands, make sure you have an escape plan. Typically an alarm clock would suffice—for anything other than the Dreamlands. Once a storm of irony starts washing across the fantasy land of your dreams, there is no doubt the alarm clock will fail. But, if you have a friend give you a telephone call, or drop by, then you'll always have an exit. And again, that's what friends are for.

escaped. Or mostly escaped. Once free of the confusing maze, he found himself in the ancient city of Sarkomand.

Unfortunately for Carter, Sarkomand was a stopover where the dread black galleys lay port. And this time they had a moon-beast and its slaves among the crew. And, to Carter's horror, they were torturing the group of ghoul-friends who'd helped Carter escape from the gug city.

NOT DEAD, BUT DREAMING

## When Ghouls Attack

Back when Carter had visited the ghouls, he'd learned they were allied with the night-gaunts—somewhat—who understood the ghouls' meeping, gibbering language. So, given the dire circumstances, and because he was quickly running out of friends in the Dreamlands, Carter decided to help the prisoner ghouls. He managed to attract the attention of a night-gaunt guarding the area. Once the fiendish night-gaunt had grabbed him, Carter communicated the situation to the dark creature (after a quick bit of tickling). The night-gaunt carried him back to the land of ghouls—which was pretty close. Carter, the ghouls, and the night-gaunts conceived a plan of attack. United, they assaulted the ship containing the captured ghouls and diabolical moon-beasts. The moon-beasts and friends were quickly overwhelmed, and their prisoners were easily freed.

Exhilarated by the victory, the army of ghouls pressed onward to the nearby garrison of moon-beasts, launching an all-out attack. With the assistance of Carter, and the night-gaunts (the night-gaunts could grab foes and fling them, or just tickle them to death), the force crushed the moon-beasts, and their strange slaves.

## I Scratch Your Rubbery Back, You Tickle Mine . . .

With Carter's aid, the captive ghouls were once again free. Finding some leverage in the situation, he tried to work a deal. Perhaps the ghouls would loan him a night-gaunt or two, and help him get to Kadath? It was a plan, although he didn't expect much to come of it, given the way things had been going. But to Carter's surprise, the ghouls not only agreed, they offered to accompany him into Kadath proper, and loan him the entire night-gaunt army.

Together, the group soared through the air in an impressive force, eventually arriving in Kadath. An ecstatic Carter rushed to the throne-room, only to find it empty.

## The Lights Are On, but the Gods Aren't Home

Well, not *completely* empty. Waiting for Carter was what turned out to be his nemesis, Nyarlathotep. The great messenger of the gods

NOT DEAD, BUT DREAMING

smugly informed Carter he'd been tracking the writer's progress all along. If Carter had just stopped *escaping* so much, it turns out, Nyarlathotep would have told him everything. Such bitter irony.

Finally, with Carter staying put, Nyarlathotep explained that the city of the man's dreams was quite literally a figment of Carter's imagination. Like Kuranes, Carter had created the city. It was comprised of the majestic cities of Carter's youth—bits of Boston, Providence, even Arkham. Unfortunately, Carter's city was *so* grand it had even impressed the gods. So, they packed their belongings, left Kadath, and headed to "Carter-ville."

This was all a bit much for Carter to comprehend. But before he could muster a few questions, Nyarlathotep informed him that it was his obligation, like it or not, to ensure the safe return of the gods to Kadath.

Nyarlathotep easily summoned a shantak-bird to carry Carter away. But before he left, Nyarlathotep charged Carter with the duty of visiting the majestic city and pleading for the gods to return to Kadath. Not surprisingly, and without a second thought, Carter agreed. There wasn't anything to debate if it meant he'd get to visit the great city he had sought for so long.

IT WAS ALL A DREAM . . .

But the tricky Nyarlathotep had pulled a fast one. As guardian of the gods, he could force them to return to Kadath whenever he wanted, without Carter's assistance. However, it was much more enjoyable to have some fun at Carter's expense. Instead of setting out for Carter's mythical city, the shantak-bird headed toward the center of the universe, where the great deity Azathoh waited.

By this point, it's probably obvious that Carter wasn't the swiftest horse in the race. Sometimes it took him a while to really catch on to what was happening. And luckily, the trip from Kadath to the center of the universe was lengthy. This gave Carter the time needed to contemplate the situation and find a solution. Like a blinding flash of light, the answer strobed through his mind: Wake up. Even though Carter was a man of words, on occasion he was a man of action. Quickly, he leaped from the shantak-bird, and

> ## MYTHOS SURVIVAL TIP:
> ## TRUSTING NYARLATHOTEP
>
> If you encounter Nyarlathoptep, in any of his 1,000 forms, be cautious. If you find yourself wondering if you can trust him, don't. The great messenger god is a bit of a trickster, and delights in disrupting the events in human lives—and most everything else for that matter. For the most part, Nyarlathotep is sneaky and manipulative regardless of the form he takes. Worse, he enjoys "pranks," and goes out of his way to weave elaborate tales—if it means he can have a laugh at your expense or taunt some other entity.

fell into darkness—which promptly awakened him. Instead of drifting through the void of space and time, Carter was in his bed, with a beautiful, golden sunrise peeking through the windows of his Boston home.

## NO MORE DREAMS FOR YOU

As might be expected, Carter's adventures didn't end there. As he grew older, his ability to dream faded. No longer could he spend endless dream-months on quests, or visit his cat-friends in Ulthar. Without his fantastic dreams, Carter was forced to tolerate the humdrum nature of a normal human existence. This probably made him grumpy.

As Carter trudged into middle age, his dream situation didn't improve much. But one night, while deep in slumber, his dead grandfather appeared before him. In this dream-like state, his grandfather told Carter of a silver key that would unlock Carter's lost, dream-powered boyhood. Without hesitation, Carter hunted down the key. Along with it he found a mysterious parchment covered in cryptic sigils.

Key and parchment in hand, Carter drove to his boyhood home

NOT DEAD, BUT DREAMING

NOT DEAD, BUT DREAMING

## Mythos Survival Tip:
## Meeting with Azathoth is a Bad Idea

At the center of the universe resides the deity Azathoth, who is sometimes referred to as the blind idiot god (although wisely, never within earshot). Azathoth received his "idiot" title because he basically sits at the center of the universe, doing nothing all day and night—if there were a day and night where Azathoth is. Meanwhile, amorphous forms dance around the great god, playing flutes (the sound of trouble). Fortunately for the universe, this appears to keep Azathoth content.

It perhaps goes without saying that one should avoid vast entities at the center of the universe, that when disturbed can collapse the whole of reality. Even so, try to stay away from Azathoth if you can. There are many ways this can be done, the most relevant here is by *not* listening to Nyarlathotep when he tries to make a deal.

of Arkham. But as he strolled back home, he discovered it wasn't modern-day Arkham at all—it was the Arkham of his youth. Suddenly, Randolph Carter was a ten-year-old child again.

### This is Why We Can't Have Nice Things

Back in present day, Carter's cousins swarmed around his estate, eager to declare the missing fiction writer dead. A meeting was held to discuss divvying up Carter's belongings, and while Carter's numerous and dedicated friends argued the writer was still alive, they had a difficult time convincing the cousins' sneering lawyer, Ernest B. Aspinwall.

Then, rather unexpectedly, the eccentric Swami Chandra-putra stepped forward, claiming to possess news of Carter's whereabouts. The strange swami set everybody on edge with his improbably dark eyes, monotone voice, and voluminous robe and mittens, all of which concealed his form. Regardless of all of this, the attendees patiently listened to Chandraputra's story.

## THE RED PILL OR THE BLUE PILL

After frolicking about the Arkham of his youth, Carter ventured into a dreaded cave outside of town, known as the Snake-Den. There, he practiced one of the rites he'd memorized from the strange parchment—the rite of the silver key. Suddenly, he was transported beyond space and time, confronted by a mysterious entity named 'Umr at-Tawil (don't try to pronounce it).

'Umr at-Tawil explained that Carter must pass through the Ultimate Gate in order to continue. Of course, Carter was free to turn back—now—if he so desired. But if he continued down the rabbit hole, there was no telling what might happen. Not surprisingly, Carter continued onward.

With a jolt, the adventuresome writer was suddenly experiencing many facets of his life at once. In an instant he was a young Carter, a middle aged Carter, and an old Carter. Then, from beyond the boundaries of reality, Yog-Sothoth was suddenly before him, explaining what was happening (at least Carter was pretty sure it was Yog-Sothoth, you never could tell, with all these great, godlike deity types). Impressed with Carter's adventures so far, Yog-Sothoth decided Carter was ready to learn the Ultimate Mystery of Life. That's right, the greatest, awe-inspiring mystery in all of the universes. It wasn't likely Carter was going to refuse this. And he didn't.

In that enlightening moment, a sudden realization came to Carter, with the help of Yog-Sothoth—perhaps one he'd always known, but was never confirmed. Humanity, everything in fact, were a part of something greater. Just what this "something" was couldn't be grasped by Carter. It transcended space and time. It can't be seen, and most don't know they're a part of it.

In the end, it was the understanding of the big picture that Carter came away with. He realized the different facets of himself, whether it be young Carter, old Carter—they were parts of a larger, formless entity. And in Carter's case, that entity was Yog-Sothoth.

In the Cthulhu Mythos, this is the type of knowledge which

NOT DEAD, BUT DREAMING

challenges sanity. Certainly Carter's was at risk after such a revelation. And honestly, where do you go after that?

With the secrets of the universe revealed, Yog-Sothoth offered Carter the chance to take advantage of his new ability to be many places at once. Carter immediately confessed he wished to visit the planet of Yaddith. Although it was, now occupied by slimy, nasty dholes, the planet had once been home to a mysterious and wise race, often cropping up in Carter's dreams.

So with a warning to keep his silver key handy, and his sigils memorized so he could return to Earth, Yog-Sothoth transported Carter back in time, to the planet of Yaddith.

And by sigils, Yog-Sothoth was referring, of course, to the ones scrawled on the piece of parchment—the same parchment sitting in Carter's car, back in Arkham.

## Mythos Confusion Tip: Wait, I don't Get It

Ultimate truths, by their nature alone, are incredibly difficult to understand. At best, humans can glimpse a shadow of the whole and perhaps form a rudimentary concept as to what it means. To assist in this undertaking, here is an example:

Let's say you are a corner of a triangle—yes, a triangle. As a corner, you give little thought to the lines extending away from you on either side. It's your business to be a corner—nothing more, nothing less. However these extending lines are technically a part of you, there is no awareness of them beyond your existence as a corner. In fact, you have no awareness of the triangle's other two corners. And you'll *never* have any understanding of this triangle in its entirety, or even the greater concept of a triangle and its mathematical and geometrical qualities. You are just a corner, or perhaps you prefer to be called a right angle. Makes no difference in the big picture.

NOT DEAD, BUT DREAMING

## ONE WAY TICKET

Carter's consciousness zipped through space and time, landing in the body of Zkauba, a wizard from Yaddith. Zkauba wasn't overjoyed about hosting his new co-occupant. And Carter, now trapped without a return ticket, simply wanted to go home (perhaps he should have stuck with the writing).

The two warred for dominance over Zkauba's body. Not to be outdone, Carter concocted a clever drug cocktail, which allowed him to take semi-permanent control, and spent his days researching a way to return home. Before long, he developed an ultra high-tech, metallic light-wave envelope he could ride back to Earth—albeit in the aesthetically unappealing, alien form of his host, Zkauba.

With the assistance of the rather unusual gadget, Carter finally arrived on Earth safely. With not a moment lost, he set about deciphering the sigils on his recovered parchment. His hope was the translated sigils would allow him to return in human form—not the odd looking alien shape he presently inhabited.

And with this revelation, Swami Chandraputra concluded, maybe the cranky lawyer Aspinwall would consider giving Carter a few days . . .? (I'll bet you forgot the swami was speaking.)

### MYTHOS SURVIVAL TIP: CHECK YOUR LUGGAGE

If you find need to travel across space and time, always be prepared for the return trip. Nothing's more embarrassing than arriving at your destination planet, light-years away, or eons away, and realizing that you don't have the proper tools to get back home.

In addition to any artifacts you may need, double check that you have the appropriate sigils and incantations memorized. If you're planning for an extended stay, take a written copy with you.

NOT DEAD, BUT DREAMING

## THE END OF RANDOLPH CARTER

Naturally, Aspinwall proclaimed Chandraputra a fraud. The so-called swami clearly spoke with an obvious Yankee dialect. In fact, on closer inspection it was evident the swami was wearing a mask. Obviously, the "foreigner" was attempting to scam the cousins of their rightful fortune. Charging forward, Aspinwall attempted to tear off Chandraputra's mask, in what today would be considered typical Scooby Doo fashion (again, Lovecraft was ahead of his time).

When the mask came away, everyone shrieked in horror. Before them stood—although they didn't know it—the hideous, alien form of Zkauba, the Yaddith magician. Then the real problems started. The excitement awakened Zkauba's dormant personality. In an instant, he slipped inside a mysterious, ticking device inside the room—originally assumed to be a clock. In reality, it was the space-time-traveling, metal envelope.

Zkauba—with Carter—disappeared. And from that moment onward, no one has ever seen the strange, alien creature. The same goes for the mysterious swami. As for Carter, it appears he likely resides permanently on Yaddith, imprisoned within the body of Zkauba—one can hope that, perhaps, he

## MYTHOS SURVIVAL TIP: HIDING IN PLAIN SIGHT

Always keep your Mythos goodies well hidden, and well guarded. While you might think that you have cleverly hidden your space-time traveling, metal envelope by making it look like a clock, it's not worth the risk of having someone, especially your malicious alternate personality, discover it. Put all eldritch devices out of sight—in an out-of-the-way, inaccessible, locked room. Inside the room, they should be in a chest or bureau, under lock and key.

somehow ended up in the Dreamlands instead, hanging out in his long-lost city, chatting about art with his ghoul-friend Pickman, sipping moon-wine.

At the very least he's not in a cemetery.

NOT DEAD, BUT DREAMING

# More Mythos Monsters

. . . those who described these strange shapes felt quite sure that they were not human, despite some superficial resemblances in size and general outline. Nor, said the witnesses, could they have been any kind of animal known to Vermont. They were pinkish things about five feet long; with crustaceous bodies bearing vast pairs of dorsal fins or membranous wings and several sets of articulated limbs, and with a sort of convoluted ellipsoid, covered with multitudes of very short antennae, where a head would ordinarily be.

—H.P. Lovecraft, "The Whisperer in Darkness"

The Cthulhu Mythos teems with strange and powerful creatures, some of which you may have already encountered (especially if you're working through this book systematically, as originally instructed. If you're skipping about, you may have some important creatures you are likely to encounter. Go back, and start again.)

This section will cover some of the beasts—and ancient races—not discussed in prior sections. For a complete list of *all* of the creatures, deities, and denizens of the Mythos, visit the *Cthulhu Quick Reference* section.

## THE YIG

*Ophidiophobia*, the fear of snakes, is common amongst many humans. In addition to being slimy, wriggly, and often just plain creepy, snakes are dangerous. But if you venture into certain parts of Oklahoma, be careful you don't act upon your fears.

Legend tells of the Yig, the half-human father of serpents, who hisses derisively upon anyone hurting any of his snake-children. Local Native Americans take the legend of Yig seriously—they won't even defend themselves against attacking rattlers.

### SWEET HOME OKLAHOMA

"The Curse of Yig" is one of the few tales in which Lovecraft ventured westward in the United States. In this story, a husband and wife, Walker and Audrey Davis, set out from Arkansas, along with their trusty dog, Old Wolf. The couple was looking for a better life in Oklahoma, planning to set up a farm. Sadly for Walker, Oklahoma wasn't really the best choice—he suffered from ophidiophobia (don't we all). In Walker's youth, an old Indian squaw had ominously intoned a warning—she said snakes would ultimately be the end of him.

As the two journeyed, Audrey discovered a nest of newborn snakes. She was eager not to rattle her husband. Instead, she used the butt of her rifle to smash the wriggling monstrosities to mushy bits. But Walker found her out. He grew incredibly agitated—not because of the snakes, but because of potential repercussions from the snake-god, Yig. He chastised Audrey for the rest of the trip—as if traveling to Oklahoma by wagon wasn't painful enough.

At their farm site, deep in Wichita country, the couple constructed a cabin and began tilling their land. Soon, there was a good harvest. And they quickly became friends with the neighbors, Joe and Sally Compton. Sally was of little help putting Audrey's mind at ease in regard to the snake situation—she delighted in telling Audrey the most gruesome tales of horrible snake-deaths. And Walker's frequent visits to the Wichita Indians didn't help—the tribe reminded Walker of Yig's long memory, and how

MORE MYTHOS MONSTERS

the snake-god tended to hold a grudge. It didn't take long before Audrey was worried sick about the whole snake-killing incident. As a safeguard, the couple distributed charms around the house, hoping to ward off the vengeful Yig.

## ONLY A DREAM

By Halloween, the couple had relaxed a bit. They invited friends to stop by, throwing a party to celebrate the fall harvest. Guests arrived from all of the neighboring farms. And the barbecue was one of the best in fall harvest history. Delighted couples, including Walker and Audrey, whirled about the dance floor.

The evening went a bit *too* well—when the exhausted Davises finally flopped into bed for the evening, they neglected to place their anti-Yig charms about the house.

In the deep of the night, the couple awakened with a start. A strange sound buzzed within the cabin. Walker leaped from the bed, grabbing a lantern. And there, in the light, the couple beheld an enormous, speckled mass of squirming, seething rattlesnakes.

Walker screamed and dropped the lantern. Darkness quickly draped the room. Then Walker fell silent.

Audrey responded as any caring, loving spouse would have. She lay in the bed, clamping her eyes closed, and assumed she must have been dreaming. After lying motionless for awhile, Audrey accepted the reality of her situation. It wasn't a dream. She needed to take action.

And she did. Audrey lay in the bed, motionless (maybe it wasn't an entirely new plan). But this time she understood—the horrible event wasn't a dream.

There, in the dark, she considered the situation. Audrey reasoned Walker must be long-dead by now, and beyond rescue (clearly Walker was a husband and a *friend*). So, if she could just lie still for awhile, perhaps the snakes would forget about her, and slither on their way.

Try as she might, she couldn't stay put. Knowing snakes slithered around the house was too much for her to endure. Just then, a large, formless shape grew in the darkness, slinking slowly toward her. Creeping closer. Audrey had no doubt the monstrous Yig was coming for her.

Without hesitation—surprisingly, given her previous hesitations—she grabbed the axe resting near the nightstand, and viciously chopped the attacking form to bits. No doubt the creature had it coming for killing her dear, late husband Walker.

## My Bad

At sunrise, concerned neighbor (and obviously a good friend) Sally Compton arrived to check on the Davises. But she was stunned and horrified at what she found. The dog, Old Wolf, lay in a disgusting heap by the fireplace—puffed and swollen from the poison of repeated rattlesnake bites. And Audrey lay on the floor, hissing like a snake.

Nearby, the butchered remains of Walker Davis showed no evidence of a single rattlesnake bite.

The situation was regarded as the most unfortunate case of mistaken identity *ever.* Walker had fainted upon spotting the mass of wriggling snakes. When he regained his senses and began groping about in the dark, a paranoid Audrey mistook him for Yig. It could happen to anyone.

Though no one had an explanation for the barely-humanoid, hissing, wriggling children Audrey gave birth to nine months later. Shortly afterward, she died.

## Horrors Underground

In "The Mound," Lovecraft returns the reader to Oklahoma. And it turns out that Oklahoma suffers from more than just a snake problem. Outside of Binger, in Caddo County, a large mound rises up above the plain. The mound is rumored to be haunted—onlookers report spotting a ghost-like, Indian man, pacing the mound during the day, and a headless squaw by night.

Plenty of curious people have investigated the legends of the mound, over the years—resulting in death and insanity (big clue there). And while most investigators disappear, go mad, or both, one unfortunate man named Captain Lawton (after disappearing,

## MYTHOS SURVIVAL TIP: DON'T PANIC!

The actions of Audrey Davis show what happens when you're not thinking clearly. When dealing with the Cthulhu Mythos, or just a typical night prowler, hasty decisions bring about dire consequences, such as chopped-up spouses. If you encounter a Mythos monster, don't turn into a jellied mass, or start shrieking. Take a deep breath. Relax. Count to five. And hope your friend has offered himself or herself in an attempt to spare your life. Regardless, remaining calm allows you to make smart decisions. Besides, any Mythos creature managing to kill you *before* you finish counting to five, likely would have caught and killed you anyway—friend or not.

*and* going mad) was discovered a week later, near the mound—but his feet had been removed (even bigger warning).

But not heeding dire warnings is what investigators do best in the Cthulhu Mythos—as do those who are not well informed about the Cthulhu Mythos. As it turns out, there was one determined investigator who continued snooping around the mound, ignoring the locals' cautioning. And, it seemed to pay off. He unearthed an odd, magnetic cylinder buried in the dirt. The cylinder contained a yellow scroll with the narrative of Pánfilo de Zamacona y Nuñez (yes, *that* Pánfilo de Zamacona y Nuñez).

It seems, Zamacona had been part of Coronado's expedition team, which headed north from Mexico in 1540. According to the scroll, Zamacona discovered an ancient, subterranean city called K'n-yan.

## ALL ABOUT THE OLD ONES

The expeditionary team had heard rumors of the Old Ones, alien creatures who had once lived upon Earth, but truly had little knowledge of the Cthulhu Mythos. Reports had these Old Ones living in colonies, and even trading with humans way back in the day. But then something mysteriously caused the land to sink beneath the water. Blaming Earth's inhabitants, the Old Ones grew reclusive and antisocial, moving their cities underground. The great mounds, like the one near Binger, were believed to be caved-in passages leading to the Old Ones' ancient cities.

It was believed that due to their age and advanced understanding of technology, the Old Ones possessed a variety of nifty powers—they could animate dead corpses, and utilized this to create an entire slave class (poor Herbert West, the things he could have learned). The Old Ones also communicated telepathically, and allegedly could materialize and dematerialize at will. Zamacona was stunned by the tales of the Old Ones and their powers, and decided to locate one of their underground cities. Exploring the land of the mysterious mound in Oklahoma, he discovered an opening, and immediately descended toward the interior.

## MOVING UNDERGROUND

Zamacona traveled for many days, and finally stumbled upon an eerie underground landscape, lit by a misty blue light. And from this location, in the distance, Zamacona spotted glittering cities. To his delight, the cities were constructed entirely of gold. And although fame, fortune, and a solid retirement plan were nearly within Zamacona's grasp, it was not to be—the Old Ones hunted Zamacona down.

The Old Ones resembled the local Indians of the area—particularly the guardians who kept watch at the mound, day and night (although it was harder to make out a resemblance with the squaw, her being headless). They communicated telepathically with Zacamona, explaining he had, indeed, discovered the ancient realm of K'n-yan. The Old Ones also explained why they were so darned antisocial.

Long ago, they arrived on Earth from beyond the stars, led here by the great god Tulu (aka Cthulhu). But when most of the land abruptly sunk underneath the ocean, imprisoning Tulu in his watery city of Relex (aka R'lyeh), they assumed evil space-devils

## WHAT TO DO WHEN YOU'RE ATTACKED BY A MYTHOS MONSTER

There's a clear lesson to be learned from the mistakes of Audrey Davis and her encounters with the Yig. Keeping a level head during a crisis makes all the difference:

1. If you think you're being attacked by a Mythos creature, *never* assume it's a dream. In this instance, being wrong is always safer. After all, if it is a dream, you'll just wake up (hopefully). But assuming it's a dream does nothing to help the situation. You might as well put on some ruby slippers and wish yourself away, if you think that'll help. Re-read the information box *More on Friends, Partners, and Loved Ones in the Mythos.* Avoid mixing these. No matter how it's approached, the outcome is painful—assuming there is an actual emotional attachment. If not, then have at it. In that case, the "partner" is a glorified friend who is all the more willing to sacrifice his—or her—self to save you.

2. If you believe a friend or loved one has been attacked by a Mythos monster, don't assume they're dead. Always *check*—assuming it doesn't place you in harm's way. If you're stuck in one of those regrettable partner/friend relationships, attempt to help the person. And know that sometimes surviving isn't always the best option. As Audrey's offspring are proof, occasionally in the Cthulhu Mythos, there are far worse things than death.

3. When a frightening form looms over you in the dark, it's sometimes a good idea to make sure it's actually a monster, before attacking. Consider calling out to your friend/partner: "Hey, <friend/partner's name here>, is that you, or are you a nasty <Mythos monster name here>?" However, don't wait too long for a reply. And when in doubt, flee.

CONTINUED . . .

were at work. Anyone allowed to remain on the surface must have been in league with such devils. Closing their city to the outside, the Old Ones went into hiding, imprisoning and killing anyone who attempted to enter. Bad news for Zamacona.

## You Know Too Much

Sometimes knowing the answers comes with a price. After Zamacona's questions were answered, he learned he'd never return to the surface. So, the Old Ones escorted Zamacona to Tsoth—to start the first day of the rest of his life. During the journey, the Old Ones informed him of the layout of the land—a great cavern sat below K'n-yan—once filled with great cities, and now only ruins and dust. And below that, the lightless cavern of N'kai, home of the Great Old One Tsathoggua. The giant, amorphous Great Old

## Mythos Survival Tip: Stay in Shape

In addition to going insane, an excellent method of escaping a Mythos horror is to run away from it. Many Mythos monsters are horrifying to behold, but sometimes slow to react. A nimble runner is more likely to survive Mythos perils than a couch potato.

As part of your survival training, consider preparing for a marathon, or any endurance race. This type of training will appear "normal" to your peers, since it is socially acceptable (preparation against possible Cthulhu Mythos monster attacks, less so). You'll be rewarded with better health, toned muscles, and the ability to dodge some of the slower Mythos beasts.

If you're in a time crunch, be sure to skip all the extra fitness stuff, like weight training and martial arts. Being quick is all you need. If you fail to outrun a Mythos monster, your wicked martial arts skills aren't going to save you.

## WHAT TO DO WHEN YOU'RE ATTACKED BY A MYTHOS MONSTER (CONTINUED)

4. There are means of protecting yourself against Mythos monsters—other than friends. Charms, amulets, incantations, sigils. All of these are useful forms of defense. Even knowing the name of the offending creature can prove helpful (particularly with the incantations). Overall, it is best to keep a few of these defenses prepared. Stock drawers with charms and amulets. Draw sigils beneath beds and carpets. And always keep a silver dagger nearby.

5. It is possible to kill a Mythos minion. These are the servants of the greater Mythos creatures. For instance, a mass of writhing snakes might be in the service of Yig. Dispatching the snakes, while not entirely easy, is far more likely than destroying Yig. Honestly, there is pretty much no hope of destroying the greater Mythos creatures. Holding them at bay is the best one can hope for. And this is why, once again, friends are so important. Consider them place holders in a deadlock with a greater Mythos monster.

6. While it is not entirely fruitless, there is a last ditch option that works on occasion. If cornered, friendless, and the moment of your demise appear imminent, try engaging the Mythos creature in conversation. Some of them like to chat. And a few love to reveal insane secrets (meaning the secrets drive a victim insane). In reality, all this does is buy time. But as unexpected events often save people in the Cthulhu Mythos, there's nothing wrong with hoping you'll be saved by a wandering night-gaunt.

7. If you've ever been warned about a curse or an unfor-tunate early death by a mystical person—including

CONTINUED . . .

MORE MYTHOS MONSTERS

One resembled a big, fat, sleepy toad, but wasn't much of a threat to the Old Ones, as he didn't get around much.

Zamacona listened to the Old Ones' tales, and after a few attempts at pronouncing these names, most likely Zamacona understood why the Old Ones were telepathic.

Stuck in Tsoth, Zamacona spent his time attempting to visit ancient N'kai, and devising escape plans. Eventually he befriended a noblewoman named T'la-yub. She claimed to know of a passage that led aboveground, and together the two planned to escape. They set off for the surface.

But in a moment of notoriously bad planning, the pair decided to camp—just prior to reaching the surface—and the Old Ones recaptured them before they could break free of their subterranean prison.

## Mythos Survival Tip: Become a Survivalist

In addition to being in top physical shape, you should always be prepared for escape from situations guaranteed to strain the limits of your endurance. You need to be able to survive any situation, without relying on anything but your wits and the most basic necessities.

Over time, you can gradually teach yourself how to get by with little rest, and subsist on a minimal supply of food and water. Make sure you watch every episode of those survivalist shows—where a guy gets dropped in the wilderness and has to stay alive for a week, armed with nothing but a can of spray paint and an electric hair dryer (and maybe a small camera crew who has plenty to eat with them).

Hopefully, with training, you'll fare better than Zamacona. If you find yourself trapped in a subterranean city for four years, you won't screw up your one chance for escape by taking a needed rest when you're almost at the surface.

## WHAT TO DO WHEN YOU'RE ATTACKED BY A MYTHOS MONSTER (CONTINUED)

Native American shamans, cultist priests, wandering gypsies—don't ignore the warning. Rest assured that the fate revealed to you will come to pass. Take this into account when relocating or traveling to a new land.

8. Assuming you've completely ignored rule #7 of this list, keep a close eye on your friend/partner. In fact, it is good to garner a promise from the person that he or she will not attack and destroy any of the potential servants or minions of the Mythos deity that you've been warned about. Also, it's worth the time to secure a promise that the friend/partner will adhere to rule #2 in this list. Having safety precautions are pointless if you end up being killed by your friend.

9. Just because very few or no Mythos tales have been set in a location you're considering settling does not mean the area is safe. H.P. Lovecraft's Cthulhu Mythos has been expanded by many writers over the years. This means pretty much every location, be it land, sea or air, has been covered. The monsters of the Cthulhu Mythos are not bound by lines on a map. This is a human hubris. These abominations lurk everywhere.

10. When all else fails (and it inevitably will), remember you can always hasten your demise by poking the monster with a stick.

The Old Ones understood Zamaconca's plight, and were even sympathetic to his yearning to return home. As a result, they restrained themselves when it came to his punishment. As for T'la-yub, she should have known better—the Old Ones immediately transformed her into a corpse-slave, chopping off her head, and sending her up to the surface for night-time guard duty. Hopefully her headless form would serve as a deterrent to

MORE MYTHOS MONSTERS

future explorers. And if not, well, she could always scare them off with her torch.

Even though the Old Ones refrained from the dire punishment of Zamacona, no one really knows how he fared. All that remains of him is his odd, metallic cylinder, discovered close to the surface. Perhaps he eventually escaped.

## I-Go, You-Go, We All Go with the Mi-Go

One of the more fascinating and complicated creatures of the Mythos canon, other than Cthulhu, of course, is the fungoid race of the Mi-Go. In "The Whisperer in Darkness," Lovecraft returns to the East Coast, where we encounter these terrifying beasts.

Albert Wilmarth, instructor of literature at Miskatonic University, decided to investigate strange legends whispered in southern Vermont. Witnesses offered accounts of weird claw-prints discovered in the mud, and strange, crab-like creatures, spotted floating downriver, after a great flood. The crab-things were reported to have many legs, and enormous, bat-like wings.

Wilmarth noticed a similarity between the legends in Vermont, and those of a creature known as the *Mi-Go,* located in Nepal. He thoroughly researched the tales of the Mi-Go, and eventually published a series of articles, debunking the sightings. He was quite proud of himself—until he began receiving correspondences from Henry Wentworth Akeley.

Akeley, too, had been conducting his own research. He had snapped a series of photographs of the odd claw-prints left by the creatures. One night, while investigating, he heard droning, buzzing tones, and realized the beasts were conversing with a group of human cohorts. Akeley managed to capture the odd buzzing on a phonograph recording. And to seal the deal, he discovered a peculiar black stone in the woods, covered in ancient hieroglyphics that could have come straight out of the *Necronomicon.* As Akeley continued to send evidence to Wilmarth, the professor slowly came to accept the veracity of Akeley's accounts.

MORE MYTHOS MONSTERS

## DANGEROUS INVESTIGATIONS

Working together through correspondence, Akeley and Wilmarth investigated the Mi-Go. But their work was often derailed—letters waylaid, disappearing shipments of evidence, and faked telegrams, supposedly from Akeley, urging Wilmarth to abandon his examinations. An anxious Akeley realized the Mi-Go, and their human cohorts, were aware of Akeley's and Wilmarth's collaboration. Eventually, Akeley was certain the Mi-Go had launched attacks upon Akeley's house. Frantic letters poured into Wilmarth's mailbox about the nightly assaults—the steady, buzzing drone, and beating of wings, always outside. There were even gunshots, fired at Akeley's residence. The constant supply of guard dogs Akeley imported from neighboring Brattleboro kept vanishing, or dying. Something was clearly amiss.

## VISITING VERMONT

Just as things appeared to be at their worst, Wilmarth received a calm correspondence from Akeley. In the letter, Akeley exhibited (you guessed it) a complete change in personality/demeanor.

Akeley explained his new understanding of the Mi-Go, who had decided to sit down with Akeley and have a nice chat. The Mi-Go, it turned out, were quite friendly (the killing attempts were simply a grave misunderstanding). In fact, Akeley grew to be fast friends with the intelligent alien race, and wanted to introduce Wilmarth to them. They could learn from each other. Perhaps, Akeley concluded, Wilmarth would consider coming to visit in Vermont. And, of course, bring every shred of physical evidence with him.

Wilmarth, suspicious, sent a telegram in reply. And his apprehension eased when Akeley responded cordially to this new correspondence. Clearly, if Akeley was capable of sending and receiving telegrams, he *must* be fine. So Wilmarth set off for Vermont.

## IT ONLY HURTS FOR A MINUTE

Upon his arrival to Brattleboro, Vermont, Wilmarth was not greeted by his friend Akeley, but by one of Akeley's friends,

Mr. Noyes. Noyes informed Wilmarth that due to a bout of asthma, Akeley was not able to venture from his home, and instead waited for Wilmarth at his residence. Probably utterly confused by the friend-pawn maneuver, Wilmarth followed Noyes. But when he arrived, he found Akeley in the downstairs study. Akeley's near-immobile body was confined to a chair, and draped in a dressing gown, scarf, and hood. His expression

MORE MYTHOS MONSTERS

## MYTHOS SURVIVAL TIP:
## REMEMBER WHO IS THE FRIEND

On some occasions in the Cthulhu Mythos, there is "friend confusion." Or as it is better known: Friend reversal. This isn't surprising, given the importance of having a friend in eldritch situations. Sometimes, a person believes he or she has befriended a person, only to learn that he or she is the friend—you know, the one to be sacrificed. This is why it's important to always confirm who is the friend and who is the befriended. Do this in letters, conversations, and even the occasional test such as saying, "Be a friend, and get me a cup of tea."

Even with these precautions set in place, it goes without saying that any sudden change in demeanor or personality is always a bad thing. Most likely the friend has been lost. But even when personality changes aren't involved, remain suspicious of friends, and never trust anyone whom you've never met in person but claims to be a friend. Realistically, it's best to never trust anyone.

And of course, if you receive a message from a friend asking you to bring any and all evidence with you, don't go. But if you must for some insane reason, do remember to make copies first. Also make sure you have an escape plan. It might turn out that you're the friend, in which case your friend can't be trusted.

was rigid, eyes glassy. And he spoke in a hacking whisper (this was a critical case of asthma).

But he seemed excited enough as he informed Wilmarth of his new friends, the powerful Mi-Go. The intelligent aliens had volumes of knowledge to share. And while they may not have seemed particularly forthcoming and friendly in the past, they eagerly wished to work with their new human friends. In a gesture of good faith, the Mi-Go extended an open invitation to Wilmarth to visit their home planet of Yuggoth.

However, there was one tiny catch. In order for Wilmarth to travel to Yuggoth, the Mi-Go would need to remove his brain and place it in one of their space-traveling brain cylinders.

MORE MYTHOS MONSTERS

215

## MI-GO HOME

While the Mi-Go had developed advanced space travel technology, it turns out they could only transport brains—and only when encased within special strange cylinders. Of course, the body could be kept alive indefinitely for the brain's return. Akeley assured Wilmarth the process was safe. In fact, the procedure was painless, and before he knew it, Wilmarth would be on Yuggoth. To further illustrate his case, Akeley suggested the professor should converse with a brain-cased human, who happened to be on the shelf—in the corner. Under Akeley's guidance, Wilmarth hooked the brain case to its associated hearing/listening/speaking devices. The encased brain informed Akeley, in its flat, metallic tone, of the thrills and excitement Wilmarth would experience, after having his brain severed and stuffed into a cylinder.

Wilmarth expressed his excitement over visiting Yuggoth. He was due for a vacation anyway. And as for the brain surgery—no problem. Since Akeley appeared to be mighty tired, Wilmarth

### IC DEAD PEOPLE

One doesn't have to look any further than the Mi-Go's highly advanced brain cylinder technology for proof of their superior intellect. The concept of the brain cylinder is, in many ways, similar to the concept of a personal computer. Sure, the brain might not be comprised of IC (integrated circuit) chips and transistors per se, but a Mi-Go brain cylinder offers compact processing power and a streamlined carrying case.

Brain cylinders have their own set of peripherals—a speaking device, a listening device, and a sight device. Add to this the brain cylinder's inherent portability (it was designed for space travel, after all), and its built-in brainpower (literally), and you may just have the perfect computing machine.

MORE MYTHOS MONSTERS

agreed to further discuss their travel plans in the morning.

At which point Wilmarth pretended to go to bed, and started devising a way to get the heck out of this crazy house.

As Wilmarth planned his exodus, he overhead voices downstairs—Noyes, the buzzing Mi-Go, and a brain-cased human. While he couldn't make out anything definitive, even so, the conversation still gave him the creeps. When the meeting wrapped up and the house grew silent, Wilmarth decided it was the best time to sneak downstairs.

Naturally, he was concerned about his friend, so he checked on Akeley. But Akeley wasn't there. It appeared he'd disappeared. Well, there was Akeley's empty dressing-gown on the chair. And, to Wilmarth's horror, also on the chair were Akeley's head, and his severed hands.

And then Wilmarth spotted another brain case in a corner— that of Akeley. Suddenly it came to Wilmarth. He realized Akeley had occupied the brain case all along, while the Mi-Go impersonated him, using discarded Akeley body parts.

Wilmarth promptly fled the farmhouse, and eventually found his way back to comfortable Arkham. The Mi-Go didn't bother him again, and Wilmarth decide to give up the debunking business, and go back to teaching literature.

## In Search of the Great White Ape

Many Lovecraftian stories describe great, white, apelike creatures—some dwelling deep in ruins, others underground, and others in caves. Actually, they find all manner of places to live. But all of Lovecraft's white ape tales share an even closer theme—a disturbingly close connection to humanity and family.

These mysterious white apes have been spotted all over the world. In "The Beast in the Cave," a hapless tourist accidentally separated from his tour group in Mammoth Cave in Kentucky, and quickly became lost. As the lost tourist's torch gradually flickered out, he grew certain that he was being stalked by a wild creature—possibly a lost mountain lion.

Not wishing to end up as lion-dinner, the tourist snatched

a few heavy rocks, and as the mysterious predator drew closer, the tourist pegged it a few times—breathing a sigh of relief when the creature dropped with a satisfying *thunk*. As good expedition guides do, he hunted down the lost traveler, having searched for nearly four hours (lost tourists look terrible on the annual performance review).

Together, the two men ventured back to discover what manner of creature had attacked the tourist. And what they found was a large, white ape, with long, rat-like claws. When the repulsive creature flipped over, expelling its last breath, it emitted a series of strange sounds—and the two men were even more horrified to discover an uncanny resemblance—this clawed, ape-like creature had once, not long ago, been human.

## It Runs in the Family

Lovecraft often described humans who devolved from their original human form, into white apes. This might be a good time to revist the eugenics information box for a refresher.

Sometimes this devolving process happened over generations. On other occasions, such as the beast in the cave, the process was more immediate. And then there were those cases where it ran in the family.

In "The Facts Concerning the Late Arthur Jermyn and His Family," poor Arthur Jermyn descended from a long line of slightly crazy Jermyns—ranging from a *tell-weird-tales-about-the-Congo-while-in-your-dressing-gown* kind of weird, all the way up to a *murder-your-entire-family-upon-getting-news-from-the-Congo* sort of weird. So it probably didn't come as much of a surprise when, one night, Arthur soaked himself in oil and set himself on fire.

In addition to being weird, many of the male members of the family had an unnatural fascination with white apes. There was Wade Jermyn, who traveled to the Congo to find a mysterious and legendary gray city, rumored by the Onga tribe to be chock-full of white apes. He didn't have much luck, but he did return from the Congo with a weird and violent bride who pretty much liked to hide away from visitors and the public, and eventually returned to the Congo.

Then there was Alfred, who ran off to join the circus. He selected an especially pale gorilla to train and perform with in the show. And all went well, until he decided one day for no reason to bite the gorilla in the neck.

So it seemed only natural that Arthur, Alfred's son, and last of the Jermyn line, would set off to the Congo to pursue Onga legends of the lost city (think of Michael Crichton's novel and film *Congo*). Unfortunately, he learned the white apes had been wiped from existence by the warlike N'bangu tribe. The tribe also made off with a stuffed white goddess, believed to be a great princess, which had been worshiped by the pale apes.

Luckily, Arthur met a Belgian trader who promised to procure the stuffed goddess. Arthur returned home, eagerly awaiting the box containing the white ape-princess. But after opening the box, he screamed, ran from the house, and turned himself into a human torch.

Folks who later examined the box found a white ape inside (no surprise there). But the Jermyn family resemblance was undeniable, as was the Jermyn coat of arms she wore about her neck.

## It Runs *Even More* in the Family

I know what you're thinking . . . more white apes? Yes, more white apes. While the whole ape/human thing doesn't seem to be very popular with many fans of the Cthulhu Mythos, there is no denying it was popular with Lovecraft. This in part might be due to the common, pop cultural misunderstanding in Lovecraft's day that it was possible for humans to devolve into a far more primitive state (consider the "wild children" found in the 1800s). Of course, it all comes from hereditary troubles, and the greatest fear being no one truly knows what happens in their family history.

This doesn't mean we should ignore the "atavistic" tales of Lovecraft. Maybe the "ape" isn't important, but the devolving is—remember the Marsh family in "The Shadow over Innsmouth?" Frog/fish people, or apes, it's the same premise. Anyway, if you take anything away from these white ape tales, it should be: Don't worry so much about being a great white ape; just accept the fact that if you don't run into one, or are related to one, you'll eventually turn into one.

In "The Lurking Fear," one man took it upon himself to investigate tales of trouble on Tempest Mountain in the Catskills. Tempest Mountain, named for the strange storms constantly swirling about its peaks, was also home to the spooky and long-abandoned Martense mansion. The peculiar Martenses had always been disliked in the area, and were well known by a common trait shared by many family members—one brown eye, and the other blue.

It was in the early colonial days when the Martenses settled on Tempest Mountain. And with the centuries, their wealth and family's reputation faded. Eventually, there was nothing but a ruin left of the once majestic mansion—and no Martenses to be found.

When a sudden thunderstorm settled over the area (it was Tempest Mountain, after all), fear swelled to a frenzy when a lightning bolt struck near a squatters' camp, causing the homemade structures to collapse, and resulting in the death of all seventy-five inhabitants. All in all, it wasn't too bad as the dead people were nothing more than poor, homeless squatters—low on the gene pool in Lovecraft's day. Actually, it wasn't the death of the squatters that inspired terror, it was how they died. When the location was visited, all that remained were clawed and chewed corpses, and parts of corpses (seems that squatters were low on the food-chain as well). So one man, a self-described "connoisseur in horrors," decided to investigate further. The investigator enlisted the help of two companions, George Bennett and William Tobey. All three ventured up Tempest Mountain. But the three men were unexpectedly caught in a storm (yes, on Tempest Mountain). In need of refuge from the rain and lightning, they entered the remains of the Martense house. Within an hour of entering, all men grew curiously drowsy.

After a quick nap the investigator awoke, discovering his companions missing. This was followed by a brief lightning-flash, which revealed the terrifying form of an ape-like creature. And as quickly as the lightning had strobed, the creature vanished. Of course, Bennett and Tobey were never found again.

Even with his newfound and recently lost friends missing, the investigator was undeterred. He returned to the nearby town and hooked up with a reporter named Arthur Munroe. They bonded immediately, quickly becoming pals. And together, they roamed the countryside, hunting for information about Martenses. But, to their surprise, another violent storm struck, and the pair was forced to take refuge in a cabin. As lightning crashed nearby, Munroe peered out the window to assess the damage. Big mistake. Almost as quickly as the investigator had befriended Munroe, he was dead. When the investigator checked on Munroe, who stood, motionless, at the window, he found the reporter with his face chewed to shreds.

But if anything, Cthulhu Mythos investigators (even when they don't realize they are such) are a strongheaded group. Another death didn't discourage the investigator. Instead, he continued exploring—after the storm—and eventually unearthed the grave of Jan Martense. Luckily, before Munroe died, he'd uncovered a number of Martense family records. It seems the Martense family had crushed Jan's head in with a skull of some sort. Now things

## MYTHOS SURVIVAL TIP: STAY AWAKE

As it is apparent from this tale written in the 1920s, staying awake isn't a modern problem. And for investigators of the Cthulhu Mythos, it is an extremely important matter. Remember to remain alert at all times. When venturing into caverns, forests, ruins, or escaping from the ancient city of the Old Ones, it is important to be wide awake and full of energy. Sleep is often a co-conspirator in the Mythos. It settles upon a person at the most inopportune moment. This means one should always keep a steady supply of caffeinated drinks and energy shots on-hand. It's also not a bad idea to carry a taser. (Sure, they hurt, but you're guaranteed to stay awake after you zap yourself with a taser. Also handy on a small number of Mythos creatures).

were clear to the investigator. The simplest explanation was that Jan Martense had become a vengeance-seeking ghost, and was able to ride lightning bolts down to Earth in order to attack his unfortunate victims. All right, maybe not the simplest, but certainly fantastic in nature and worthy of further investigation.

## LIFE IS SELDOM SIMPLE

Doggedly, the investigator tore into the earth, looking for some sort of clue, any clue that might support his seemingly simple hypothesis. But all he received for his efforts was falling into an underground passage. Frightened, he scrambled to the surface and safety. But as he did, he saw a terrible claw, and two hateful eyes, gazing at him from the blackness below.

After a short reprieve, and some time to collect himself,

## MYTHOS SURVIVAL TIP:
## KNOW WHEN TO CUT BAIT

Determination is a quality admired by many—particularly hungry monsters. Sometimes when investigating the Cthulhu Mythos, diligence rewards. Other times it doesn't. Knowing when to run and when to press onward can be difficult. Honestly, it comes down to a person's desire to live. Usually, the greater the desire, the sooner one flees. But risk takers know peril sometimes pays. Sadly, the investigator in "The Lurking Fear" is a poor example, as in the end he only had the satisfaction of destroying a group of "degenerate" humans. Although in his day, this was reward enough. And actually, there are few other examples of great reward in the Cthulhu Mythos, unless you count learning secrets and going insane, or gathering vast knowledge and being lost in time as rewards.

Overall, it is probably better to flee than to push onward. However, for those who are headfast and determined, there is some sort of reward—fleeting as it may be.

the investigator returned to Jan Martense's grave site. What he expected to find wasn't there. The odd tunnel had collapsed due to more storms. Even so, he knew there had to be another entrance, as the underground passage seemed quite lengthy. He strolled the grounds of the Martense mansion, intrigued by the vast number of mounds littered across the land. Then, like an unexpected lightning bolt from a storm on Tempest Mountain, it struck him. Each of these mounds were links in a vast honeycomb of tunnels beneath the surface. In fact, they were a bit like oversized mole mounds. Excitedly, and seemingly oblivious of the dangers awaiting him, he staked out one of the mound entrances. He didn't have to wait long before a horde of ape-like creatures streamed from the mound entrance. They were terrible, white apes with scissor-sharp claws. Some even had one brown eye and one blue eye—the Martense "look." Being short on friends, the investigator promptly fled. But he wasn't going to be outdone. As soon as possible, he returned with several local men. He also brought plenty of explosives. Not wanting to wait until the ape-like creatures sprung from the mounds, the investigator and the locals planted the explosives and destroyed the network of mounds and tunnels. These also (hopefully) killed what was clearly the surviving descendants of a devolved Martense family.

# What to Do When You Meet Cthulhu

*This was that cult, and the prisoners said it had always existed and always would exist, hidden in distant wastes and dark places all over the world until the time when the great priest Cthulhu, from his dark house in the mighty city of R'lyeh under the waters, should rise and bring the earth again beneath his sway. Some day he would call, when the stars were ready, and the secret cult would always be waiting to liberate him.*

—H.P. Lovecraft, "The Call of Cthulhu"

At long last we've arrived—the denouement of the book, and perhaps of the planet. But we can't rush into things. All of the previous chapters have led to this one. So if you've skipped through them, you're not likely to survive long enough to meet Cthulhu. This is a good opportunity to jump back and at least skim those previous chapters.

And if you've been diligent and scoured all of the preceding text, then you know there are many threats in the Cthulhu Mythos. Unfortunately, most, if not all of them, are likely to appear before the Great Cthulhu awakens. Stop to consider that Cthulhu is a creature beyond human comprehension (not unlike most other Mythos critters). His, or her, dreams are powerful enough to influence and invoke insanity in humans. Imagine his waking thoughts. Arguably, he doesn't see the world as humans do. In fact, he probably doesn't even see reality as humans do. Most likely, he views multiple realities, and all of time, simultaneously. Imagine the headache Cthulhu will wake up with—no wonder everything will get destroyed.

But we can't actually blame Cthulhu. Rather, humans, and every other creature on the earth, are mere specks. This Great Old One is interested in the really big picture. So it is unlikely he'll even give humanity a second thought—or a first. Quite honestly, he might not even notice us at all. Even so, our fate is sealed. All is lost, and doom awaits us.

If this sounds nihilistic or apocalyptic that's because it is. Really, the goal isn't to outwit or thwart Cthulhu, the best plan is to survive until he awakens, and then maybe slip away unnoticed and undamaged. Or, at the very least, embrace the inevitable fate that awaits humanity. Although, there is no need to put the cart before the horse at this moment. Things will be much clearer (maybe) once we examine the H.P. Lovecraft story that started the entire "Cthulhu" business.

Without a doubt, one of Lovecraft's most popular tales is "The Call of Cthulhu." Without this story, most likely you wouldn't even be reading this book. And even more likely, this book wouldn't have been written. And an entire genre of literature and films would be tentacle-less. As a culture, we owe much to Lovecraft and this wonderful tale.

## Cthulhu, R'lye—Who the What, Now?

In "The Call of Cthulhu," a set of papers belonging to the late George Gammell Angell, a professor of Semitic Languages at Brown University, set things into motion. The papers were found by his great-nephew, Francis Wayland Thurston, along with a strange bas-relief, depicting a bulbous-headed, tentacled creature with wings.

In addition, there were references to a strange "Cthulhu Cult" (yes, he has one). In the notes, it is revealed that a young, excitable fellow named Henry Anthony Wilcox called upon Professor Angell after creating the peculiarly tentacled, bas-relief sculpture. It seems Wilcox suffered strange dreams prior to making the hideous-looking bit of art. In these dreams, he found himself inside a Cyclopean city that dripped with green ooze, and was walled by black onyx stonework. And when he was there, from deep below the surface, a great voice rumbled the mysterious words "Cthulhu" and "R'lyeh."

Oddly, the enigmatic expressions sounded familiar to Professor Angell. In an attempt to learn more, he requested regular dream-reports from Wilcox. Happy to oblige, Wilcox described the great walls of the vast city. Inscribed upon the walls were hieroglyphs. And when he said "tall walls," he meant they were often several miles high. All of this gave professor Angell plenty to consider—at least until Wilcox stopped dreaming of the mysterious city. As it turns out, Wilcox's weird dreams started not long after a great earthquake shook the ground in late February/early March. And newspapers reported accounts of people around the globe who'd had similar experiences. Often, these dreams inspired artists to create amazing works. Others caused insanity, or death.

And then, about a month later, all of the weird dreams abruptly stopped after a huge storm.

### Inspector Legrasse, on the case

Angell's interest in the bas-relief stemmed from seeing a similar depiction, and hearing the name Cthulhu before (a name not easy to forget, let alone spell). Years prior, he'd attended a meeting of the American Archeological Society. At the time, an Inspector

John Raymond Legrasse brought forth a statuette and asked the assembled archeologists to identify it. The statuette had been discovered in New Orleans during a raid.

Prior to the raid, several squatters had gone missing from the area (not surprising). When Legrasse and his team investigated, they discovered a weird cult, worshiping the bas-relief idol. Apparently, the creepy cultists revered Great Old Ones who'd come from beyond the stars. The Great Old Ones were forced to take refuge underground, and underwater, due to great cosmic forces, thereby preventing their reign upon the Earth—for a limited time. But the cult believed when the stars were ready, Cthulhu, priest of the Great Old Ones, would rise again from his underwater city of R'lyeh. And when he did rise, his cult would be standing by—whether it be to sacrifice humans in his honor, or to offer themselves as sacrifices.

## IÄ, IÄ IS RIGHT!

As you've likely noticed, there's a great deal of chanting that appears in the Mythos, often in the form of indecipherable names, and words with far too many consonants than are typically found in English words. Sometimes these chants are preceded by the words, Iä, Iä! (Generally pronounced as: *Eee-yuh, Eee-yuh*). Some sources believe it translates to "Yes, yes," or "Hey, hey," but is also believed to mean: "I hunger, I hunger!"

Sometimes "Iä, Iä" is strung together with other words and phrases. Given the increased attention to Cthulhu in popular culture today, it is possible to find a number of phrases—many quite clever, but unrepeatable, in this book. However, perhaps the most popular is "Iä, Iä Cthulhu Fhtagn." To see just how popular it is, if you're reading this book in a public place, try calling out the phrase. Most likely you'll get a response. And if you're at a game, film, comic, or other similar convention, give the phrase a shout. You'll certainly be the star of the show.

## You Have Gumballs in Your Mouth

Most of the archeologists at the conference didn't recognize the bas-relief. But Professor William Channing Webb, from Princeton, vaguely recalled a creepy cult similar to the one described by Legrasse. The cult worshiped a similar statue. And, as in the Louisiana gathering, the members had chanted the strange phrase: *Ph'nglui mglw'nafh Cthulhu R'lyeh wgah'nagl fhtagn* (you're on your own here).

---

## Old Ones, Great Old Ones, Elder Gods, Outer Gods, or Other Gods?

Don't know whether the creature in front of you is a Great Old One or an Elder God? No matter. The following list should clear things up.

### Old Ones, aka Great Old Ones

These terms refer interchangeably to the extra-terrestrial beings that arrived on Earth from beyond the stars, long ago. The Great Old Ones live underground, or are imprisoned underwater. Some of them eagerly wait for the stars to be right again so they can return to the surface of Earth and wreak havoc.

### Great Ones

These are weak gods of Earth that cavort about the Dreamlands (and, as you may recall, wandered off to live in Randolph Carter's mystical city, until Nyarlathotep put a stop to it).

### Other Gods, aka Outer Gods

Lovecraft used the term *Other Gods*, but the label *Outer Gods* is often used today. Lovecraft's Other Gods are powerful deities within the Mythos—more powerful than the Old Ones (hey, they're not trapped underwater, for one thing). These powerful deities mostly ignore humanity.

### Elder Gods

There are some folks out there who distinguish between

**CONTINUED . . .**

Fortunately for everyone attending the conference, Webb managed to translate the inhuman-sounding phrase: "In his house at R'lyeh dead Cthulhu waits dreaming."

With this final bit, Professor Angell's notes came to an end. Angell's great-nephew, Thurston, the fellow who'd uncovered all of this, was left intrigued, but with no ending to the tale of Cthulhu.

---

## OLD ONES, GREAT OLD ONES, ELDER GODS, OUTER GODS, OR OTHER GODS? (CONTINUED)

Elder Gods and Other Gods, but Lovecraft used the two terms interchangeably. So we'll go with that. Deities such as Nodens and Hypnos are designated as Elder Gods.

### BRINGING SOME OF IT TOGETHER

The Great Old Ones, being not entirely of flesh and blood, can only exist when the stars are *right* (also known as when the stars are *ready*). If the stars are *wrong*, the Great Old Ones remain in a dormant state—not dead, but not alive, either. Since the Great Old Ones are not quite dead, they can communicate by means of telepathy. So they can invade the thoughts of humans in dreams, and whip up cultists into a frenzy. Hence, the Cult of Cthulhu and their persistent desire to awaken the Great Old One.

It's not all sleeping and dreaming for Cthulhu. While in his subterranean slumber, he keeps the Great Old Ones preserved—and in stasis—using special spells; overall, they remain protected until the stars, and the earth, are ready for them. And when that time comes, Cthulhu and his Great Old One friends will arise from R'lyeh, resume reign over Earth, and serious chaos will ensue.

If this explanation didn't clarify things for you, no problem. When you encounter one of these beings, trying to figure out what to call them will be the least of your worries.

## Remain Vigilant

Deciding it was better to know than to live in ignorance, Thurston investigated the Cthulhu Cult further. At first he had little success, and nearly abandoned the quest. But then he stumbled across a newspaper article regarding the freighter *Vigilant*, which had arrived in port with the yacht *Alert* in tow.

The only survivor of the *Alert*, Norwegian sailor Gustaf Johansen, recounted how his schooner, *Emma*, had been attacked, unprovoked, by the *Alert* and its suspicious-looking crew. But the crew of the *Emma* boarded and overtook the yacht, killing the evil men.

Then, the *Alert's* new crew landed on a small, uncharted island, and something *really* bad happened. And given it was so horrible, Johansen didn't really like to talk about it. Naturally, this left the worst part of the events to be created by everyone else's imagination.

## Putting the Puzzle Together

After reading the newspaper article, Thurston had an epiphany. The unconnected clues in Professor Angell's notes fit together in Thurston's head. The earthquake and subsequent storm in late

### What Does It Mean, "The Stars are Ready?"

It's hard to say when the stars will be *ready*, or what this means. Some believe certain celestial bodies must align in order for the stars to be considered "right." Others claim great, cosmic forces, beyond humanity's understanding, are at work and will bring about an end time.

In any case, it's guaranteed the world will end, at the hands (or claws) of the Great Old Ones. And it's become quite popular to say, "The Stars are Right." Give that one a call-out. It's another line that'll get an answer if enough people are within earshot.

February caused a portion of the ancient city of R'lyeh to rise. With R'lyeh closer to the surface, and Cthulhu's slumbering brain closer to humanity, the Great Old One's malign thoughts tumbled into the nightmares of men.

Knowing this, the crew of the *Alert*—who were actually cultists of Cthulhu—ventured into the ocean to protect R'lyeh. It just so happens that the members of the *Emma* bested them (cultists are better on land than water).

In late March or early April, when another storm swept the area, R'lyeh was submerged once again. The weird dreams around the world suddenly and inexplicably (well, now explicably) halted.

## You're not Really Going to Open the Door With the Monster on It, Are You?

Thurston was certain he had deciphered the puzzle surrounding the Great Cthulhu. But his theory lacked one essential element: Evidence. However, this little bump didn't stop him. Thurston hunted down a manuscript written by the late Johansen. In the document, it described the events on the terrible island—the things Johansen couldn't bring himself to talk about in public. After landing, the sailors found an odd, alien city, comprised of eerily non-Euclidean angles (not a surprise). As they descended into the ruins, they came across a door marked with a squid-like, winged creature on it. So, of course, they tried to open it. And who should they find on the other side but a very grumpy Cthulhu (having just awakened).

In the horrifying events following the encounter, all but Johansen eventually died (he had a shipload of friends). They were grabbed by squishy tentacles, simply dropped to the ground from fright, or died later on the yacht; it was difficult to recall. Regardless, Johansen had scurried back to the *Alert* and started the engines, pushing them to top speed. But even going that fast, he knew it wasn't possible to outrun the gigantic creature pursuing him. As a last ditch effort, he reversed direction, and careened straight into Cthulhu's tentacled head.

To Johansen's surprise, the monstrous head popped like a sack of gelatin. Even so, it immediately began to reassemble into its original form.

But that was time enough for Johansen to gain speed on the monster and escape. Later, Johansen was rescued and lived happily ever after (if that's possible).

And it was a simple conclusion that the following great storm sent R'lyeh back to the depths of the ocean, and Cthulhu with it—likely realizing the stars weren't quite right.

## Preparing for Meeting Cthulhu

For the readers who were diligent and read this book in its entirety—or had a friend read it aloud—then everything from Azathoth to Zoogs have been covered. This means on a scale of 1 to 10 of preparedness, the diligent reader is nearly at 10. It should also be pointed out that if a friend read the book aloud, then the

### Mythos Survival Tip: So You Think You Can Beat Cthulhu?

"Beat" is a relative term here. In all fairness, in the case of Johansen, Cthulhu was caught offguard, and most importantly, the stars were just not ready. And let's not forget, the Great Cthulhu clearly didn't want to move or think much. If so, he could have easily called upon other minions, used spells, telepathy, or myriad other weapons at his disposal to destroy Johansen.

Still, it does reveal that if Cthulhu is encountered before the appointed time, a clever person might slip away mostly unnoticed—maybe along with the assistance of some foul weather.

Many will take this tidbit as a gleam of hope. Don't waste too much time on it. The odds of the same thing happening again are pretty slim. And let's not forget, Johansen used every friend he had to pull this trick off. So, unless you literally have a ship loaded with pals to keep Cthulhu's attention, things look pretty gloomy.

friend is probably planning the old "friend reversal" trick at this moment (and has neglected to read the previous statement). Good for you, clever friend!

When it comes to meeting Cthulhu, the answer doesn't rest with how to beat him in a fight, or cast him out of this reality. What's more important is to understand when he makes his debut to humanity, how to see the signs, and how to be prepared, and how to stretch out those remaining days on Earth. Most likely, one of the countless other Cthulhu Mythos creatures will rip through the barrier between realities and wreak havoc long before Cthulhu reawakens. Most of these creatures can be handled with the proper knowledge and tools (e.g. friends).

## How To Prepare For The End

1. Reading this book is the best starting point. Honest.

2. Jump on the Internet and join as many social networks as possible. Think about it. Do you think Facebook became so popular just because people liked posting personal comments, and other people (better known as total strangers) liked reading those comments? Nope. When looked at properly, "Friending" becomes something completely different thanks to social networking. So get things rolling. Add a few thousand friends to your life.

3. Silver daggers are useful in nearly all rituals related to the Mythos. But they can be dangerous. This means a silver dagger should only be obtained after the proper safety training. It is rather pointless to accidently kill yourself when preparing to prevent a death from the Cthulhu Mythos. Get the silver dagger, but be careful.

4. Chalk, salt, charcoal, silver dust, and a variety of other items are useful for drawing protective sigils. Needless to say the best one to learn is the Elder Sign. Don't use the one on the spine of this book. Besides being trademarked, it isn't the one you're looking for.

5. Some might think that as the end approaches, finding a copy of the *Necronomicon* might be wise. This is the worst thing one

can do. It won't help. Most likely it will spread insanity, panic, and then be stolen by someone else. Avoid that tome and all those of a similar nature. Too much insight is unhealthy. This is why doctors make bad patients. They know too much.

6. Consider relocating to a remote area with a very high altitude. Unfortunately, this means the location is probably snowy and mountainous, and filled with caves—and therefore, flying polyps; although, most people find them easy to avoid unless provoked. In either case, the higher altitude protects against rising waters, most thunderstorms, lost travelers, and a vast number of Cthulhu Mythos creatures not inclined to visit low atmospheric, low temperature areas.

7. Once relocated, build two abodes. Make sure one is hidden, and the other is in plain sight. This ruse fools most everyone as no one builds two houses and lives in the hidden one. Also, the advantage of the decoy house is the convenient aspect of inviting unwanted guests and then vanishing in the middle of the night to the second house. Don't return. Leave them to believe you've been killed or abducted. Handy notes and splashes of red paint assist in this. Or, if you're very creative, make or purchase a Mi-Go brain cylinder off the Internet and leave it sitting empty on a shelf. Nothing says "gone" like an empty brain cylinder.

8. Food and water. This one seems obvious, but think of all the disaster films where people overlook these necessities. In fact, if you start hoarding now, there will be plenty for bargaining later—even with the hungry Mythos monsters you will inevitably encounter. And as always, a bargain is a bargain. Find all those folks who bought into the Y2K end of the world scheme and purchase their military rations and stored goods at rock bottom prices—but don't reveal why; they are just looking for another apocalypse to justify their previous purchases.

9. Make sure you have a variety of clothing. No one really knows what environmental disasters await the reawaking of Cthulhu. This means being dressed for survival success is essential. Be it hot or cold, have the clothing for both. Also, make sure you

have a quantity of robes of varying colors, along with thread and needles for stitching emblems. It is possible the world will be swarming with cult members. Having the appropriate robe allows you to blend into the group.

10. Cell phones. Don't bother with them. Once things reach the end, there is nothing more useless than a cell phone. In fact, they become a great risk as countless people in a dire panic will be searching for signals when there are none. Those people are better known as Victims of Mythos Creatures. While desperately running in circles, waving a cell phone, some horrendous creature will lurk up on them and have a snack. Just accept that coverage will not exist in the end times, and lose the phone. Can you hear me now?

## How Not to Line Up For the End Times

It's apparent the Cthulhu Mythos is fraught with danger. And one important danger is the destruction of our planet—cute little blue-green Earth. And now, after having encountered Lovecraft's works, albeit third-hand, it's clear the planet, and its inhabitants, teeter upon the precipice of destruction. This makes the question more "When" than "If." Even so, it leaves a little room for "How?" All right, perhaps that was confusing, so let's rephrase it: How does it all end?

To be blunt, no one knows. But after having read this book, it is apparent there are a handful of scenarios that are most likely. This means the odds favor them (not the gods). Knowing these scenarios allows for improvision and adaptation, the very trademarks of humanity. Memorize these scenarios so they can be readily identified and provide you with plenty of time to adapt:

1. A crazy cult or backwoods family summons an Other God, who arrives upon Earth, squashing it into oblivion. True, this isn't the Great Cthulhu reawakening, but no one said humanity would be here when his nap ended. All that is promised is if humanity's around, and Cthulhu re-awakens, then things are pretty much over. In other words, don't put all of your magical

amulets in one basket. Be prepared for another Mythos entity to bring about a swift and fearsome ending to the world.

2. A mad scientist creates a device that stimulates the pineal gland and the barriers between realities are rent asunder, allowing all manner of monstrosities to stream into our universe. If such a thing happens, and it nearly did in one of Lovecraft's tales, then not only will the planet be overrun with hideous creatures, but also countless humans with excited pineal glands. It is unclear to experts which is the greater threat—squirming, wormlike abominations with razor-sharp teeth or humans using their third eye to pry into and control other people's lives (a great risk for those with vast supplies of friends).

3. Someone in the Dreamlands dreams an opening into this world. Until this point, most travel has been one way with the Dreamlands, and usually this requires dreaming on the traveler's part. But there are many humans who've found themselves trapped in the Dreamlands, and now long to come home. This means it is certainly possible for them to dream-up some method of opening a door between the Dreamlands and our reality. Once this happens, night-gaunts, cats, moon-beasts, ghasts, gugs, zoogs, and every other entity found in the Dreamlands will be on our doorstep.

4. Randolph Carter returns. Let's face it, this fellow was enough trouble the first time around. But now, in all likelihood, he's lost in space and time, battling it out with some alien body he's inhabited. This unfortunate writer of weird fiction has caused trouble on Earth (though mostly in cemeteries), in the Dreamlands, and even on the planet Yaddith. Overall it spells bad news. It wouldn't be surprising if he returned with the whole of some alien race in pursuit, and most of the creatures of the Dreamlands as allies. And this time there will be no relatives to send him away.

5. Zombie infestation is a great threat. Remember Herbert West? Of course, you do. And we all know he's dead. But think about it, he was a reanimator, and he made notes, and he attended Miskatonic University. Obviously, his notes have been found,

and that explains why crowds of zombies dwell in shopping malls. The next step is the suburbs and inner cities. Except these reanimated dead are all out for revenge upon the person who returned them to an undead state. Nothing but chaos and an unhappy ending can result from this.

6. The Yith return en masse. It is important to remember that the Yith are masters of time. They typically protect themselves by jumping from one time to another, and to make things worse, they send their consciousness into a human body in yet another time. Since they can travel through time, there is no doubt they know when the end of the world comes. As a result, when they encounter it, they'll pop into another, safer time—except when all of the Yith do this at once, it spells the end of humanity (a very unimportant fact to the Yith). So keep an eye out for changes in personality/demeanor in public figures and friends. These are early warning signs.

7. The Deep Ones invade! Don't think being beneath the ocean prevents these devious creatures from returning to the surface. They already occupy many towns around the world—with the only clue being the "Innsmouth Look." And to make matters worse they worship both Dagon and Cthulhu. Undoubt-edly they'll start the invasion by proffering gold trinkets and baubles, proclaiming that everyone can be rich (just watch late night infomercials to spot their advance guard). And while humanity is lost in a shopping frenzy, millions of Deep Ones will spring out of the waters and sacrifice every living thing on the surface.

8. We go with the Mi-Go. If it wasn't evident from Lovecraft's tale of warning, the Mi-Go are not here because they are friendly. And it's likely they're not here to mine some rare mineral, as it has been supposed. Rather, they like humans, or more specifically, human brains. This group of aliens has already landed upon Earth, and like the rest of us they need more computing power, more memory, more versatility from their PDAs. However, unlike the Mi-Go, humanity uses silicon based technology. The Mi-Go use human based technology—

namely human brains. There is little doubt they are looking for the smartest smart phone, and the brainiest supercomputer in the universe. And with a planet ripe for harvesting, the Mi-Go are a great threat—and clever, as they've learned to use friends against friends.

9. Shoggoths attack. Remember the Elder Things? They were the aliens visiting primordial Earth. In fact, many argue they are the progenitors of all life on the planet. They loved to dabble with genetics. As it turns out, they were fond of slaves, and created the amorphous shoggoths. However, the shoggoths weren't very fond of being slaves. They revolted, the Elder Things fled, and then all was peaceful. What this really means is the shoggoths have had hundreds of millions of years to reproduce and prepare to destroy humanity. While it could be said that humans and shoggoths are siblings (having the same parents, so to speak), it appears the shoggoths prefer to view humans as "food." Since these Mythos creatures can alter shape, and can potentially imitate human forms, it is merely a matter of time before they attack—or come looking for a quick snack.

10. The Great Cthulhu awakens. This is the big one. If the stars are ready (or right), and it is time for Cthulhu to wake from his slumber, then the game is over. Score: Cthulhu 1, Humanity 0. There are plenty of warning signs, as seen in "Call of Cthulhu." The earliest indications will be increased funding for arts in public schools and universities. The world will be overrun by a wave of great writers, composers, sculptors, and painters. And then Cthulhu rises from the depths of the ocean and everything comes to an ugly end. If possible, avoid this scenario, or at the least, hope the Great Old One has so many other things going on that he overlooks your existence.

At first blush, all of the above scenarios might appear hopeless, but that's mostly because they are. However, they are not entirely devoid of hope. Consider Johansen in "The Call of Cthulhu." This guy found Cthulhu, used a shipload of friends to keep him busy, rammed a yacht into Cthulhu's head, and then managed to escape. At the very least, if Cthulhu awakens, he'll be looking for Johansen's descendants first. But even more important is that when face-to-face with one of the greatest threats the Cthulhu Mythos offers, humanity managed to slip away like a frightened mouse. Repeating this is not entirely impossible. Once again, being prepared, knowing the signs, understanding what to avoid, and who to have at your side is essential to surviving an encounter with even a creature as powerful as Cthulhu.

## WHAT TO DO WHEN YOU MEET CTHULHU (AND WHAT NOT TO DO)

Regardless of what mild hope has been offered up to this point, most everyone agrees that what you do when you meet Cthulhu is die. So, it's best to avoid any personal meetings. And if forced into an encounter, offer up all of your friends at once (none of this one-at-a-time-stuff), put on your game face, nail him in the head with the largest object you can find (a ship would be a good start), then flee.

In reality, what you do when you meet Cthulhu isn't as important as what you don't do. As a rule of thumb, it's best not to raise the ire of a Great Old One. Nothing good ever comes of it. And unlike the long list of other giant creatures that climb out of the ocean, Cthulhu won't limit himself to one or two major cities, grow sleepy and return to a watery bed. Once Cthulhu is really awake, he'll be staying around to wreak havoc, so here is a list of things to avoid or not avoid:

1. It should be apparent from the number of times Godzilla has attacked that there are no number of guns, tanks, electrical lines, missiles, planes, bombs, and clever traps that can stop him. This translates easily over to Cthulhu. All of the mentioned items have less of an effect on Cthulhu. Like all other giant monsters from the ocean (and Cthulhu is far more than that), standard military weapons are useless. Avoid using them, and it's possible Cthulhu won't go on a rampage.

2. Multi-Chamber Human Launcher (MCHL). The name says it all. But, of course, many people are likely to think this is a cruel

and inhumane weapon. This attitude exists mainly because it is a cruel and inhumane weapon. But in order to create any type of diversion, sacrifice is necessary (ask any cultist). Essentially what the MCHL attempts to do is pacify Cthulhu by offering him bite-sized human snacks. Think of how many people enjoy "Buffalo Wings." It's just as likely that Cthulhu will enjoy them as well—except humans are the morsels. No, this weapon won't send him away. But it may distract Cthulhu, and allow for time to hide. And if enough snacks are offered up, he might just remember something else more important that he has to do in a different reality.

3. One thing that is right off the list is filming Cthulhu. Sure, a giant creature invades New York City, your friends are dying, and you have a digital camera with a few hours of battery. The best thing that can be done is to hand the camera to a friend, and flee. Let the friend stay behind, attempting to get close-ups of the non-photogenic Cthulhu. In all probability, the first clear sight of Cthulhu drives the friend insane, and now he's on a mission to get more footage. Meanwhile, Cthulhu's rampaging, and very interested in destroying the human with the camera who keeps running through subways and climbing collapsing buildings to get a better angle.

4. Joining a cult might be a good option. It is important to make sure you join the proper cult. If you already have the "Innsmouth Look," or your last name is one of those on the Innsmouth watch list, then find the nearest coastal city, and there will be a cult waiting. But, for those less fortunate, simply find a major metropolitan city, or an out of the way rural town, and there will be a proper Cult of Cthulhu. Submit to their demands and become a member. While there is no guarantee this will protect you, it does provide an immediate increase in the number of "friends" who may be consumed first.

5. Although no one has seriously suggested it, probably because no one has seriously suggested Cthulhu as a real threat, building a mecha-Cthulhu is just plain silly. Don't even think about it. One Cthulhu is enough. Bringing a second Cthulhu-like

thing is asking for trouble. Honestly, how else can a Great Old One respond to a cheap knock-off of himself with anything but contempt? And that contempt isn't limited to the creators. No, it covers all of humanity. So encourage all of your friends away from building mecha-Cthulhus as well. This is one option best ignored.

6. Summoning Nyarlathotep is worth a chance (have a friend do this). It is clear this Cthulhu Mythos deity is a trickster, and any deal made with him is going to have a bad outcome. But, because he's unpredictable, he might create so much confusion and havoc that at the very least, you can find a safe haven.

7. It is quite feasible that even after Cthulhu awakens, he'll return to the ocean depths for one reason or another—really, no one can divine his plans or thoughts. If this does happen, don't count it as a sign that all is well. And tempted as humanity might be, do what you can to help prevent the military from chasing across the ocean and launching depth charges in a feeble attempt to kill Cthulhu. Think about it. If military weapons on land have no effect, what are weapons underwater going to do? This doesn't work in classic giant monster films, and it certainly won't work in this case. Also, this rules out attack submarines, torpedoes, underwater mines, and nuclear weapons. Just forget about the weapons. Unless it is the MCHL.

8. Consider becoming a human computer. There's an upside to this. Remember the Mi-Go? They need processing power, and humans can provide it. While Cthulhu is ravaging the Earth, any human who agrees to place his or her brain in a Mi-Go brain cylinder can be traveling across the universe to safety. True, life after that will be very much like being a brain in a vat. But that's because you'd be a brain in a vat. But a live brain.

9. Broadcasting a signal across space in hopes that an alien race, or some equally giant monster will arrive to save the Earth is utterly ludicrous. It would be great to point out a best case and worst case scenario here, but there are none. All are worst cases. At worst, an entirely new Cthulhu Mythos alien race discovers

Earth, and waits until Cthulhu departs. Once the place is clear, the new aliens arrive and enslave the few remaining humans who managed to survive. Or worse yet, a second, horrible, Cthulhu Mythos creature arrives and pals-up with Cthulhu to make sure no one is left behind—in this case meaning no survivors are left behind.

10. Start sleeping. This is a long shot, given the amount of explosions, screaming, yelling, chanting, growling, and howling winds going on about you. But, if you're persistent, you might fall into a slumber and sneak into the Dreamlands. Now mind you, things are not going to be much better there. And if Cthulhu desired it, he'd easily enter that reality. Still, there is a slim chance that since the Dreamlands are a creation of the human mind, they might not be visible to Cthulhu. Sure, Nyarlathotep and a number of other Cthulhu Mythos critters are there, but they're a little different. Most of them stay in the Dreamlands or some other reality. Nyarlathotep, naturally, is the one that jumps around a lot, but using guideline #6 before entering the Dreamlands might keep Nyarlathotep busy enough to forget about the place until things settle down.

When dealing with the Cthulhu Mythos, there are never guarantees. In fact, quite often there is little hope for success. However, for those readers who've managed to absorb the material in this book, either by reading, or by osmosis, the odds of surviving a disastrous encounter with the Cthulhu Mythos have been increased ever-so-slightly. Rest assured, those odds have barely increased, but again, when dealing with the Cthulhu Mythos, sometimes all it takes is a sliver of a chance to succeed (or fail).

From this point on, the book offers handy references. Even though you might have absorbed the contents in their entirety, the chance of forgetting something important is highly likely. This means a quick reference section could be all that stands between you and an abysmal end at the claws of some Mythos creature. So take the knowledge in the prior pages, refresh it with the forthcoming pages, make plenty of friends and always anticipate that which cannot be anticipated.

# Cthulhu
## Quick
# Reference

So now you've got the appropriate background material covered. You've absorbed numerous tricks and tips to help you survive on a day-to-day basis. You know the details from many Mythos stories, and are prepared to sound like a know-it-all at the meeting of the local Lovecraft Fiction Club.

But let's face it. When you're running away, screaming from a Mythos monster, it sure would be handy to have a reference to determine what is about to devour you.

So here's a quick reference to help. For each entry, there's also a threat level, and a *What To Do* section to help avoid un-necessary pain and suffering.

### AZATHOTH

Shapeless Outer God sitting in the center of the universe. Azathoth rules over all other Outer Gods. It is sometimes referred to as the Blind Idiot God (although if you encounter Azathoth, try not to call it that).

The massive Outer God has an entourage swirling around it, dancing, and playing flutes. Pretty good life.

THREAT: Low, Azathoth is hard to get to unless you own a really fast spaceship (and if you do, please come see me).

WHAT TO DO: Take some dance lessons, and learn how to play the flute.

### CTHULHU

Enormous, green, squidlike Great Old One with tentacles and wings. Cthulhu slumbers in the underwater city of R'lyeh. One day, when the stars are ready, Cthulhu will return to Earth and make all of our lives miserable.

THREAT: High, especially if you're big into snorkeling.

WHAT TO DO: Consult the previous chapter.

### DAGON

Dagon is an ancient god of fish and fishing, possibly a Great Old One. It is worshiped by the Esoteric Order of Dagon.

THREAT: Medium

WHAT TO DO: Stay inland

### DEEP ONES

Frog-fish creatures that live in the sea. They enjoy a human sacrifice or two, on occasion, and have no qualms about mating with humans. The Deep Ones have bred with the folks of Innsmouth for many years, resulting in a town full of freaky-looking, fish-eyed Deep One hybrids.

THREAT: High

WHAT TO DO: It's generally best to stay out of Innsmouth after dark. And stay out of the water around those parts, as well.

DREAMLANDS

Alternate dimension existing on top of our own. The Dreamlands are primarily entered through dreams. Some people are rumored to be able to "dream up" portions of the Dreamlands.

THREAT: Low, unless you take drugs to get there. Don't do drugs! The Dreamlands can also be a threat if you decide to embark upon endless quests to find a pretty city you once dreamed about.

WHAT TO DO: Don't spend too much time in the Dreamlands. You don't want to end up as a permanent resident, like King Kuranes.

ELDER GODS: SEE OTHER GODS

ELDER SIGN

The Elder Sign is a symbol, sometimes depicted as a star with an eye in the center, or as a branch-like symbol. It is namely used to ward off threats from beyond.

THREAT: None

WHAT TO DO: Learn how to draw the Elder Sign. Any and all versions. Never hurts.

ELDER THINGS

Barrel-shaped, winged beasts found in Antarctica. These creatures came to Earth a billion years ago (give or take), and used to live on the surface, until the surface became inhospitable. Now they are rumored to live underwater in great cities. The Elder Things bio-engineered the slimy shoggoths.

THREAT: High

WHAT TO DO: Don't dissect them, that's a good start.

FLYING POLYPS

Flying polyps are an alien race that came to this planet, long ago. When the Yith arrived on Earth, they fought with the flying polyps, driving them underground. Later, the flying polyps surfaced, annihilating their foes.

It's rumored that the flying polyps still reside underneath the long-dead city of Pnakotus, in Australia.

THREAT: High

WHAT TO DO: Run

FUNGI FROM YUGGOTH: SEE MI-GO

## GHASTS

Large creatures that live in the Dreamlands. They hop around on large, kangaroo-like legs and look like nose-less humans. Ghasts like to hunt in packs.

THREAT: Low (they live in the Dreamlands; you can always wake up)

WHAT TO DO: The ghasts are primarily after food. Carry a bag of rib-eye steaks as a possible alternative, or trick the ghasts into chasing your best friend instead.

## GHOULS

Ghouls are humanoid creatures with sickly, almost rubbery skin. They can be found in both the "real" world and in the Dreamlands. Their faces are canine in appearance. Contrary to popular belief, ghouls can be friendly toward humans, and in fact, some humans have been able to learn the ghouls' gibbering language, and communicate with the creatures.

THREAT: Low

WHAT TO DO: Make friends with them, and learn their language. Ghouls can be quite helpful.

## GREAT OLD ONES (ALSO: OLD ONES)

Extra-terrestrial beings that came from beyond the stars, in ancient times. Some of the Great Old Ones, such as Cthulhu, are colossal in size, whereas the Old Ones from The Mound are smaller, resembling Native Americans.

Today, the Old Ones live in underground cities, or are imprisoned underwater. Some of them await a cosmic condition in which the "stars are ready" so that they can return to Earth's surface and cause chaos. To this end, they enlist cults to worship them (and, if the Great Old Ones are lucky, the cults will hopefully bring this "stars are right" condition to fruition).

THREAT: High

WHAT TO DO: Depends on the Great Old One. Generally, it's best to stay out of the way of the Great Old Ones, if you can.

## GREAT ONES

These are weak gods of Earth that cavort about the Dreamlands (and, as might be recalled, went off to live in Randolph Carter's mystical city, until Nyarlathotep put a stop to that).

THREAT: Low

WHAT TO DO: Don't try to hunt them down to ask them questions. You might not run into issues with them, but their guardian, Nyarlathotep, is likely to show up and cause trouble.

## GUGS

Gugs are enormous, unfriendly, furry creatures inhabiting the Enchanted Wood of the Dreamlands. Highly unattractive, their fang-filled mouths open vertically (and are just large enough to eat you up in a single gulp). Gugs like to snack on their nearby friends, the ghasts.

THREAT: Low (Again, it's the Dreamlands—just wake up)

WHAT TO DO: Only travel through gug-infested lands when gugs are sleeping. Luckily gugs like to nap after a big meal, such as after feeding on a ghast. So feed them a ghast.

## HASTUR
### (ALSO: HIM WHO IS NOT TO BE NAMED, THE UNSPEAKABLE ONE)

Whoops. Guess we shouldn't have named him. Apologies.

*Him Who is Not to be Named* is a dangerous deity of the Cthulhu Mythos. It's not certain exactly what *Him Who is Not to be Named* is, but many consider him to be one of the Great Old Ones.

THREAT: Depends. Did you name him, or read a book naming him?

WHAT TO DO: Well, don't call him/her/it by Hastur, for starters.

## HOUNDS OF TINDALOS

The Hounds of Tindalos appear in Frank Belknap Long's story "The Hound of Tindalos," but they are mentioned indirectly by Lovecraft. The spooky hounds live in the distant past, and experience time differently than humans do. They are not fond of anyone who attempts to transcend the boundaries of time. If they catch a whiff of you traveling through time, they'll hunt you to your death. Once the Hounds of Tindalos have your scent, they can follow you back to your dimension, and enter your plane of existence through angles and corners. So if you've angered a Hound, make sure you stay clear of . . . well, most everywhere.

THREAT: High, if you're a time traveler

CTHULHU QUICK REFERENCE